A Deal with the Devil

A Romantic Comedy

Abby Matisse

A Deal with the Devil
by Abby Matisse

Cover Artist: Pish Posh Design
Design and Layout: Debbi Stocco

ISBN-13: 978-0-9859612-1-3

LITTLE
Black Dress
PRESS

Discover other titles by the author @ www.abbymatisse.com.

Fan or Friend Abby on Facebook
Follow Abby on Twitter and Pinterest

Table of Contents

Chapter One

She needed a do-over. Big time.

The realization struck Amanda Wilson like a thunderbolt during hour four of what should have been a two and a half hour drive to Lake Geneva. Unfortunately, it was too late for a do-over. Also unfortunately, she was utterly and completely lost.

For the last ninety minutes, she'd driven aimlessly through the unmarked roads of backwater Wisconsin, cursing Google Maps and whacking her ill-functioning Garmin on the dashboard of the car. The fact that neither high-end GPS technology could locate the place was probably some sort of sign; a universal warning of impending disaster. As a city girl, going off the grid for a weekend alone may not be the smartest thing she'd ever done.

The car rolled to a stop.

Amanda put it in park, picked up the Google directions and studied the map for the umpteenth time in the past few hours. According to the worthless piece of paper in her hand, she had arrived. She dropped the map in her lap and looked out the passenger window, frowning at the dilapidated wood fence peeking out from under a tangled mass of weeds. She could only imagine what sort of ramshackle dwelling might sit on the other side of those trees.

She shook her head in dismay. If this was the place, she needed to turn right around and hightail it back to Chicago as fast as her Audi A4 could take her. And as soon as she got there, she needed to sit Kate down and demand an explanation, because this felt like a sick joke. And after the day she'd had—no, make that the past few months—she was in no mood to be toyed with.

This area appeared to be about the furthest thing from luxury she could imagine. Of course, if she decided to head back, finding the highway again would be no small feat. She had no earthly idea where she was and it was entirely possible she was stuck here. Permanently. A very sobering thought.

She much preferred her urban and ultra-chic West Loop neighborhood to this critter-infested, overgrown locale. Rustic, Kate had called it. Amanda's lips curled in disgust as she surveyed her surroundings. Rustic didn't even begin to describe it.

It was hard to imagine Kate venturing anywhere near a place like this. It looked scraggly and abandoned and downright filthy—exactly the sort of horror movie location where you ended up after you ran out of gas in the middle of the night and just before you met Freddie Krueger.

She leaned forward and peered up through the dirty windshield. In the past hour, the sky had turned an ominous shade of white—not a good sign given the weather bulletins she'd tried to ignore all week. If she was going to leave, she'd better get on it because it looked like they were about to get a winter's worth of snow dumped on top of them.

Amanda flung the map onto the passenger seat and flopped back as she contemplated the best course of action. She needed a cocktail and an hour-long shower, not a three-hour drive back to Chicago.

She expelled a long, exaggerated sigh and turned her head. Despite the dull overcast day, a shiny piece of metal caught her eye. She sat up straight and then leaned forward, peering intently. Wait a minute. She squinted and glanced up and down the road. The mailbox! This *had* to be the place.

Amanda yanked the car in gear. In her excitement she hit the gas harder than intended, spraying a long fountain of gravel in her wake as she executed a U-turn that would make a NASCAR driver green with envy. She skidded to a stop in front of the mailbox and leaned over the passenger seat to peer at the name. Connelly.

She smacked her palms on the steering wheel. Finally.

Thank God the chichi mailbox had caught her eye. Kate's place featured an ornate wrought iron and steel number—so different from the beat-up metal contraptions nailed haphazardly to rotted wood posts that adorned other driveways up and down the lane. As she turned into the driveway, she vowed to ignore her earlier misgivings about Freddie Krueger and going off the grid. She was here. That had to mean something.

She stopped the car and got out, stretching lazily as she studied the wide logs that formed the walls of the cabin. Her eyes drifted up to the stone chimney that jutted skyward from the cedar shake roof. Kate had declared the cabin 'rustic with an urban twist.' Whatever that meant. The exterior didn't look too promising, but to be fair, Kate said they had focused on the interior and wouldn't tackle the outside until next spring. Given the decrepit look of the front porch, the sooner the better.

A large, puffy snow flake drifted down and landed on her cheek, melting instantly. She looked up at the sky and two more landed on her forehead. It was starting. Amanda brushed the moisture off her face and strode toward the back of the car. After popping the lid on the trunk, she hauled her suitcases out. The larger of the two landed on the ground with a dull thud.

Good grief. How many suitcases do you need for three days alone in a cabin?

Apparently two plus one tote bag stuffed with every beauty product she owned. To be fair, what she'd done couldn't technically be considered packing. She'd just tossed random items into a few bags without giving it much thought, which was completely out of character. Amanda was a planner and an obsessive organizer and normally when she traveled, she packed by checklist. But she had been too preoccupied to bother planning and so she'd brought one quarter of her closet and every item in her bathroom vanity.

A do-over would be pretty sweet though. She'd give anything to go back and undo the last six months. Even the past three would suffice. Too bad it wasn't possible. The only thing she could do now was come up with a plan to crawl out from under this massive cluster of a situation. And she needed to do it soon. She only had another month or two at most before her financial house of cards would collapse around her.

A familiar lump of dread formed in her stomach at the thought. Drastic measures were called for or she'd face bankruptcy—an option she refused to consider. At least for now.

She dragged bag number one up the porch steps while trying to talk herself down. No point getting all worked up. She had three whole days to figure something out, which was plenty of time to come up with a plan.

When she got everything into the cabin, she plopped down on the larger bag, huffing and sweaty and trying to muster the strength to haul the bags upstairs. The bottle of Shiraz she'd stowed in the smaller suitcase tempted her, but she resisted. No cocktails. At least for the next hour. She needed a shower and then she planned to get busy on her strategy for resolving this mess. Cocktails could come later.

After she lugged her bags upstairs, Amanda strolled into the bathroom, laid her robe on the counter and turned on the water. Then she peeled off her uncomfortable suit—which she would have changed out of at the office had she known she'd get lost—opened the beveled glass door and stepped into the slate-tiled, multi-jet dream of a shower.

Kate hadn't oversold it. The bathroom—and everything else in the newly redecorated cabin—looked magnificent. The place might be tiny but it absolutely oozed luxury. Not even the teensiest detail had been missed. No big surprise given her best friend's reputation as one of Chicago's hottest interior designers, but completely unexpected if you went by the broken down look of the exterior.

As the warm spray hit her from all sides, Amanda sighed and stood there, soaking it in. Then she reached out and twisted the temperature dial. The water grew hotter and her eyes drifted closed as delicious moist heat seeped into her stiff muscles. She relaxed into it for several minutes and then reached for the over-priced shower gel she'd bought on a whim the weekend before. It had beckoned from its fancy table-top display at Nordstrom and practically leapt into her hands as she and Kate wandered by.

She wiped the water from her eyes and examined the label. Tahiti in a Bottle. Her mouth twisted. Its claims of instant stress relief sounded absolutely ridiculous, but she'd purchased the shower gel anyway. She always did, even though her career as a brand marketer should make her impervious to merchandising gimmicks. But when it came to beauty products, she fell for them all, finding it impossible to resist the promise of discovering magic in a bottle, a face cream, a hair conditioner or pretty much anything else. It was one of the few areas in her life where she could be considered an optimist.

As she squeezed a dollop of lavender-scented magic into her palm, the scent wafted upward. It reminded her of why she'd found the product so irresistible. Wild promises aside, the fragrance alone had been worth every penny. She drew in a long appreciative breath and sighed. Heaven.

Amanda lingered until she used every last drop of hot water, but when she stepped onto the rug, her shoulders still seemed level with her ears. She needed to chill—a tall order given her money problems—and it would take something more drastic than a few blobs of expensive bath gel.

With her salary and position, she shouldn't experience money issues. Granted, she definitely splurged on occasion and she certainly didn't consider herself a genius budgeter. But she managed expenses okay, aside from the random irresistible beauty product or occasional afternoon of power shopping with Kate. Those little luxuries hadn't caused her problems, though. Rob had. And after ten years of care-taking her younger brother, she should have known better.

Amanda shook her head as she dried off. Given their history, she should have known Rob's requests wouldn't stop with the first loan. If she'd cared to really look at it, she could have guessed he'd come begging for more. But she hadn't. And he had.

Now she found herself on a one way street, headed straight for financial ruin. Hence her weekend at the cabin. Sam and Kate had insisted she stay at their newly refurbished place and—aside from being free of charge—its location in the middle of nowhere seemed the perfect setting to plot a life reinvention. A hundred grand in debt sounded serious by anyone's standards and it would take a serious plan of attack to get her out from under it.

She slipped into her cheetah print bathrobe and tightened the belt. As she glimpsed her reflection in the half-fogged mirror, she scowled. Leaning closer, she traced her fingers over the contours of her face. She looked like crap. Not surprising given her money problems and her thirtieth birthday, which loomed just around the corner, wasn't helping matters. She dreaded the upcoming milestone as it would highlight her current reality as a spinster and possibly the biggest loser she knew.

Snap out of it. Debbie Downer mode wasn't going to solve anything. Three days sounded like an eternity, especially when they came with no irresponsible brother, no crazy branding job, no phones and no friends. With no distractions, she could work miracles in that amount of time.

She'd been so excited about her weekend of solitude, even news reports of a November snowmaggedon couldn't scare her away. She needed this time alone. Hell, she deserved it. And on Sunday night she'd have it all figured out.

As Amanda reached for the hair dryer, glass shattered downstairs.

Her stomach lurched and she froze mid gesture, holding her breath as she strained to listen. She was afraid to move; afraid to do anything but stand there, still as a statue.

After what seemed an eternity, she allowed herself to breathe again, expelling a long sigh as she collapsed against the counter, weak with relief. Thank God. On top of everything else going on, she didn't need to battle a crazed serial killer. A tree branch had probably just knocked against a window.

As if on cue, the winter wind whistled outside, banging the shutters against the house. Definitely a tree branch. Besides, Kate's cabin lay so far off the beaten track; Amanda doubted a criminal could even find the place. And considering the overcast, frigid weather, any sane serial killer would be home and curled up in front of the fireplace with a glass of wine—which was exactly what she planned to do as soon as she dried her hair.

Her thumb moved to the power switch just as a door slammed.

Amanda jumped two feet in the air. *Holy Crap!*

Her fingers tightened around the dryer and her heart stopped for a beat, maybe two, and then thumped so hard, she felt lightheaded. She fought a wave of blackness. *Don't be a wimp. Do something!* She shook her head and tried to think.

Heavy footsteps clomped across the wood floor below.

She slapped a hand over her mouth to muffle a scream and every instinct compelled her to run.

But to where?

Adrenaline pumped as Amanda set the dryer on the counter and did a quick Fred Flintstone-like tip toe to the door. She opened it with caution, grimacing as the hinges creaked and groaned. Then she peered down the hall and calculated the distance to the bedroom. At least there, she could hide in the closet or maybe cram herself under the bed. The tiny bathroom left her too exposed.

The footsteps paused at the base of the stairs and then started up, one heavy thud at a time.

Amanda bit her knuckles to stifle another scream. She'd never make it. She was trapped! Her heart pounded as she eased the door shut and spun around, her eyes darting about in search of cover. With nowhere to hide, she lunged for the counter and snatched up the dryer.

Where the *hell* was her cell phone?

She wracked her brain. Crap. She'd left it on the bedside table. In the bedroom she didn't have time to get to. Perfect.

Don't scream. Do. Not. Scream. The screamer is always the first to go in slasher movies. She rolled her eyes. *Slasher movies? What the hell! Get a grip and do something.*

Amanda tried to ignore the approaching footsteps, ticking through her options at lightning speed. The self-defense advice she'd recently Googled rushed back. When faced with immediate danger, the blogger had advised, launch an offensive and then run like hell.

Sounded like a plan.

The dryer appeared to be her only potential weapon, so she mustered her nerve, gripped the dryer like a baseball bat and assumed a stance that would've made Hank Aaron proud.

Google had never let her down before. Well, except for the bad directions to the cabin. But to be fair, Garmin hadn't found the place either, so Google should get a pass. She rolled her eyes again. *Who gives a crap about Google or Garmin? Take control and say something, anything, damn it!*

Amanda cleared her throat and felt a little dizzy as she shouted, "Who's there?" She'd done her best to channel the I'm-in-charge-here tone—the one she trotted out during boardroom altercations—but she didn't quite succeed and so she added a fib for good measure. "I'm not alone in here!"

Lame. Super lame. Everyone knows the horror movie chick who claims she isn't alone, is. Why did I let Kate drag me to so many horror movies?

Amanda drew in a sharp breath and—as the footsteps went ominously silent—she envisioned Jack Nicholson in The Shining, limping down the hall and dragging his bloody ax.

She stifled a shriek, which came out sounding more like a kitten's mew.

Out of options, Amanda made a deal with her maker. She'd never complain about her thirtieth birthday, ever again. Hell, she wouldn't even whine about her mountain of debt. Just let the crazed serial killer turn around and leave.

He can take whatever he wants, but it would be great if he left the wine. Oh, and my laptop.

Still posed like Hank Aaron, she shuffled away from the door, resisting an urge to cower in the corner. *Please don't let me be chopped into little pieces. Big pieces either. No pieces.*

A familiar male voice drawled, "Well if you've got company, then I suggest you make yourselves decent or this is about to get really embarrassing...for all of us."

The door swung open.

Amanda blinked and her stomach dropped. Jake Lowell. *What the hell? He's supposed to be in Iraq.* Given a choice, she'd rather face the serial killer or have a Here's Johnny moment with Jack Nicholson.

Amanda let the blow dryer drop to her side but her grip on the makeshift weapon tightened as he sauntered in. He made a show of glancing around as he said, "You look alone to me"—he gestured toward the vanity—"unless you shoved your friend into one of those cabinets."

No, no, *no!* Amanda squeezed her eyes shut. This was too much on top of everything else going wrong in her life. Maybe her debt problems had finally gotten to her. Maybe she was having a nervous breakdown. What was a nervous breakdown, anyway? If it meant conjuring up the image of your ex—otherwise known as the devil incarnate—the man who should be half a world away at the moment, then yes, she experienced a nervous breakdown.

Just before she opened her eyes, she incanted a silent prayer that she'd imagined him, like some sort of dark illusion. She opened her eyes and frowned. The flesh and blood Jake—all six foot one hunkified love 'em and leave 'em inches—stood before her, looking immensely pleased with himself.

He smirked as he leaned against the wall. "Happy to see me?"

Happy was not the word she would've chosen.

"What the hell Amanda"—his was the tone you'd take if scolding a naughty five-year-old—"I know you turned off your cell because Kate and I have called nonstop for the last two hours. And I noticed you unplugged the phone downstairs. Nice." He raised a brow. "So have you stopped answering doors now, too?"

Between friends, his attitude could be considered teasing. But since they weren't friends—weren't *anything*—his amusement seemed to mock her. And, it pissed her off.

"Please." She folded her arms. "When did *you* start breaking and entering? You might've tried ringing the doorbell." Or not coming at all.

"What do you think I've been doing?" He shoved his hands into the pockets of his jeans. "I've been outside freezing my ass off for the last fifteen minutes, knocking, ringing the doorbell, yelling like a total fool. When you didn't answer, I had no choice but to break in." He pointed his thumb toward the first floor kitchen. "You're paying for the window, by the way."

Her eyes narrowed. *In your dreams.*

As she studied him, her mood grew darker. He seemed far too cocky and comfortable for her liking and she didn't even attempt to keep the edge out of her voice as she said, "What are you doing here?"

His expression hardened and judging from the look in his eyes and the set of his jaw, she could tell he meant business. "I'm bringing you back to Chicago."

"Bringing me..." her voice trailed off as she stared at him, incredulous. She cleared her throat and tilted her head. "You're kidding, right?" She hadn't seen him in a year—not since the night he'd dumped her. So why would he barge in and ruin her weekend? And nearly give her a heart attack.

If he was back on a few weeks leave, surely he could think of better things to do with his time. Like breaking hearts or destroying dreams. He was good at that.

"I'm dead serious. It's not safe here with this storm on the way. If you haven't figured that out, clearly someone needs to point it out for you."

His smirk hinted that he'd guessed the direction of her thoughts. Her eyes narrowed. *I'd like to kick his ass.* Her lips curved up as she considered a few potential methods.

"Kate sent me. Sam would've come, but his plane got delayed in New York." He shrugged. "So, here I am."

Her smile faded, her suspicions confirmed. Her BFF had turned traitor. Or she'd lost her mind. Maybe both.

"By the way"—he gestured to the hairdryer still grasped in one hand but now dangling by her side and his tone matched his wicked grin as he said—"were you planning to hit me with that thing?"

Her mouth twisted. Whoever had said that time healed all wounds had lied. Or maybe her wounds were still too fresh. All she knew was—while she'd never been the violent sort—she was pretty sure giving him a good whack would do wonders for her mood.

Rather than follow through with that twisted fantasy, she calmly set the dryer on the counter and battled the simultaneous urge to dash for her cell. She had a few choice words to share with Kate and it was all she could do to restrain herself.

"As soon as you dry your hair, we'll get out of here." His tone conveyed the confidence of a man accustomed to command.

It raised her hackles even more.

She drew in a long breath and counted to five before she said, "I just got here and I'm not leaving until Sunday night, but I'll be sure to lock the door behind *you*." This would be right after she shoved him outside.

Jake's voice chided her in that slow, maddeningly rational tone she detested so much and which he had always pulled out during their most heated arguments. "Amanda, this is a serious storm. We're going to get three feet of snow." He held up three fingers to emphasize the point as he repeated, "Three feet."

I know how many fingers three is.

Somehow, she resisted the impulse to point that out. Instead, she placed one hand on her cheetah-clad hip and waved the other imperiously as she said, "Oh please. I heard those weather reports too, but it's November." She arched a brow. "Do you seriously think we'll get that much snow?"

Jake's eyes bugged out. "Have you looked outside in the last hour?"

She ignored him and maintained her resolve despite the tendrils of wet hair stuck to her face and rivulets of water dripping down her back. As a wayward droplet trickled down her cheek, she flicked it away and lifted her chin.

He started to speak but she cut him off. She wasn't listening to any more lectures.

"Look, I'm sorry you drove all the way up here." In truth, she wasn't the least bit sorry, but she was trying to be polite. In her view, he should have known better than to come. "I suggest you head right on back to Chicago. I can take care of myself," she said. Then she bent over and towel-dried her hair with enough force to make herself wince as she plotted the revenge she'd unleash upon Kate.

Jake strode to the window and pulled aside the curtain. "Stubborn as ever I see."

He had no idea.

She shot him the evil eye, partially concealed behind her curtain of dark curls. Then she stood up straight, flinging her wet tresses back in dramatic fashion. Droplets of water sprayed onto the mirror as her gaze came to rest on the chiseled profile that had so captured her the night they met. While he held top billing as the last man on Earth she ever wanted to see again, Amanda couldn't make herself look away. He had shattered her romantic illusions of a future together twelve months before, but there was no denying Jake Lowell was still a total hottie.

Her job, brother, money problems and impending doomsday birthday had her resembling the walking dead but somehow, spending the last year in a war zone had made Jake even hotter. Life was not fair.

Jake turned and his lips curved up as he caught her staring.

Amanda's cheeks grew warm and to hide her embarrassment, she grabbed her overnight bag and dug around inside. "When did you get back?"

"This morning," Jake said, as he scratched his jaw and watched her dig—a hint of a smile lit his eyes. "Need some help?"

She always fidgeted when nervous and hated that he knew her so well. To dispel what she felt sure he was thinking—that his presence had gotten to her—she grabbed the first thing her fingers encountered and held it up like a trophy. "Here it is!" Then, she picked up the dryer. "Now, if you'll excuse me"—she arched a brow and eyed his reflection in the mirror—"I'm going to dry my hair and then curl up with a glass of wine."

Determined to ignore him, she stared straight ahead and turned on the dryer. But despite best efforts, her eyes locked on his broad shoulders as he ambled out the door. She forced herself to look away and, as her gaze drifted back to her reflection in the mirror, she scowled.

What the hell was wrong with her? Why was she standing there looking like a weak wimpy lovelorn loser? The man was a womanizer. A breaker of hearts. A destroyer of dreams. She knew this. So why moon over him like a love sick teenager?

Stop it. Moon over Chris Hemsworth. There's an US Weekly tucked in your tote bag downstairs and your boy, Chris is on the cover in full Thor regalia. Forget about Jake Lowell. The man is the devil.

As irritated by her own weakness as she was by Jake's uninvited presence, she called, "Drive carefully!" Her calculated tone—all faux sweetness and insincerity—made her feel better. Sort of. Given the way he'd dumped her, he deserved a whole lot worse.

As his footsteps retreated, Amanda expelled a long, exasperated groan. Jake Lowell was in town. Great. And Kate had sent him to rescue her. *Rescue* her. She shook her head in disgust. While consistent with the sort of retro romantic delusions she'd come to expect from Kate, she still found the notion hard to believe. She wasn't rescuing material and after a decade of friendship, Kate should know this.

Amanda scraped the brush through her hair so hard; it pulled out a small clump of curls. She slammed the brush on the counter and rubbed her head as she tried to determine who to blame for ruining her weekend.

Jake should have refused when Kate asked him to come. After all, sparing feelings and rescuing ex-girlfriends wasn't something a commitment-phobe like Jake would typically place much value on. And while she was creative, even her wild imagination couldn't concoct a logical excuse for Kate's behavior. Of course, nothing about Kate could be considered logical. Her southern belle roots ran deep—especially where romance was concerned—and so, staging a dramatic knight in shining armor rescue would be right up her alley.

Come to think of it, she should have suspected Kate's motives the instant her friend offered up use of the cabin—especially since she'd just finished the redecorating job. She and Sam hadn't even stayed here yet. She sighed and vowed to deal with Kate later.

Jake was the more troubling part of this scenario. Granted, he never missed an opportunity to rescue, but his Navy SEAL instincts—finely honed after thirteen years with the elite fighting force—must have kicked into protector overdrive to make him go this far out of his way. When they'd been together, she had thought his protectiveness cute and his alpha male ways super sexy—at least most of the time. But now, his caretaking attitude just irritated her.

Did he really imagine—a year after dumping her—that he could charge in like a knight on a white horse or something?

The over-the-top rescue scenario held all the hallmarks of a Kate intervention and she could've guessed her friend's involvement even if Jake hadn't fessed up. But her friend had missed one important little detail. Amanda didn't need anyone's help and most especially, not his.

She'd rather be buried alive in the three feet of snow they were predicting, then stuffed and put on display like those animals in the Natural History Museum who'd instantly frozen during the onset of the last Ice Age. She could envision her bedraggled, cheetah robe-clad body, stuffed with a placard underneath that read: Twenty-First Century Spinster Frozen Alive. Or some other equally depressing label. Hopefully they'd style her hair and use a good makeup artist and maybe leave out about five pounds of stuffing, preferably in the upper thigh area.

Amanda pursed her lips. She wasn't going to let Jake Lowell ruin her weekend. He needed to leave. Now. And then he needed to stay out of her life forever. He shouldn't find it too hard as he'd long ago made it perfectly clear it's exactly what he wanted.

Chapter Two

Half an hour later, Amanda flounced into the living room and wasn't surprised to find Jake lounged on the sofa, his long legs stretched out as he watched the evening news. Listening had never been one of his strengths.

She breezed by, glaring at the back of his head but determined not to let him see the extent to which his continued presence irritated her. Remembering his earlier comment about the weather, she stopped in front of the living room window and lifted a slat on the wood blinds.

Her eyes grew round and she reared her head back in surprise. In the hour since she'd arrived, the world had turned white. There must be at least three inches of snow on the ground and it was still coming down so hard she could barely make out the silhouette of her car in the driveway.

Amanda chewed the inside of her lip. This was not good.

Sure there'd been storm warnings, but she'd dismissed them. Midwest Novembers typically brought any number of false weather alarms and like every other Chicagoan she'd figured *what's a little snow*? She'd envisioned flurries—the picturesque kind that blew about like a shaken snow globe, but never really accumulated. The kind they usually got in November. Clearly, not a good move.

She turned and tried to sound composed as she said, "Wow. It's getting bad out there."

"Really? I hadn't noticed." He laced his fingers behind his head and crossed one foot over the other which only added to his I-told-you-so attitude.

She bristled, but before she could respond, the TV reporter mentioned the weather. Jake lifted the remote and turned up the volume while Amanda perched on the arm of a nearby chair, her eyes glued to the fifty inch flat screen.

The massive storm had dumped more than two feet of snow in Minneapolis and was headed to the Lake Geneva and Milwaukee areas where it was expected to deliver up to three feet over the next few days. The highway patrol's weather advisory warned drivers to get to their destinations and stay off the roads until the storm passed.

Amanda chewed on a fingernail. If she didn't leave now, she might get stuck here and that was a complication she could live without. Her work schedule for the coming week could best be categorized as a nightmare and her money situation was simply too out of control. She literally couldn't afford to disappear for a week.

She gazed broodingly into the empty fireplace, silently cursing the weather gods responsible for ruining her weekend. After a few minutes, she turned to Jake and said, "I guess we should head back."

He didn't even glance in her direction. He didn't need to. She could sense the internal gloating from across the room.

Forty-five minutes later, he had boarded the window smashed during his break-in, stowed her bags in the trunk and was five minutes into what she feared might be an endless lecture on safe snow driving. It took every ounce of self-restraint to resist rolling her eyes, but finally—just before she lost it completely—Jake's lecture mercifully ended. And the instant it did, Amanda didn't hesitate. She opened the front door and stepped onto the porch, pulling her coat more tightly around her as she eyed the snow with trepidation. The storm seemed to have picked up steam in the past hour and there looked to be at least six inches on the ground. She felt a small stab of fear as she contemplated the dangers they might encounter on the road. Still, given the alternative, she'd rather take her chances.

She glanced at Jake, who looked about to launch into driving lesson number two and decided she'd endured enough. She held up a hand to stop him and then, teeth rattling, she hugged her waist while shifting her weight from one foot to the other. "Jake, I'm from Chicago. I know how to drive in the snow. Besides, it's too cold out here to stand around. Let's go before it gets even worse."

Amanda stomped down the steps and marched toward her silver Audi A4.

"Just follow me," he shouted above the wind as he trailed behind. "I'll drive slowly. Remember to keep a safe distance, but always have me in your—"

She slammed the car door, turned on the ignition and cranked the heat to full blast as she watched Jake trudge to his SUV.

He took the protector thing to a whole new level, which probably came with the territory for a SEAL. But given their break-up, she found his caretaking attitude irritating as hell. She'd always been super independent, but since the night her parents had died—she'd been just nineteen—she'd grown even more self-sufficient. She hadn't been given a choice. In the blink of an eye, she'd gone from big sister to single parent.

In her opinion, she'd done a pretty good job, too—especially considering she'd been a kid herself when she'd taken on the responsibility. She'd maneuvered through a million difficult situations and, when she looked back, was proud of the way she'd handled most of it. So pretty much the last thing she needed right now was her ex-boyfriend swooping in for a dramatic rescue that didn't even need to happen.

She didn't need Jake's help—or anyone else's—with anything.

Amanda adjusted the rearview mirror. Having made peace with her decision to leave, she just wanted to get the hell out of Dodge or Wisconsin or whatever. She couldn't imagine anything worse than getting snowbound with the man who had kicked her to the curb.

The lights on Jake's black Escalade flipped on as his engine fired up. Amanda buckled her seatbelt and focused on following at a safe distance, though he drove much faster than she would have liked.

The combination of the pitch-black night and her Audi's extra bright headlights turned the snow into a blinding white swirl. But they made steady progress for several miles until, suddenly, Jake's brake lights blazed and, without warning, his truck jerked to the right. The maneuver caused his SUV to fishtail.

Before she could react, the cause of his problem came into view. Her eyes grew round and she sucked in a sharp breath when she saw the thick branch lying across the road, blocking her path. Operating on pure instinct, Amanda yanked the steering wheel hard to the right, barely missing it. The action sent her car into a skid. Panicked, she hit the brakes harder than she should have and the car started to spin.

Amanda held her breath and squeezed her eyes shut as she spun toward Jake's SUV. Somehow they avoided a collision, but she opened her eyes just in time to see Jake's Escalade slam into a ditch on the other side of the road.

Pulse racing, she took her foot off the gas, guided her car onto the shoulder and put it in park. After peeling her fingers from the steering wheel, she rested her head against the back of the seat, panting harder than she had after climbing Heart Attack Hill during her first—and last—5K run.

She hated running—almost as much as she despised her lingering feelings for Jake. He'd dumped her, so why was she still lusting after him? It was time to get over his worthless, womanizing ass.

Amanda drew in a long, shaky breath and, as her breathing slowed, she peered through the smeared window and driving snow, expecting to see him headed across the road. As a SEAL, a little fender bender wouldn't stop him.

But as several seconds passed with no Jake, she grew concerned. Something was wrong. Her fingers shook as she unbuckled the seatbelt and opened the door, her eyes glued to his vehicle. Still no Jake. She felt sick as she tightened the belt on her coat. Then she held her neck scarf across her face to block the sting of the wind, and half ran, half slid across the slick, unplowed road.

Jake's vehicle was wedged in the ditch, but the driver's door looked accessible. Amanda struggled through knee-deep snow drifts, falling twice as she made her way over the uneven terrain. As she got to the driver's side door, she paused for a moment and took a deep breath as she mentally prepared for the worst. Then she grabbed the door handle and yanked it open, stepping onto the running board and hoisting herself up so she could see inside.

Jake sat in the driver's seat, holding his left temple as he tried to restart the engine.

"Are you okay? What's wrong with your head?" Her eyes scanned his face and then the cab. She couldn't see any broken glass. No blood. All good signs.

"It smacked against the window." He stopped fiddling with the keys and leaned back in the seat, fixing her with his killer blue eyes. "I need to get out of this ditch."

I need you to stop looking at me like that.

Amanda swallowed hard and looked away, trying to sound cold and pragmatic as she said, "I've got news for you. You're stuck." She turned and glanced at the driver's side window. It wasn't cracked, but she supposed he could have a mild concussion. "Let me see." She took hold of his sleeve and pulled his hand away. Then she reached out and touched the skin above his left temple, which felt like a tiny zap of electricity. She yanked her hand back and leaned forward to visually inspect the area. Then she cleared her throat and said, "It's a little red. You'll probably get a bruise. What happened?"

"You're kidding, right? You saw that branch. I almost flipped over."

"That's a tad dramatic, don't you think?" She arched a brow and tried to squelch an illogical, but nearly uncontrollable, urge to giggle. "It wasn't that big a deal. I just zipped by it." She couldn't resist the exaggeration—especially since he fancied himself the fount of all knowledge on safe winter driving.

"Yeah, I noticed," he said, his voice sounding flat. "Your zipping ran me off the road."

Of course he'd blame her.

She didn't bother to hide her amusement as she said, "Maybe you should've followed your own safe winter driving tips. Personally, I found them very helpful."

His eyes narrowed. "You think this is funny?"

She shook her head and pulled her lips inward to stifle a giggle as she said, "Of course it's not funny." Hysterical might be a better description—especially with the wounded-pride expression on his face. Plus, she *loved* to be the one rescuing Mr. Tough Guy from the ditch.

He glared at her. "I slammed on my brakes and nearly flipped over trying to avoid that branch and then had to do it all over again to dodge you."

"We both did, but only one of us ended up in the ditch. Maybe you shouldn't have been driving so fast. If I recall correctly 'slow and steady' was safe snow driving rule number two." Amanda hopped down and grinned up at him. "Just sayin."

He glowered at her as he unbuckled the seat belt and dropped to the ground. He shut and locked the door and they tramped across the road. He cast a last regretful glance at his wounded Escalade. "I hope my truck is okay. I literally just drove the damned thing off the lot on my way up here."

When they got close, Jake headed toward the driver's side door.

She grabbed his sleeve and shook her head. "Whoa there, big fella. This is my car and I'll do the driving, thank you very much." She stole a peek at him as he stomped around the back of the car and slid in beside her. From the set of his jaw, he didn't look pleased. Too bad. Her car was sort of new too and no one but her would be putting it in the ditch.

"Should we keep going or head back to the cabin?" Amanda cast a sideways glance at Jake as she switched off the hazard lights. "I can't decide." She really didn't want to go back to the cabin, but she feared what they might encounter down the road if they kept going.

"We need to head back to the cabin," Jake said, his tone making it clear he'd broach no arguments. "There's nothing to speak of between here and Chicago and we can't risk running into more trouble."

More trouble. Like that was even possible. Her blissful weekend of solitude was not off to a good start. So far, it was decidedly short on bliss and could no longer be considered solitary.

They were quiet on the drive back and Amanda's mood grew as black as the moonless night. She poked along at a snail's pace, which caused their return trip to take nearly an hour. The silence was broken only by Jake's occasional sighs, which she guessed to be related to her driving skills.

Despite his apparent disapproval, at least she hadn't put them in the ditch, which she would've pointed out had he dared to challenge her. He didn't.

When they arrived, Jake carried her bags back into the cabin and built a fire. Then he sacked out on the couch, watching sports highlights. He held a bag of frozen peas to his left temple, which now sported a large purplish red knot similar to the one she might have inflicted had she whacked him with the blow dryer as she'd been dying to do earlier.

She glanced at him surreptitiously and stifled a giggle. You can't outrun karma, big boy. Clearly the universe agreed with her. Jake deserved to be punished.

Amanda allowed herself to feel a small measure of satisfaction as she sidled up to the fire, rubbing her palms together and working on her attitude. She felt cursed. Aside from Jake's bump on the head, which she considered a mark in her column, the fates appeared to be conspiring against her. There could be no other explanation for her recent run of bad luck. She'd just wanted a weekend alone. Had that really been asking too much?

She peered over her shoulder. He looked ridiculous holding that bag of frozen peas against his head. If she hadn't been in such a foul mood, she would've been tempted to sneak a quick pic with her cell phone. The Facebook posting and resulting comments from her girlfriends would have been priceless.

Amanda turned back to the fire. A year ago, she would have considered being snowbound with Jake to be pure heaven, but given the brutal finality of their break-up, this situation had disaster written all over it. She watched the flames lick greedily at the dry kindling. After he'd dumped her, she'd vowed to avoid him at all costs. That had been pretty easy to do while he served in Iraq. Not so easy now. The cabin only consisted of four rooms.

Her stomach grumbled—a not-so-subtle reminder she hadn't eaten since noon—so she headed to the kitchen in search of food. She peered into the freezer, moving items around until she found two steaks and some frozen asparagus. Coupled with the bottle of Shiraz she'd brought, her find should make for a very nice dinner.

Forty five minutes later, she loaded two plates and carried them to the living room, returning a few moments later with the wine.

"Thanks," Jake said, gazing up at her in surprise. "I figured I'd have to fend for myself."

She shrugged and gestured to the bag pressed against his temple. "I thought you might like a steak with those peas."

"Hilarious." He set the vegetables on the table and eyed the steak with lust. "Have we declared a truce?"

"Let's not get carried away." She poured the wine and handed him a glass. "I considered tossing this at you, but it would be a shame to waste such a good bottle of wine."

He grinned. "Given your attitude the last couple of hours, you seemed more likely to stab me with this fork than to cook me a steak." Jake waved the fork, then picked up his knife and dove into the meal with gusto.

She sipped at her wine and watched him devour his food. Her appetite had vanished and she planned to drink dinner. She couldn't believe just three hours had passed since he'd sauntered into the bathroom. Earlier, she'd fantasized about shoving him out the door and dead-bolting it behind him. But since they were stranded together, she figured she should at least try to get along. She drew a long, fortifying breath and tried to convince herself he wasn't really the devil. It just seemed so—especially when women, commitment or feelings were involved.

"How long are you in town?" She sipped her wine. Hopefully not long.

"I got out." He shot her a quick sideways glance and then looked away, taking a big swig of wine.

Her mouth dropped open as his words slapped her across the face. But she recovered quickly, fixing her features into a cool façade and tapping a fingernail on her wine glass.

So...he'd followed through with their plan. He'd left the Navy and had returned to Chicago for good. Oh well. What did she care? Granted, she'd assumed he'd chuck their idea just as he had their relationship, but apparently she'd been wrong about everything concerning Jake Lowell.

"Interesting," she said, keeping her tone as nonchalant as she could manage. She didn't want him to assume his decision to follow-thru with their plan bothered her. "How does it feel?" As her dreams of a happily-ever-after as Mrs. Jake Lowell flashed back, she knew how she felt. Miserable.

Her eyes zeroed in on the tanned, muscular forearm protruding from the rolled up sleeve of his white button down. Maybe she *should* jab him with the fork—just enough to draw a little blood. She could patch him up afterward. Surely Kate kept a first aid kit somewhere in the place. She eyed her fork and her lips curved up, but she restrained herself and instead, took another sip of wine.

"I can't tell yet. It's still too new." He shrugged. "I'm excited about my plans, but you know how it is between my grandfather and me." He grimaced and then popped a bite of steak in his mouth.

"I'm sure it'll be better between you two now that you're out."

He scoffed. "Right. Clearly you don't know him well."

"He just wants you to be happy. I don't know why you can't see the truth." She tried to figure out why she always jumped to defend Jake's grandfather. The problem between the two men had nothing to do with her and yet, she could never resist.

Jake shook his head. "I do. Max wants to control me, just like he controlled my father."

"I don't believe that."

"Believe whatever you want," he said. "It's true. I've only been back a few days and he's already up to his old tricks, but this new twist takes his game to a whole new level." She thought she detected a glimmer of admiration in his eyes. "And I've got to figure out a way to outsmart him." Jake took a swig of wine. "He's trying to blackmail me into marry..."

Amanda stopped paying attention, too busy contemplating Jake's messed up relationship with his grandfather. She didn't approve of the way he dealt with Max and they'd battled endlessly on the subject while together. Granted, his family situation wasn't perfect, but whose was? Her situation with her brother was totally whacked out right now and yes, he royally pissed her off on occasion. But she refused to let money problems or the irresponsible phase Rob seemed stuck in, to ruin their relationship. In her view, Jake should be grateful he still had Max—especially since he'd already lost both parents.

Amanda looked up and noticed Jake staring.

She picked up a napkin. "What? Do I have something on my face?"

He opened his mouth and then twisted it into a wry grin as he shook his head and swallowed a generous amount of wine, nearly draining the glass.

She frowned as he continued to stare. "Tell me." She kept the napkin poised at her mouth and waited for him to respond.

He laughed and set his glass on the table. "No, no...I just—" He shook his head again and then picked up his silverware and cut another bite of steak. "Never mind."

She dropped the napkin and eyed him with suspicion, suspecting she might need the strength of alcohol when he replied. "*Tell me,*" she said. Then she took a nice long sip, swishing the wine around in her mouth as she'd learned to do on a recent business trip to Napa.

"Okay." Jake set down his silverware with deliberation, one piece at a time, and then leaned back in his chair. His blue eyes locked with hers and he paused for a long moment and then said, "We should get married."

Chapter Three

Jake uttered his on-the-fly proposal at the precise moment Amanda swallowed. She only got part of the wine down. The rest she spat out.

He watched as she grabbed a napkin and held it to her mouth, her eyes watering as quick gulps of air interspersed with deep, rattling coughs. "You okay?" He stood next to her, looking down with concern.

She shook her head and kept coughing.

"Excited about the prospect of marrying me, huh?" Jake smacked her gently on the back with his palm.

"It went down the wrong pipe," she said, her voice a raspy croak. "Water."

Jake trotted into the kitchen, filled a glass with water and set it on the table in front of her. She coughed and reached for the water while he settled on the stone hearth. As she sipped at the water, he tried to figure out what had compelled him blurt out a half-baked idea before he'd even begun to think it through.

Jake tapped a thumb on his thigh and wished he could jump in his Escalade and drive until he found himself a few thousand miles away. Unfortunately, with his SUV nose down in a ditch, he wasn't going anywhere anytime soon.

He rested his head against the stone fireplace and gazed up at the ceiling. No matter the situation, he never blinked under pressure. So what the hell was his problem? Granted, he'd been shocked when the family attorney called on his way up here to tell him about the change to his trust fund. But it still didn't excuse his behavior. Iraq must've been harder on him than he'd imagined.

On paper, Amanda might seem a perfect solution for a fake engagement scheme. It's not like there would be any messy emotional complications because in the past few hours, she'd made it crystal clear she was over him. Still, actual experience told him anything involving the two of them would likely be difficult, impossible—maybe even disastrous. He had concluded this a year ago, which had been a key driver behind the break-up and which made his dumb proposal even dumber.

His gaze drifted back to Amanda. She appeared royally pissed off. He looked away and tapped his thumb harder, wishing he could take the words and shove them back in his mouth. But now he had to let the situation play out. Who knew? Maybe she'd go along with the idea. Hell, maybe it could even work, though he knew it wouldn't be easy. Still, after several hours of obsessing about his potential options, he still hadn't come up with anything better. And, if he wanted to avoid his grandfather's marital trap and still get his business started as he'd planned, he needed to figure something out; and soon. His entire future now hung in the balance.

Amanda cleared her throat and Jake looked up.

Judging from her narrowed eyes and the set of her jaw, she had readied for battle. He didn't blame her. If the situation had been reversed, he would've thought her crazy. In an effort to avoid the tsunami of questions headed his way, he stood and turned his back. As he reached for the iron poker, his hand brushed the other tools and knocked them so forcefully, they clanged. He grabbed the poker, thrust it into the fire and stabbed aggressively at the logs. With each jab, the self-recrimination grew louder.

It wasn't like him to say or do stupid things. And as ideas went, this idea ranked at the top of the stupid meter. He sensed her glare, but refused to turn around and the long silence amplified the crackle pop of the logs as they—and maybe his sanity, too—reduced to ashes.

"Wow." Her tone seared the silence. "You must've hit your head harder than I thought."

He stoked the fire and tried to keep his cool. "My head's fine." But privately, he wondered if he'd literally gotten the sense knocked out of him when his head had smacked the window.

"So if your little bump on the head didn't precipitate the proposal, what did?"

Jake set the poker back in the stand and turned to face her. He shoved his hands into the pockets of his jeans and tried to come up with words to explain the unexplainable. "It wasn't an actual proposal. More like"—he paused and searched for the right word—"an observation."

Her eyes flashed, suddenly the color of a dark, stormy sea. "Oh, *really*." She folded her arms and leaned back into the sofa cushions.

He tried to ignore how hot she looked all riled up. "I proposed a business deal." He kept his voice calm, his words pragmatic. "We'd just *pretend* to be engaged, we wouldn't actually get married."

Her expression changed from anger to confusion. "And why would we do that?"

He cleared his throat, hating to make himself vulnerable—especially to her. "My grandfather changed the terms of my inheritance and now I can't access my trust until I set a wedding date."

She raised a brow and spoke each word with slow deliberation as she said, "Let me get this straight: you want *us* to pretend to be engaged so *you* can get access to your trust fund?"

An array of potential responses flashed through his mind, but he decided to keep it simple. "Yes."

She scrunched her face like an angry toddler. "And why would *I* help *you* with *your* trust fund?"

"Well I c—"

She waved a hand and sighed. "Never mind; I'm sure I don't want to hear the answer." She drummed her fingers on the sofa and studied his face. "Why do you need access to your trust fund so badly? I thought you wanted to make your own way in life. If you need the money, why not just work for your grandfather?"

He choked back a bitter laugh. He'd go to work for his grandfather about two seconds *after* hell froze over. "I'm starting a company to help veterans. I planned to use my trust to get the business off the ground while I look for investors." He saw a spark of what might have been curiosity light her eyes, but it extinguished almost as quickly as it appeared.

"Why choose *me* for this grand plan?" She spread her arms wide and her voice grew louder. "We broke up, remember? I do. *I* recall the scene with great clarity."

He wasn't about to play into her drama or let her rehash their breakup, so he provided the most logical explanation he could think of. "Because if it's you, my grandfather will believe it's real."

Her eyes widened, her voice just below a shout as she said, "So you want to *use* me to—"

"No!" He said. "No. My plan wouldn't be using you. It's just… you know…he's always liked you."

She scoffed. "Like I said, you're *using* me."

"I'd put it another way. I *chose* you because you're the only way a fake engagement will look real." She looked about to let loose a fiery response, but he held up a hand to stop her. "And it's not *using you* if there's something in it for you too." He figured it couldn't hurt to try some reverse psychology at this point, so he added, "Look, you don't want to marry *me* any more than I want to marry *you*. So trust me, if you agreed to fake an engagement, I'd make it worth your while."

Amanda lowered her gaze and brushed her palms on her jeans. A few moments later, calm and composed, she stood and fixed him with an icy stare. "Sorry Jake. The answer's no."

"You'd be very well-compensated." He tried his best to sound persuasive as she started toward the stairs. "Name your price," he called after her, hating the desperation in his voice. "*Seriously,* just name it."

She maintained her composure and kept walking.

Jake strode to her side and reached for her arm as he pulled out the only card he had to play. "Mand, this could be your ticket to that year in Paris you always dreamed of."

She snatched her arm away and anger erupted behind her eyes as she said, "What did you say?"

He swallowed hard, but didn't blink. He couldn't back down now. His entire future now seemed to ride on her agreement. "I know how much Paris meant to you and your mother. It's your chance to live the dream—for both of you."

She glared at him.

He smiled and tried to sound persuasive. "You have to at least consider it."

"I have to..."

Sparks shot from her eyes. And not the passionate ones he remembered so well. If he'd been within reach, she probably would have slapped him. Instead, she smacked him down with her tone.

"You're an ass."

"How does my offer make me an ass?"

"You know how I feel about Paris. Mom and I always dreamed of it."

He shrugged and spread his arms wide. "I know. That's what makes this idea so perfect. You had to put the plan aside when your parents died. Now you can live your dream. How often do you think someone gets a second chance like that?"

Her chin lifted and she sniffed, "Paris isn't important enough to me to fake an engagement with *you*." Her mouth twisted. "And besides, it's a dream I'd realize only after I lie to your grandfather and pretty much everyone else I know; a lie that would mean I have to deal with *you* for the next year." Her laughter sounded harsh and hollow. "Thanks, but I'll take a pass."

Amanda stalked up the stairs, her back ramrod straight and with every step, Jake felt his own dream slip farther from his grasp.

At the top, she leaned over the rail. "Your family's millions can't buy me! I'll get to Paris—and whatever else I choose to do in life—

on my own dime. I don't need your help with *anything*. And don't you *ever* mention my mother again!" She stomped into the bedroom and slammed the door so hard it rattled.

Jake stared at the closed door for several minutes and then flopped onto the sofa.

Smooth Lowell...*real* smooth.

He needed to give the idea more thought. Faking an engagement with Amanda might not be his only option, but it's the best he'd come up with so far. Granted, she didn't seem too open to the idea, but he'd figure out how to persuade her. He had to. Whether it made any sense or not, Amanda Wilson now appeared to be his only real option.

* * *

When Amanda woke up, the bedroom looked dark and gloomy. It perfectly suited her mood.

She'd barely slept and exhaustion only added to her bad temper. She snatched her cell off the nightstand and pressed the display button to check the time. Noting the ten missed calls from Kate, Amanda tapped the phone against her lips and contemplated the wisdom of calling her friend back. She shouldn't. Not until she calmed down a little. Still, she was pretty sure her mood would only worsen until she gave Kate a piece of her mind. It was payback time.

Amanda rearranged the pillows against the chocolate colored padded headboard as she plotted the verbal tongue-lashing she'd deliver. Ever since they'd met freshman year at Northwestern, the girls had been as close as sisters, but Kate's upper crust southern belle ways frequently clashed with Amanda's practical Midwest middle class upbringing. It kept things lively to say the least.

She burrowed into the deliciously soft high thread count Egyptian cotton sheets and pulled the down-filled duvet around her waist as she punched in her friend's number.

Kate answered on the second ring. "When did y'all get back?" Her sugary Alabama drawl sounded bright and cheery and just a tad devilish—the tone she always used when up to no good—and it only irritated Amanda further.

"When did *you* lose your mind? Because I can't think of any other reason you would've sent *him*."

Kate continued, sounding unfazed by Amanda's crankiness. "I called all night long. Why didn't you pick up?" Her voice lowered to a conspiratorial whisper, tinged with mischief as she said, "He's still there, isn't he?"

If Kate had been in the room, Amanda might have strangled her. "Thanks to you, we're *both* still here."

She heard Kate's sharp intake of breath. "Why are you still at the cabin? He promised to bring you right back."

"We tried to leave, but it didn't work. I won't even go into that whole dramatic series of events. Suffice it to say we're stuck here— and for God only knows how long." She expelled a long-suffering sigh. "Seriously Kate, what were you thinking?"

"I was worried about you." Kate sounded wounded.

Amanda knew better than to fall for Kate's southern belle routine—all syrupy sweetness and feigned innocence with a hint of the martyr thrown in—she'd known her for too long. "Worried? *You* got me into this! *I* wanted to stay in Chicago, remember? If it weren't for you, I'd be home in my comfy little condo right this minute, screening calls and ordering takeout from Mr. Wong's."

"You needed to get away and the cabin seemed perfect. Isn't the décor fabulous?"

It was fabulous, but just then Amanda couldn't have cared less. "It would've been perfect if *he* hadn't come." Her anger faded and silence stretched between them for several moments as Amanda tried to figure out why she always let Kate off the hook so easily. She sighed and then said, "Please tell me this isn't some horrifyingly elaborate attempt to get us back together."

"You're crazy," Kate giggled. "I swear, Mand, where do you get this stuff?"

"Where do I get it?" Amanda looked up at the ceiling and began the count. "Hmmm, let's see. First, we experienced Drunk Guy. Then, Klepto Guy—"

"You don't *know* he's a kleptomaniac."

"The police who cuffed him seemed to think so. But you're right; I took a pass on the trial, so who knows?" Amanda said. "Oh, and then we have my personal favorite—Married Guy."

"He didn't *seem* married when I met him in Dominick's." Kate sounded defensive.

"Just because a guy wanders through the produce aisle, isn't wearing a wedding band and lets you have the last ripe avocado, it doesn't mean he's single," Amanda sniffed. "It also doesn't mean you should fix him up with your best friend. His mere presence in the fresh produce section should've been the giveaway. Bachelors don't tend to buy perishable items."

"Now you're stereotyping."

"Maybe," Amanda said. "But clueless as I may be when it comes to men, even *I* know; if you want to find single guys at the grocery store, you look in either the beer or chip aisles. Any other aisle and they're likely either gay or married."

"You really think I'd go to this much trouble."

"*Think*? I *know* you would. I was forced to date those three winners in just the last six months. Do we really need to sashay down memory lane?

"Whatever," Kate said breezily. "I won't let your negativity bring me down."

Her friend never owned up to her ever-present matrimonial plotting. "You should've opened a matchmaker service instead of an interior design business," Amanda said. "You'd be loaded by now. Or have your own reality show on Bravo. You know how you'd love to whoop it up in the Bravo clubhouse with Andy Cohen."

"Don't try to change the subject," Kate said. "I swear; I'm not trying to get you two back together. If so, I'd just invite you both to dinner now that he's back."

"No you wouldn't because you know neither of us would show up," Amanda said. "Oh and by the way, thanks for *telling* me he was back."

"I didn't find out myself until yesterday." Kate said, without a hint of artifice in her voice. It made Amanda wonder if her friend might be telling the truth. If she wasn't, Kate would've attempted to justify her actions. "Jake surprised us all. He didn't even tell Sam. He just showed up on our doorstep yesterday."

"Really," Amanda said, unable to keep the disbelief out of her voice as she tried to figure out whether to believe her.

"Yes." Kate switched tactics and went on the offensive. "Besides, I *could've* told you if you hadn't turned off your phone," Kate said, her voice dripping with disapproval. "I *tried*. And if your phone had been *on*, I also could've warned you about the snow and I wouldn't have *needed* to send Jake."

"I wanted to get some peace and quiet, remember? Besides, given your history with set-ups, I'm sure you can understand why I'd suspect your motives. You have to admit, getting snowbound with my ex sounds like a scenario only *you* could dream up."

Kate sighed. "It does sound romantic."

"Pregnancy has turned you into a sap," Amanda said. "And I suppose it would be romantic if we were still *together*!"

"I swear, Mand, I didn't plan this. It's just…I heard the snow would get bad and when I called, I couldn't get you. Sam's plane got delayed in New York. I *had* to send Jake. I couldn't think of anyone else."

"You could've called my brother."

Kate was quiet for several beats and her voice sounded uncharacteristically flat when she finally said, "You can't be serious."

"He would've come." Amanda liked to think so, but in truth, she wasn't so sure.

Kate's silence conveyed her opinion of Rob and Amanda knew this wasn't a topic she wanted to get into with her, so she took a deep breath and moved on. "Anyway, believe it or not, Jake proposed."

Kate squealed. "I *knew* he'd come to his senses once he got back from Iraq. You guys are *perfect* for each other. You have to tell me *everything*!"

Amanda rolled her eyes. "Before you get carried away, it wasn't an actual proposal. He wants us to *pretend* to be engaged so *he* can get access to his trust fund. I guess his grandfather changed the terms or whatever."

"I don't get it. Why does he think you'd go along with a dumb idea like that?"

"Exactly," Amanda said. "He claimed he'd make it worth my while. He even brought up Paris, saying I could live the dream for my mother or some crap like that."

Amanda heard Kate's sharp intake of breath. "He didn't. What a *jerk*."

"I know, right? Using my mother to try to manipulate me into agreeing to his dumb plan may be a new low for him," Amanda said. "But hey, it's all good. His bone-headed proposal might've cured me of him once and for all." She hoped so anyway. Seeing Jake again had been harder than she'd thought.

"I'm disappointed in him," Kate breathed.

"I passed disappointed eleven months and two days ago." Not that she was counting.

Kate said. "He absolutely *ruined* your twenty-ninth birthday. I could just *strangle* him."

"There's an idea. Maybe I'll get around to that this afternoon." Amanda plucked at the bedspread. "For now, I'm going to avoid him and as soon as the weather even hints its letting up, I'm getting the *hell* out of here—even if I have to walk back to Chicago."

Silence stretched between them. When Kate finally spoke, her voice took on a familiar edge. "Mand, I have an idea."

Amanda knew those words and that tone well and also knew the combination usually meant trouble. "The last time you said that, we nearly got arrested and we would've been if I hadn't seriously groveled."

"Ancient history," Kate sniffed. "Let it go."

"It was *last year*. St. Patrick's Day on Rush Street, remember?" She still wasn't over the incident and not inclined to let it drop.

Kate ignored her comment and said, "What if you agreed to do it?"

"What if I agreed to do what?"

"You know; what if you agreed to do the fake engagement deal?"

"*What?*" Amanda cried. "Are you *insane*?"

"Shh! Hear me out. You have a bunch of debt, thanks to your brother."

"Yes, b—"

"Amanda Wilson"—the southern belle morphed into the steel magnolia—"you *listen* to me."

Amanda blinked, stunned by Kate's instant transformation from airhead to commander-in-chief.

"You have a ton of debt, you want out of corporate life so you can do your own thing and—not to harp on a sensitive subject—but before your parents died spending junior year in Paris seemed a foregone conclusion. If you negotiated right, this situation could be the answer to all your problems."

"Or it could mean that a whole new boatload of trouble just docked."

"Stop the negativity." Kate said. "*Think*. All your debts paid off in one fell swoop—gone, pfft, finito."

"For some reason, the word finito sounds less convincing when spoken in Alabaman—something to keep in mind for the future."

"No," Kate said, sounding breathless as her enthusiasm picked up steam. "Really think about it."

Amanda often found it hard to stand firm in the face of Kate's over-the-top gusto. As irksome as her perkiness could be, she possessed a childlike zeal that, at times, could be irresistible.

Now was not one of those times.

"I get it. In theory, if I agreed to Jake's deal, the money could pay off my debts." But this wasn't theory, this was her life. And she wasn't going along with it. The theoretical payoff would come at too high a price.

"Yes, which is the reason you went to the cabin in the first place." Kate's fervor increased. "If you negotiate well enough, you could quit your job and figure out what you *really* want to do with your life while enjoying everything Paris has to offer. Just *imagine…..*" Kate clapped and emitted a squeal. "I can't *wait* to come and visit with my daughter!"

"I thought you didn't want to know the sex of the baby in advance. Did you decide to go ahead and find out?"

"No, I just *know* I'm having a girl."

Amanda rolled her eyes. Undoubtedly, in Kate's posh Birmingham world of debutante balls and beauty pageants, southern belles only gave birth to *little* southern belles. "I'm sure you have the tiara all picked out, but don't get carried away. You'll go into labor."

"No, I still have two more months," Kate said.

Amanda reminded herself that—in her friend's unique and irritatingly meddlesome way—she'd only been trying to help. "Listen, I know this engagement deal could end my financial problems if I negotiated right," Amanda said. "And it's tempting. It *is*. But do I want to lie to everyone I know in order to get the payoff?"

"That's definitely a downside," Kate conceded. "But you'd only have to lie to Jake's grandfather. And honestly, I think he sort of deserves it. He should've been more upfront about his decision to change the terms of Jake's trust fund instead of springing it on him the way he did."

"Can you blame him? He probably wants to ensure Jake settles down with one woman instead of following the same destructive path as his father."

"Probably, but more importantly, this could be the answer to all your problems," Kate said. "Jake would be generous, I'm sure of it. Remember, his grandfather's *absolutely* loaded."

"I'd rather *die* than take Jake's money. "There has to be another way."

"*This way* just arrived on a silver platter. You can't ignore that," Kate said.

"Yes I can." Furthermore, she intended to.

"Chances like this don't sashay by every day. The door opened. You *have* to walk through," Kate said. "It's a sign."

At best, it was a sign she should *sashay* for the hills. Jake broke her heart and almost a year later, the pieces were still scattered about. She hadn't even attempted to gather them back up let alone put them back together again. "My gut tells me if I try, the door will either slam in my face or smack me in the ass as I walk through."

"I swear. You're such a Negative Nellie today. Can you at least pretend you're capable of positive thought?"

"I prefer to think of myself as realistic. Unlike you, Miss Scarlett, your tomorrow-is-another-day philosophy doesn't work for me. Certain things are better left in the past."

"Whatever," Kate said and Amanda heard Sam calling Kate's name. "I have to run, hubby's waiting. Think about it and call me later."

Amanda hung up and tapped the phone against her chin as she stared at the ceiling. Maybe Kate was right and Jake's proposal could solve her money problems. Maybe it *was* a sign. She pondered the possibility for a few minutes and then shook her head. She didn't believe in signs *or* happy endings. She hadn't since the night her parents died. That night, she'd become a hardcore realist. But two years ago, she'd met Jake at Kate and Sam's wedding and their instant attraction had fueled dreams she hadn't allowed herself since she was a young girl. Unfortunately, the dreams died when Jake dumped her, claiming they were too different to make it work.

He'd been right about that. They were different. His family was loaded; she'd been raised solidly middle class. He rolled out of bed looking like a Greek god. It took her an hour plus twenty different beauty products just to make herself barely presentable. He chewed women like her up and spit them out on a fairly routine basis. She was an idiot when it came to men and had been far too naïve to understand she meant nothing to him until it was too late.

But he'd taught her an important lesson. Going forward, her dreams would be firmly rooted in reality. When she married, she'd choose a nice, safe, reliable, normal guy. Not some over-the-top, unattainable commitment-phobic freak like Jake. Now, she knew better.

Kate couldn't be more wrong. Jake's proposal was a bad idea. Besides, listening to Kate is what had gotten her snowbound in the first place. No. She'd stick with her original plan and develop her own way out of this mess; a way that didn't rely on Jake Lowell. Her approach might take longer, but at least she wouldn't get burned.

Chapter Four

Amanda swung her legs over the side of the bed and hopped down. She shoved her feet into her slippers and padded to the window, pulling aside the white chintz curtains so she could peer outside.

It wasn't snowing as hard. At this rate, they might be able to leave later that day. Hope stirred at the thought. But for now, she had her plan for the day. She was going to head downstairs, grab a cup of coffee and her tote bag and haul it back upstairs. The overcast, snowy weather offered the perfect excuse to lie around and craft her plan of action and doing so would be a great way to avoid Jake.

She slipped on sweatpants and a white V-neck sweater and plodded into the bathroom where she splashed cold water on her face and brushed her teeth. Then she pulled her thick brunette hair into a ponytail and headed for the stairs.

When she got to the top, the sound of Jake's off tune whistle stopped her in her tracks. She had loved his whistling when they were together. It had given her an odd sense of comfort.

Amanda gave herself a mental pep talk. *You can do this. Tune him out.* Still, as she started down the stairs, her pulse raced and a confusing mixture of excitement and dread percolated inside. *The man is the devil. Keep your distance.*

The cabin lights flickered. She stopped and gazed about in bewilderment as the lights flickered three more times. Then, they shut off completely. She clutched the stair rail and called down, "What happened?"

"I don't know," Jake called back. "I'll check the circuit box, but since they all went out at the same time, I doubt the breakers are the issue."

Grasping the rail for dear life, Amanda descended the rest of the way with care. Once her feet were on solid ground, she padded into the utility room and peered over Jake's shoulder while he flipped switches and muttered a few choice words.

"Like I thought; the electricity went out." He swore under his breath as he shut the door on the circuit box. Then he strode into the kitchen, where he opened and closed cupboards until he located a stockpile of candles and matches. In a nearby drawer, he found a stash of flashlights and some batteries. He piled the loot on the kitchen counter and strode toward the foyer.

Amanda traipsed after him and chewed a fingernail as she watched him pull on hiking boots. "Where are you going?"

"To the garage," he said. "Hopefully, Sam keeps a gas-powered generator out there. Damned electrical heating," he said as he yanked his boot lace tight. "If the power stays off, we'll need a way to keep this place warm. I'm not sure the fireplace alone will do it, but it may be all we have." He slipped on his coat and gloves. "I'm also going to haul more wood up to the porch. The pile out front looks a little low."

"I'll help." Amanda spun around and trotted upstairs to change. Jake's shout of laughter caused her steps to slow. She turned and tilted her head. "What's so funny?"

His lips twitched, but he made an obvious effort to keep a straight face as he said, "I'll handle it. You stay inside."

"What." She arched a brow. "You don't think I can carry wood?"

His smirk said it all.

"I work out, you know." She balled her fist and flexed a bicep, displaying the small round bump she'd worked so hard to acquire the past few months. "I even hired a trainer for a while." Before Rob's antics had brought her to her financial knees, that is. The trainer was long gone.

"Impressive," he said, eyeing her bicep in a way that clearly conveyed it was anything but.

She put a hand on her hip. "You really think I'm a high maintenance cream puff, don't you?"

Jake's broad grin softened his strong, aquiline features and caused the corners of his eyes to crinkle. He flipped up the collar of his coat and winked as he drawled, "If the stiletto fits..."

* * *

High maintenance cream puff. He couldn't have said it better himself. She sure was a cute cream puff, though. But right now, he had other, more pressing matters to contend with.

He pushed Amanda from his thoughts and lowered his head to block the wind. The snow had blown into drifts higher than his knees in some places and looked even deeper in front of the garage. He had to give the barn-style garage door a few good yanks, but finally got it open. Then he walked inside and tore the place apart in his search for a generator.

Ten minutes later, he accepted defeat. No generator. Nice going, Sam.

Jake strode outside, vowing to have a few choice words with his ill-prepared friend. Sam should know better than to buy a place in the middle of nowhere with all electric heating and no generator on hand. Now, their only source of warmth was the fireplace and since the wood pile looked low, he needed to haul up several armfuls to get them through the next day.

As he turned toward the side yard, Amanda came up beside him.

"What are you doing out here," he shouted above the wind and pointed to the house. "Go inside."

"I came to show you a woman can carry wood," she shouted back. Her blue eyes flashed and her dark hair blew around her face like a storm cloud.

His eyes studied her rosy cheeks and flashing blue eyes and he felt a sudden urge to lean down and kiss the tip of her pert little nose. But he forced himself to look away as he said, "I'm not going to fight with you. Go back inside."

"Don't talk to me like I'm a child."

He'd never thought of her as a child, but with her lower lip pushed out in that way, she did have a major little-girl pout going at the moment. He supposed he shouldn't point that out, so instead he said, "Then stop acting like one."

Jake turned toward the wood pile and tried to remember if she'd always been this difficult.

He had barely taken a step when he felt a sharp thud in the middle of his back. Snowballs. Really? He rolled his eyes and turned to confront her, but before he could speak, a wet icy ball smashed in his face. "What the hell?" He wiped globs of snow from his face and shook his gloved hands to flick it off.

"Consider it payback for your chauvinistic views."

"A chauvinist?" Given a choice of unsavory shingles, he preferred being called an ass. At least he could agree that one fit on occasion.

"Just because I'm a woman, you think I can't carry wood?"

"A lot of women can carry wood. I just can't see *you* doing it."

"Why?"

He eyed her boots and arched a brow as he said, "Heels in a snowstorm. Seriously?"

She glanced down and cocked her foot to the side. "They're kitten heels. Only two inches."

Kitten heels. He shook his head. No need to say anything more.

She squatted to gather more snow. "I didn't pack for frolicking outdoors, but I'm improvising."

He frowned and watched her pack another snowball. Did she really think he'd let her lob another one at him without retaliation?

She reared back her arm. "Heels or not, I still throw a mean snowball." She took careful aim and then threw it with all her might, emitting a delicate grunt as it left her hand.

Jake dodged it and decided retaliation couldn't wait another minute. He launched himself toward her, taking care to adjust his weight so he wouldn't hit her straight-on. He didn't want to hurt her; merely to teach her a lesson.

Amanda's blue eyes grew ever rounder as his two hundred ten pound frame flew toward her. He grasped her around the waist and she screamed as they collapsed together. The blanket of snow buffered their fall and Jake rolled until he'd pinned her beneath him.

"Now," he propped himself up on an elbow and gazed down at her. "Say you're sorry and I'll let you up."

She opened her mouth, but instead of the verbal onslaught he'd anticipated, she shoved a handful of snow in his face and then collapsed in a fit of giggles.

Jake grabbed her hands and pinned them above her. She squealed and her eyes grew round as saucers. Then he shook his head and showered her with icy droplets.

Amanda shrieked and scrunched her eyes closed.

"Say you're sorry," he commanded again.

Her laughter faded as she opened her eyes. In them, he saw pain— a pain he knew he'd inflicted. He felt a pang of guilt.

"*You* say you're sorry," she said, her voice husky as her eyes searched his face.

"What am I sorry for?" He knew what, but pretended not to understand.

"How about an apology for the '*it's not you, it's me*' lame-o break-up line?" Her blue eyes flashed. "Or maybe you can apologize for your timing, since you dumped me the night before my birthday."

A wave of shame washed over him as he rolled onto his back and gazed up at the huge white flakes drifting down around them. "I'm sorry, Mand."

"Why?"

Jake turned and studied her, his attention drawn to her stubborn little chin. Then he looked back at the sky. "Does it matter now?" Why revisit ancient history? They'd been over a long time.

"Guess not." Her tone sounded as frigid as the snow beneath them. Jake stood and extended a hand to help her up.

She ignored him and struggled to her feet. She brushed the snow off her jeans and then stuck her chin in the air as she marched toward the wood pile. Jake trailed behind and tried to ignore the sting of shame he felt at having one of his lesser moments thrown back in his face. Still, while the break-up hadn't been his best moment, it had been the right move—for both of them. She must have realized it too. Towards the end, their relationship had devolved into an endless stream of arguments, peppered with less frequent bouts of hot make-up sex. Plus, they'd been over for almost a year so it was time she got over it.

Actually, the fact that they were over was the very thing that made his fake engagement idea so brilliant. He'd thought of little else the night before. He'd barely slept on that hard-as-a-rock excuse for a sofa Kate had chosen for the living room. Or maybe it had been the thought of Amanda asleep upstairs that kept him tossing and turning. Whatever the cause, he'd analyzed his proposal a thousand ways from Sunday and now, he considered the idea a flash of pure genius. So long as they kept their agreement all business, no one would get hurt, he'd get his business started and she'd get to experience the year in Paris she'd always dreamed of. It was the perfect win-win scenario.

He loaded her arms with as many logs as she could carry and then grabbed a stack for himself. As they slogged toward the house, the wind whipped around, slowing their progress. When the porch came into view, Jake eyed the glossy sheen of the stairs with concern. "Mand, watch the step. It looks sli—"

His warning came too late. Amanda's foot lost traction and skated over the icy surface. She cried out as her body twisted and contorted in what looked like dramatic slow motion. She waved her arms as she struggled to stay on her feet and then collapsed in a heap at the base of the stairs as wood logs rained down around her.

Jake muttered a curse, threw down his stack and rushed to her side. "Are you okay?"

Amanda nodded, her face flushed. He didn't know if from pain, cold or embarrassment—perhaps all three.

"Here let me help."

He extended a hand, but she swatted it away. Instead, she grabbed the rail and hauled herself up, wincing as she tried to put weight on her right foot. He reached for her elbow but she pushed his arm away and hobbled up the stairs on her own. She nearly fell again when she stepped onto the porch. Her wobbly legs gave her the look of a new-born colt attempting to walk for the first time, but she managed to stay on her feet.

Jake held the door as she limped across the threshold and a last whoosh of cold air followed them inside as he closed and locked it behind them.

He watched her hop across the living room on one foot and flop onto the sofa. "Tell me," he said, his mouth twisting into a wry grin. "Do you find it hard to accept help from everyone or just from me in particular?"

* * *

"The correct answer would be B—you in particular." She grunted as she pulled off her boot. She was done trying to be nice.

Jake kicked off his own boots and tossed his coat and gloves onto a nearby chair. Then he sauntered over and reached out to touch her ankle, but she smacked his hand away.

"You need to do something to stop the swelling." He stepped back, gazing down at her. "What can I do?"

She glared at him. You could walk back to Chicago. But she kept the thought to herself and turned her attention to her ankle, which indeed looked swollen. She poked at it, wincing as pain shot through to her toes.

"Stop messing with it. You're making it worse."

"Stop telling me what to do," she grumbled. She hadn't thought the situation could get any worse, but she supposed it would if she couldn't walk tomorrow. She needed to do something to stop the swelling. Embarrassed to utter her next words after the way she'd teased him the night before, Amanda tipped her head down, causing her curtain of dark hair to swing forward, partially concealing her face. "Can you bring me the frozen peas?"

Jake ambled off to the kitchen, whistling that familiar off key tune. The sound only made her feel worse. And she was frowning when he walked up beside her and set the frozen vegetables on her ankle with flourish.

He shot her a knowing smirk as he said, "The peas aren't so funny now, huh? Anything else I can do?"

She lifted her chin and feigned an air of superiority as she said, "Bring me my cell. It's upstairs on the night stand."

Jake executed a mock salute and sprinted up the stairs to retrieve her phone. He handed it to her and said, "Will there be anything else, my queen?"

She tossed her hair over a shoulder and avoided his gaze. "I'll let you know."

Jake turned away, whistling as he headed toward the kitchen.

She glared at the TV, trying to figure out what she'd done to deserve an injury. He's the one who'd been collecting bad karma.

A few minutes later, Jake returned and handed her a mug of piping-hot coffee. Then he moved to the fireplace and starting stoking the logs.

"Thank you." She blew on the steaming beverage while eyeing him with suspicion. She took a sip and her lips curved up as the coffee slid down her throat, warming her from the inside. He'd gotten the mix just right—no small feat since she'd elevated her coffee doctoring skills to the level of fine art. She cast a sideways glance at Jake. "You remembered," she murmured. She wasn't sure if she'd said it loudly enough for him to hear and didn't care.

Jake threw more logs onto the fire and stared straight ahead for a long moment, his expression stoic. Then he said, "One scoop of sugar, one and a quarter shots of milk and a sprinkle of mocha."

His words warmed her even more than the coffee had, but she checked herself. The perfectly-mixed concoction amounted to little more than attempted bribery; an attempt to seduce her into going along with his fake engagement idea. Well she had news for him. It would take a lot more than a bag of frozen peas and a cup of perfectly mixed coffee to get her to agree to *that*.

Jake threw a last log onto the fire and jabbed at the stack with the iron poker. Sparks shot high into the chimney and with a look of satisfaction; he returned the tool to the stand. "I better get a shower in while there's still hot water left." He headed for the stairs. "Hopefully Sam left some clothes. I didn't exactly come prepared to stay."

"Save some hot water for me," she called over her shoulder as he bounded up the stairs, two at a time. She eyed the stairs with concern, wondering how she'd hobble up the stairs with her ankle in such sorry shape. But she'd worry about that later.

When he got to the top, he glanced down at her. "You're welcome to join me if you'd like."

She shot a dark glance over her shoulder.

"What?" Jake shrugged, his face composed into a mask of faux innocence. "Who knows how long we'll be here. We need to conserve hot water."

Amanda rolled her eyes.

Her cell phone buzzed.

She picked it up and glanced at the display. Rob. *Crap.* She cast a nervous glance over her shoulder. Given their bitter fights about her parenting skills, or lack thereof, the last thing she needed was for Jake to overhear her conversation. So she waited until he closed the bedroom door before she answered.

"Hey," she said, trying to forget that Rob only called when he wanted something and lately, the something tended to be money.

"I stopped by your place. Where are you?"

"I'm at Sam and Kate's cabin in Lake Geneva."

"What're you doing all the way up there?"

The frown in his voice caused her to tighten her grip on the phone and she tried not to speculate about what he might want. "I needed to get away. We discussed my trip last week, remember?"

"I forgot." He sounded distracted. "Great timing since we're about to get dumped with a mountain of snow. Was that the plan?"

"No. Kate convinced me to use the cabin and the snow is worse than I anticipated. Now I'm stuck here." She didn't mention Jake. Rob idolized Jake and if he knew he was here, it would lead to too many questions. Questions she didn't feel like answering.

Rob chuckled. "You should know better than to listen to her. Kate's always getting you into hot water."

He'd done a pretty good job with the hot water thing himself the past few months, but she kept the sentiment to herself. She slid a pillow under her ankle and repositioned the peas. Then, she nestled back into the sofa cushions and waited for Rob to get to the point.

She didn't have to wait long.

"Listen, Mand,"—he hesitated for a moment and then said—"I need another twenty thousand."

Amanda shot to her feet, the peas plopped to the floor and a stabbing, searing pain blasted through her right leg. She flinched and shifted her weight to her left foot. "Twenty thousand dollars!" Her shout—fueled in part by outrage and part by the pain radiating from her wounded ankle—echoed back from the cabin walls.

The door opened upstairs. Jake poked his head out and called down, "Did you say something?"

Damn! For a second, she'd actually forgotten about Jake. Amanda flopped back onto the sofa and covered the phone so Rob wouldn't hear her response. "No, sorry," she called. "I was just playing with the volume on the television."

Jake closed the door and a few moments later, the shower turned on. Amanda put the phone back to her ear. "Sorry."

"Who was that? Is someone there with you?"

Amanda groaned inwardly and repeated her lie. "No. I was just playing with the volume on the TV."

"Then why—"

"Don't try to change the subject," she said. "I'd love to know where you think I'd get the money."

"Yeah, I know it's sort of a lot." Rob sounded sheepish.

The lame admission wasn't enough for Amanda; not after their endless discussions on the subject. "Sort of a lot? I'd say twenty thousand equates to a *hell* of a lot—especially on top of the money I've already given you."

"You know I wouldn't ask if I didn't really need it."

She knew no such thing. She tried to stay calm, but couldn't mask the undercurrent of anger in her voice as she said, "Rob, I've cleaned out my savings *and* taken on a second mortgage. You know there's nothing left. I recall being quite clear about my financial situation when I gave you the last loan."

"It's expensive starting a restaurant. There are unexpected costs."

Apparently there were a *lot* of unexpected costs; for *her*.

She drew in a long breath and tried to harden herself to his pleas. "What about your partners?"

"Tapped out," he said. "They've put in even more than I have."

"In that case, you and your partners need to apply for a business loan."

"It would never get approved. No one wants to loan money to a bunch of guys right out of college."

She couldn't have said it better herself. So why had she done it? She'd asked herself the same question hundreds of times the past six months and still couldn't figure it out.

Almost immediately, guilt stirred and she could hear her mother's voice, clear as day, reminding her to take care of Rob on his first day of kindergarten. As big sister, her job was to watch over him, to protect him. And since he was all she now had, she took her role very seriously. She didn't consider it her job to question the wisdom of his hopes and dreams. She needed to be supportive. Her mother would undoubtedly tell her as much if she were still alive. And that— more than any other reason—is why she'd loaned Rob the money. She wanted to be there for him in the way her parents would've been.

Still, her financial well had run dry. Any future support would have to come without monetary reinforcement. "You know I don't have any money, Rob."

"Will you at least consider it?"

Say no. She heard Kate's voice, clear as day, inside her head.

I am saying no. He's not listening.

She hated how she always felt compelled to justify her actions to Kate—whether in person or when she popped up inside her head as she seemed to do with increasing regularity. Kate's evil twin—as Amanda liked to think of the disembodied voice—seemed hell-bent on harassing her every time she spoke with her brother and she was tired of it. She got lectured by the real Kate far too often already.

"Please?" Rob prodded her.

Amanda felt her resolve weaken as it always did, which was precisely how she had ended up in this mess. "Sure, I'll think about it."

Think about it. Amanda sighed. There was nothing to think about. She could ponder her financial status nonstop for the next three years and the answer would be the same; she had no money. Rob's tenacious quest for cash seemed akin to a consistent drip of water on the forehead. Eventually you'd cave—if for no other reason than to get the torture to stop. "I'll call you when I get back."

Apparently dissatisfied with her answer, Rob pressed for more. "When will that be?"

"Hopefully I'll be back in a day or two. It'll depend on the weather."

"You're the best, sis."

You're a pushover, Kate's evil twin whispered.

She was exhausted—that's what she was.

Amanda muttered a curse as she disconnected the call and flopped back on the cushions. Her brother might as well have asked for a million bucks, because that crazy sum would be as easy to come up with as the twenty thousand. Her financial well had run dry. The ATM was out of service and the sooner Rob understood that, the better.

Chapter Five

Amanda pulled a worn spiral notebook from her tote bag and flipped to the dog-eared page with her budget. Then she sank back into the sofa cushions, waggling her pen as she scrutinized each line item entry. It wasn't necessary. She already knew the contents by heart. But for some inexplicable reason, she obsessively reviewed her catalogue of debts several times a day—as if by doing so, she'd magically discover a way to make them disappear. So far she hadn't.

Her bills consumed every last penny of her income, which made saving impossible. Her 401K was zilch, she'd maxed out every credit card with cash advances and her meager rainy day account had long since been drained. She'd even taken out a second mortgage on her new condominium. Despite her generous salary—and even with her recent promotion—the money she'd given Rob had wiped her out.

She glared at the page. She detested every single line and number on it; hated anything that made her feel helpless and vulnerable and out of control. But for some reason, no matter how many times she promised herself differently, she found viewing the list of bills impossible to resist.

In a sudden act of rebellion, Amanda ripped the page from the notebook with flourish, wadded it into a tiny little ball and tossed it into the fire. A smile touched her lips as the flames surrounded it, licking at it and turning the edges bright orange just before it transformed into ashes. If only she could make her debts disappear as fast.

She sat up straight and threw back her shoulders. It was time to get creative.

Amanda stared at the blank page for what seemed an eternity, clicking the pen in and out. She solved multimillion dollar brand strategy problems for a living and she didn't owe anywhere near that amount, thank God. She just needed to come up with a measly hundred thousand. Okay, maybe measly was stretching it a bit, but how hard could it be? She just needed to list out all her options for making extra money, evaluate the pros and cons, pick one and then go.

She bit her lip and racked her brain. She knew how to wait tables. That was a great option for a second job. Amanda scribbled it on her pad. She'd waited tables all through college, graduating to a gig as a cocktail waitress as soon as she turned twenty one. The higher tips had come in handy, especially since the job had been her primary means of supporting Rob after her parents died. There'd been a modest life insurance policy; just enough to pay for her brother's college education and supplement their income for the first several years until her career started to take off. Scholarships and loans had funded her own college tuition and her waitress job had helped pay for the apartment and food.

If she worked at the right place, even six months could help her power down some bills. Granted, her skills were a little rusty, but schlepping a tray with drinks was probably a lot like riding a bike. It would come back to her.

Maybe Rob could hire her once his restaurant opened. After all, she'd helped fund the damned thing. Employing her seemed the least he could do since she knew he'd never actually pay her back. Despite her foul mood, Amanda giggled as she imagined her irresponsible brother as her part-time employer.

Her laughter died away. It was impossible. Not only would she be tempted to kill Rob—which, given his status as her last living relative, she'd rather not do—the truth was her day job didn't allow her the flexibility. On a good day she worked ten hours, many days went longer and between the long hours, last minute client catastrophes and frequent travel, a night job seemed next to impossible.

Amanda waggled the pen. This little brainstorm session wasn't going very well. She couldn't even come up with another viable option beyond waiting tables, which she'd already deemed impossible. She couldn't do retail either as it would require too many hours and she'd never earn the kind of money she needed to pay off her six figure debt. She could always go for Jake's fake engagement idea. After all, he had told her to name her price, so clearly he was as desperate as she. But would he be willing to fork over a hundred grand?

Her cell buzzed.

She glanced at the display and pressed the button to connect. "Hi."

"You said you'd call with an update," Kate said.

"It's only been"—Amanda checked her watch—"an hour and a half."

"A lot can happen in ninety minutes."

Amanda set the notebook in her lap and sighed. "A lot did happen, I guess. The electricity went out. I helped Jake haul wood to the porch and, in the process, I nearly broke my ankle."

"I don't feel the teensiest bit sorry for you," Kate said, her sugary Alabama drawl enlarged her haughty tone. "Girls aren't supposed to carry wood."

Amanda rolled her eyes and tapped the pen on her notebook. "I must have missed the memo. Be sure to include me in the distribution next time."

"All women know this," Kate sniffed.

"Now you sound like Jake. But you might be right. I think I ruined my boots." And given her money situation, she couldn't afford to replace them. The thought made her even crankier.

"Amanda Wilson, do *not* tell me you traipsed through the snow in your new Stuart Weitzman boots—the ones with those cute little kitten heels."

"You always say my full name when you're pissed," Amanda said.

"And in case you wondered, it's super-irritating. Yes, if you must know, my boots are toast."

Kate groaned. "Amandaaaaaa. I could just *kill* you. I planned to borrow those next week."

"Buy your own damned boots," Amanda didn't bother to mask her irritation. It was barely ten thirty and in her view, she'd filled her quota of lectures for the day. "I need to discuss something important."

"What's going on?"

Amanda paused briefly to consider the wisdom of confiding in her friend. When the topic concerned her brother, the conversation tended not to go well. Kate's opinions of her brother had been formed early; in those first few years after her parents died. They'd been college roommates and Rob had moved in with them. Her teenage brother had not only cramped their freewheeling lifestyle, but his presence had put Kate right in the middle of Amanda's colorful and often disastrous experiments in parenting. Ten years later, Kate showed no signs of changing her mind about Rob. Of course, his recent behavior hadn't helped. Kate knew all about the money she'd given Rob and if she found out he'd just asked for another twenty thousand, her head might pop off.

Still, Amanda needed to talk to somebody and as her BFF; it was Kate's job to listen. So she drew in a long, calming breath and blurted out, "My brother called." In the uncomfortably long silence that followed, Amanda experienced the first dull throbs of a headache.

"What did he want?" Kate's voice sounded wary.

Amanda's grip on the phone tightened. She should've kept her mouth shut. But she hadn't, so she forced herself to say, "Twenty thousand."

Kate gasped. "*Dollars?*"

"No nickels," Amanda said with an exaggerated sigh. "Of *course*, dollars."

After an inordinately long pause, Kate started in, her uncharacteristically sarcastic tone making her words all the more effective. "So, after you issued your authoritative no, which of course you *always* do with your bother, *then* what happened?"

The dull throbbing ache in her temples bloomed into sharp, stabbing pain which settled behind her eyes. She needed to lie down. Amanda shifted the frozen peas from her ankle to her forehead and then rested her head on the arm of the sofa as she contemplated which body part hurt worse.

"I *did* tell him no," Amanda said. But her voice sounded decidedly more tentative as she added, "Sort of."

"Sort of," Kate repeated.

Amanda pressed the peas against her forehead and burrowed further into the cushions as she said, "I said no, but...well, you know how he is."

"Yes. I *do* know." Kate's tone signaled the return of the steel magnolia. "And I know how *you* are."

"How I am?"

"Yes. You're usually all independent and tough—or at least, you pretend to be. But when it comes to your brother, you're confused and wishy-washy," Kate said, sounding exasperated. "I don't get how someone as practical and responsible as you can be so incredibly naïve where your brother's concerned."

Probably for the same reason she bought every over-hyped cosmetics product she ran across. Like the Tahiti in a Bottle crap upstairs. When she thought of the amount she'd paid for the over-priced shower gel, her blood pressure rose. Still, she wasn't going to give Kate the satisfaction of thinking she was right. "I'm not confused or wishy-washy."

"Oh, please. You're talking to me and this brother thing has gone on for a *very* long time."

"What brother thing?" She made a silent vow to never confide to Kate about her brother ever, *ever* again. It wasn't worth it. Well, she probably would, but not for a very long time.

"Your brother wants money, or anything else, and he gets it—no matter the cost to you." Kate kicked the know-it-all tone up a notch as she added, "I'll bet you've got that raggedy old notebook and pen out right now, trying to figure out a way to find the money to give him."

Amanda frowned and glanced from the notebook to the pen. She pulled the phone away from her ear and stuck out her tongue and then pretended to pound the device into the sofa cushions. She should have known she'd get the lecture; she'd certainly heard it often enough.

When she put the phone back to her ear, she caught Kate mid diatribe, her sermon progressing in its normal track as Kate was saying, "...and the real problem is you continually ask yourself the wrong question. You try to figure out what your parents would do to support Rob. But the truth is, at this stage of the game, your parents *wouldn't* help him."

Amanda felt compelled to jump in. "If my parents hadn't died—"

Kate's voice grew louder. "If your parents hadn't died, they'd give your brother the kick in the patootie he needs and maybe he'd *finally* grow up."

She paused and then said, "I'm guessing patootie is Alabaman for ass."

"Not funny. You know I'm right."

Amanda knew no such thing. "You're wrong. My parents would support Rob's dreams, which is all I'm doing," Amanda said.

Kate made an exasperated sound. "You're *not* supporting Rob's dreams."

"Yes I am. Listen, I'll admit I'm not a model parent, but I'm doing the best I can. Plus, I'm all he has."

"Yes and because of that, he takes advantage of you," Kate said and then she raised her voice with each word she said next. "Now—and I'm saying this with love—stop...being...a...*pushover*!"

"Stop yelling," Amanda said. "You're making my head hurt."

"No. Your *bad decisions* are making your head hurt," Kate continued at a slightly-lower decibel. "Promise you'll tell him no."

Amanda pursed her lips and tried to decide if she could make such a promise.

Kate's voice took on her commander-in-chief edge as she said, "Promise me."

"I promise I'll consider it," Amanda hedged.

Kate sighed and sounded weary as she said, "We both know what consider means." She paused briefly. "Okay, where would you get the money?"

"I was just thinking that maybe I should agree to Jake's deal. I mean, it's only a *fake* engagement, right?"

"No! I suggested you go agree to his deal so you could get money to pay off *your* debts; not get more money to give to *Rob*."

"Maybe it's a way to do both."

Kate groaned. "But you shouldn't *do* both! I swear; you just don't get it. Promise you won't do anything until we have a chance to talk through your options in person."

Tired of the conversation, Amanda said what she knew her friend wanted to hear. "I promise." But in truth, she didn't have any intention of waiting. She would think it through and then she'd move forward in whatever manner she deemed best, just as she always did. And in all matters—except those involving her brother—the approach tended to work well.

It's not like she had a ton of options. At this point, Jake's proposal appeared to be her most immediate—if not only—path to zero debt.

The bedroom door opened upstairs.

"He's coming," Amanda whispered as Jake jogged down the steps. "I have to go. Call you later." She hung up just as Jake appeared beside her.

"What's wrong with your head?" He gestured to the peas lying on her forehead.

She sat up, thrust her leg onto the ottoman and moved the bag from her forehead to her ankle. "I have a headache," she mumbled.

"Need some aspirin?"

She shook her head.

Jake dropped into the chair across from her. "The snow stopped."

"Can we leave now?" She sat up straighter and the surge of hope Jake's words brought magically healed her throbbing headache.

"I think we have to. We'll run out of wood and food in the next few days and if it gets any colder, the snow will turn to ice and if that happens,"—he spread his arms wide and shrugged—"who knows how long we'll be stuck here."

Amanda didn't need to hear anything more. She shot off the couch, wincing as pain radiated from her ankle to her thigh, but she pushed through it and hobbled determinedly toward the stairs. "Let's go."

Even if they ended up in a ditch again, eventually they'd get pulled out, at which point she could find a hotel room. She wished she'd thought of that yesterday because if she had, they wouldn't have been stuck here together last night, he wouldn't have proposed and for the past hour she wouldn't have been sitting there actually considering such a ludicrous idea. Jake's engagement idea equated to sheer lunacy and she needed to get the hell out of here while she still possessed a shred of sanity and before she did something stupid, like agree to go along with it.

"The body shop called. My Escalade checks out, so we'll swing by to pick it up and then we'll head back to Chicago."

An hour later, Amanda waited in the driver's seat as Jake locked the front door. Then he jogged down the steps and slid into the passenger seat. After securing his seat belt, he pulled a slip of paper from his jacket and referred to it as he punched an address into the car's GPS system.

She didn't bother telling him the Garmin didn't work out here in the boonies. As the device tried to plot their course, Amanda put the car in drive and took off. She poked along the snow-packed country roads; her fingers gripping the steering wheel so hard, her knuckles turned white.

"Can you pick it up a little?" Jake sounded exasperated as he cast a sideways glance at her. "I think we could walk to town faster."

She kept her eyes glued to the road. "At least this way, we'll stay out of the ditch."

Out of the corner of her eye, she saw him shake his head and he turned to gaze out the window. They didn't speak for the rest of the trip. Twenty minutes later, they pulled into the parking lot of Al's Body Shop.

"This won't take long." Jake got out and zipped up his leather jacket as he strode toward the blue concrete building.

The tailored fit of his jacket emphasized his broad shoulders and lean hips and Amanda's eyes were glued to him until he disappeared through the doors. Then she turned and gazed out at the mounds of melting brown, rock-encrusted snow as her thoughts drifted to his proposal. Could it be the solution she'd gone there to find? Or would it create a whole slew of new problems? It was hard to imagine having more problems at this point, but anything was possible—especially when it involved Jake Lowell.

Name your price, he'd said. He hadn't even bothered to hide the twinge of desperation in his voice. So he must be in a pickle as well. But was he desperate enough to pay her a hundred grand? Because anything less wouldn't be worth the emotional price she'd surely pay.

Amanda rested her head on the seat and examined her peeling nail polish. She needed a manicure. But more than that, she really wanted to be out from under all this debt. It would feel pretty sweet. Not exactly the full on do-over she'd fantasized about on the way to the cabin, but pretty damn close.

On the downside, the only path to zero debt seemed to lead through Jake, which made it an incredibly risky proposition. A fake engagement with Jake sounded brutal, even in theory. The reality would probably be closer to emotional Armageddon. All things considered, she might be better off with the debt.

Still, she couldn't let go of her financial fantasy. What if she asked for *two* hundred grand? Zero debt and a hundred thousand in the bank. That level of financial security might make the inevitable emotional devastation worthwhile.

Holy crap, it's hot in here. Amanda shrugged off her coat and turned the dial to lower the heat. Hoping for a distraction, she pressed the radio button and cranked the dial to tune in her favorite station. She tapped her fingers on the steering wheel in time with her favorite Nelly tune.

Jake emerged from the building and she watched as he jogged

to his SUV. She sighed. In the year he'd been gone she had almost forgotten how gorgeous he was; almost.

Kanye West's Gold-Digger came on as Jake climbed into his Escalade. The lyrics caught her attention and she frowned as Jamie Foxx finished crooning the opening '*Oh she's a gold-digger, way over top that digs on me.*' A gold-digger.

Amanda straightened her spine and snapped off the radio. Just because she was considering Jake's deal, it didn't make her a gold-digger. This was just business. Well, business with a little heart-break and mental torture thrown in for good measure. And business that would require her to lie to pretty much everyone she knew in exchange for money. Which was technically the definition of a gold-digger, right?

Oh, who gives a crap. I'll worry about it later.

Jake pulled out of the parking lot and Amanda put the car in drive and followed him. Thank God she was headed home. After just a day in his company, she was clearly losing it.

The main roads appeared in much better shape than those near the cabin had been and, as they hit the highway, they were able to travel at close to normal speed.

A red sports car shot past with what looked like two twenty some-thing guys inside. Its back window displayed a sticker which read *No Fear*. Amanda pursed her lips and contemplated the phrase as her gaze shifted from the sticker to Jake's silhouette in the SUV ahead.

In a sudden flash of clarity, she knew what she needed to do. While there might be many ways to solve her money problems, none offered as quick or as total a solution as Jake's deal. As Kate had said, the universe delivered this way on a silver platter. Now, she needed to follow the signs, walk through the door; to show no fear.

Before she could over-think her decision—as she typically did with everything but her brother or beauty products—Amanda picked up her cell and punched in Jake's number.

She saw him glance in the rearview mirror as he said, "Everything okay?" Concern was evident in his tone.

Amanda mustered every available iota of courage and then said, "I've been thinking about your proposal."

"Really," he said, his concern morphed into surprise.

Amanda flung the words out before fear or good sense could stop her. "I'll do it, but it'll cost you."

Chapter Six

Jake settled into his favorite corner booth in Lou Mitchell's and gazed broodingly out the window. A steady stream of bundled-up pedestrians scurried past, but they didn't register. He was too busy trying to figure out the reason behind Amanda's sudden and illogical change of heart. He'd thought of nothing else for the past twelve hours; had examined it from every conceivable angle and still couldn't make sense of it. So before things proceeded any further, he intended to get to the bottom of it. Hence, the early morning breakfast meeting.

Amanda limped up to the table. "Sorry I'm late." She shrugged off her coat and slid into the booth. Her cheeks glowed from the brisk November wind, which emphasized the light sprinkling of freckles across her nose and cheeks.

He picked up the menu and pretended to study it, trying to ignore how cute she looked. "You're still limping. How's your ankle?"

"A little better. Still hurts, though." Amanda blew on her hands and then rubbed them together. "I need coffee. It's *fareeezing* out there!"

Jake smiled at her dramatic emphasis of the word and resisted an urge to nestle her hands between his the way he used to do. Instead, he set the menu on the table and lifted a hand to signal the waitress. She hustled over, filled their coffee mugs and took their order.

Jake blew on his brew and watched Amanda doctor hers.

While in Iraq, he had replayed this image over and over whenever he wanted something pleasant to think about—something more enticing than watching a bunch of filthy guys guzzle their food. She performed the task with the precision of a brain surgeon, as though life itself would cease to exist if she failed to get the taste balance just right.

Jake swigged his black coffee, in part to hide his grin.

Oblivious of his scrutiny, Amanda tasted the mixture, made a face, added a dash more cream and stirred.

His grin widened.

She tasted it again and smiled. Satisfied, she set the mug aside and pulled a piece of paper from her purse. She scanned the contents and then slid the note across the table. "We didn't have a chance to discuss the details before, so I took some time to think through my terms."

"You weren't exactly open to the idea when I first brought it up." His eyes searched her face for a clue as to what might have changed her mind.

She looked down and cradled the steaming brew with both hands. "True."

Jake studied the note and then set it aside. "Looks like you've thought it all through."

"I have."

He leaned back against the booth and studied her face. Unable to discern anything from her calm demeanor, he took a swig of coffee in part to hide his consternation and then said, "Before we get into the details, I need to know what changed your mind."

She shrugged. "Does it matter?"

"It does to me."

She studied his face and then her lips curved up. "You're worried I'll back out."

"Maybe," Jake said as his thumb tapped the table. "You've done a complete about face and for no apparent reason. You might decide to do so in the middle of our game and I can't risk that happening. I have too much riding on this. I have to know you're serious; that you'll hang in with me."

She arched a brow. "This is a game to you?"

"No. It's a game to my grandfather," he said. "Everything is. For me, this is about as real as it gets. My entire business future hangs in the balance."

She sniffed. "I won't back out. If we can come to terms, I'll see our agreement through to the end. You have my word."

She said that now, but when the situation got difficult—as he suspected it would—she might try to back out. After all, there seemed no good reason for her to agree to the deal in the first place. At least no reason he could see and he needed to ensure his partner in crime committed as whole-heartedly as he.

"I'm not thrilled about lying to Max. You know how much I care for him." She paused and then shrugged. "But the way I see it, the trust fund technically belongs to you. So we're really not taking anything you wouldn't already get. We're just speeding it up a little."

"Your reasoning is great, but it's about me. I need to know why *you'd* agree to go through with this. What changed your mind? You said Paris isn't important to you anymore and yet you've asked for a year in Paris. You don't need money, but you say you want cash."

She tucked a few strands behind her ear and looked down at her plate. "Actually, I *do* need the money."

His suspicions increased. "Why? Kate said you got a promotion."

"Why I need the money is none of your concern,"—she traced her index finger along the rim of the mug.

"It is my concern. I have to know you're committed."

She sighed. "Fine. If you must know, Rob is opening a restaurant and I need the cash from this deal to help him out. And, after I thought about it a little more, I realized Paris is important. You were right. It's a second chance to live a lifelong fantasy. I can't pass that up."

He should've known her reason had something to do with Rob. She'd always been a pushover when it came to her brother.

Before he could respond, the waitress arrived with two plates of eggs and bacon and an order of fresh banana pancakes for Jake.

Jake poured maple syrup onto his plate. "So you've got some skin in the game, too." At least there was a logical reason for her change of heart and it provided a small degree of confidence that she'd see their agreement through till the end.

"I do."

Satisfied, Jake turned his attention to his food. Since he'd only been back from Iraq a few days, every meal tasted like a Thanksgiving feast. He inhaled the heady aroma of eggs and bacon and maple syrup. Then he picked up his fork and dug in.

He'd almost cleaned his plate before he glanced up and noticed Amanda wasn't eating. He watched her as she pushed the eggs around her plate. He swallowed a mouthful of pancakes and speared another generous portion as he said, "Aren't you hungry?"

Amanda set down her silverware, picked up her napkin and dabbed at the corner of her mouth. "I want to get this settled. Are you okay with my terms?"

He swallowed another huge mouthful. "The year in Paris plus two hundred grand seems fair since you'll have to put your life on hold while our deal plays out. Who knows? If things get intense enough, you may even need some time off from that crazy job of yours."

She shook her head, causing her hair to toss back and forth. "I can't take time off work."

He shrugged. "You may have to. We'll see how it goes. I mean, this is a fake engagement, but only we know about the fake part. And knowing my grandfather, this thing is sure to come packed with parties and pretend wedding planning and God only knows what else. Once our charade starts, I'm guessing it'll be fast and furious." Jake pushed his plate away and leaned back. "This deal is more than generous, so you'll be able to afford to take off if you need to."

"Monetarily, maybe," she said, as her brow furrowed. "But there are other things to consider."

"Like?"

"Like my future career, which I can't afford to ruin just because of this deal. I'm not starting a business like you. I work for other people, remember?"

He regarded her for a long moment and then said, "I thought you wanted to do your own thing someday." His eyes searched her face. "Has something changed?"

"I do. I will. I'm just not ready to follow through on the idea yet."

He pushed his plate away. "We can deal with your job situation later. I want to discuss a few other things before we leave."

She narrowed her eyes and squared her shoulders as if readying for a fight.

Jake raised his index finger. "You need to sign a contract." He wasn't about to give her an out. If she was in, he wanted to ensure she stayed in.

"Okay." She crossed her legs and regarded him with a healthy dose of suspicion, as if she wasn't quite sure what he'd say next.

He raised a second finger. "The agreement will include an iron-clad confidentiality clause. My grandfather can't *ever* know the truth."

"Of course," she said. "I don't want word of this arrangement to get out either."

His eyes narrowed. "Be honest. Have you told Kate?"

Amanda shifted uncomfortably and started to fiddle with her napkin.

"So...I'm guessing that means yes. And if Kate knows, then Sam does too." He shook his head. "I'll have to put the fear of God into them."

"They won't tell anyone. You're paranoid."

He'd make sure they wouldn't. He planned to head over to Sam's place right after he finished here. He wasn't about to take any chances. He pointed at her. "You can't tell anyone else and that includes your brother."

She rolled her eyes. "Calm down Paranoid Pete." She stood and extended a hand. "So it's a deal?"

"Deal." As his fingers gripped her soft skin, he felt an undeniable sizzle of energy. He pulled his hand away, trying to ignore the tingle of awareness that lingered. He'd thought the months away had cured him of the instant turn-on of her touch. But a year seemed an eternity in a place like Iraq and it must have been harder on him than he realized. Jake cleared his throat. "Sam will draw up the papers and I'll stop by in a few days so we can sign them and get this baby rolling."

"Sounds good." She stood and slipped on her coat. "Thanks for breakfast."

Jake threw enough cash on the table to cover the bill and resisted the urge to take her elbow as she limped along in front of him. He didn't because he knew she'd just push him away and she'd probably give him an earful. But he still held the door open for her as they walked outside.

After they said their goodbyes on the sidewalk, Jake strode to his SUV. He pulled out of the parking space, turned right at the corner and poked along through late morning traffic, headed toward Lincoln Park.

* * *

He circled Sam's block twice before he found a parking space. He maneuvered into the tiny spot, and climbed out. Then he jogged up the stone steps, leading to Sam and Kate's townhouse and rang the bell.

Sam flung the door open, grinning ear to ear. "Hey bud. I still can't believe you're back."

"You have a few minutes?"

Sam stepped back to let him inside. "I'm about to head to the gym. You up for a workout?"

"I went earlier. This won't take long." Jake looked around. "Is Kate here?

Sam shook his head. "She's at prenatal yoga; won't be back for an hour." He headed to the kitchen. "Coffee?"

"Sure." Jake pulled out a barstool, straddling it as he sat down.

Sam poured a cup of Kate's fancy brew and pushed it toward Jake.

"According to Kate, it's been a wild few days."

Jake snorted. "I hadn't noticed."

Sam raised a brow. "Tell me I heard wrong. Tell me you don't plan to pay Amanda to fake an engagement."

Jake scowled. "I figured Kate would tell you."

"Of course she told me. She actually thinks it's a good idea because it'll help Amanda with her financial issues. I'm the one who think it's insane."

"Financial issues. You mean the loan to her brother?" Jake swigged his coffee.

"You say that like there's one loan. Make it plural and not a loan and you're closer to the truth. The kid's a vampire; he's sucked her bank account dry."

Jake set his mug down and frowned. "How much has she given him?"

"According to Kate, it's about a hundred grand and he just asked for twenty thousand more."

Jake nearly swallowed his tongue. "*What*?" He finally understood why she agreed to the deal. That kind of debt would be a strong motivator for anyone. He didn't know whether to feel relieved that she'd stick to their agreement or pissed that Rob had taken such advantage of her.

"I know. So back to the issue of your insanity," Sam said. "I get why she'd do it given her situation. What I don't understand is why you'd ask her."

Jake shrugged. "The engagement has to look real or Max will never go for it. I've only been back four days; do you think Max would actually believe I met and fell in love with someone else?"

"Probably not," Sam conceded.

"It'll be easier to convince him we got back together. Besides, you know how much he's always liked her."

Sam nodded. "And I know you're still hung up on her."

"Bullshit. I got over her a year ago."

"Uh-huh." Sam swigged his coffee.

"It's why this deal makes so much sense," Jake said. "No emotional messiness."

Sam cast a sideways glance at Jake. "I say it'll be messiness central."

"You think it's not over between us."

Sam shrugged. "An observation."

"You're wrong. It's over. Trust me. Has been for a long time."

Sam set down his mug and rested his forearms on the counter, his eyes laser-focused on Jake. "Dude, that's a load of crap I suggest you try selling to someone else. I say you're headed for trouble."

"It's a business arrangement."

Sam smirked. "Yeah, right."

"That's why I'm here. I need you to draw up the contract."

"You think she'll try to back out?"

"She might. I can't risk it."

Sam shook his head. "You should be the one backing out. After the way you ended things, I don't see this engagement sham headed anywhere this side of sane."

Jake frowned. "Did I ask your advice?"

"No, you asked me for legal assistance and as your attorney, I provided some unsolicited but eminently-wise counsel. Consider it a bonus."

"You're not my attorney. You're my friend who happens to *be* an attorney, which is the whole point. I don't want the family lawyer involved."

"Okay, here's some advice from a friend. If you really need to fake an engagement, ask someone else. She may agree to it because she needs the cash, but if you follow through with this bone-headed plan, I think it'll be like watching a car crash in slow motion."

Jake pushed his mug away and stood. "Thanks for the vote of confidence." He glared at Sam as he grabbed his jacket off the back of a chair and headed for the door.

Sam trailed behind. "Just trying to help."

Jake turned and looked Sam in the eye. "Then stop with the advice and call me when the contract is done."

Sam waved his hands in mock surrender. "Sure dude. It's your funeral."

"There's one other thing. Can you do some recon and find out what Rob's up to? I'd do it myself but it would look suspicious," Jake said. "I don't trust that kid and based on what you told me about the money, it's with good reason. Something's going on and I want to find out what it is."

"That's the first thing we've agreed on since you walked in the door."

Jake flipped up his coat collar and walked outside. "Later."

As he jogged down the steps, he heard Sam mutter something about oil and water and absolute insanity before he shut the door.

Jake grinned. What did Sam know anyway?

* * *

Amanda glanced at her watch; ten more minutes. She filled her wine glass, tipped it back and swallowed half. Then she set the glass on the counter, picked up her phone and punched in Kate's number. She tapped a French-tipped fingernail on the counter as she waited.

Kate answered, but as usual, she didn't bother with the standard greeting. She got right to the point. "Is he there yet?"

"Any minute," Amanda said. "Tell me this is a good idea."

"It's a great idea." Kate's thick southern drawl soothed Amanda's raw nerves.

"Tell me it'll be okay." Her hand shook as she tipped the glass to her lips and swallowed more wine.

"It'll be okay. It *really* will. I promise," Kate said. "Have some wine."

Amanda picked up the wine glass. "Way ahead of you."

"Before you know it, you'll be out of debt and strolling through the streets of Paris, living large and looking *fab…u…lous.*" Kate sang the last word.

Despite her nervous stomach, Amanda smiled. She couldn't recall the last time she'd dreamed of living large, or looking fabulous for that matter. Her thoughts drifted to Paris. She'd fantasized about a year abroad since childhood—it was a dream her mother had placed in her heart. She'd given up on the dream when her parents died and hadn't even thought of it in several years.

She sipped at her wine as memories of her mother drifted back. The way she'd perched on the edge of her bed and told romantic tales of the magical city where she'd met Amanda's father. Those stories had fueled her girlish fantasies and she'd been convinced her real-life prince would be there waiting for her, just as her mother's had been. Unfortunately, the dream had died along with her parents, which made it all the more exciting to once again have it within her reach. It made her feel closer to her mother, to both her parents.

"This is your chance for a total life do-over," Kate said.

A do-over; it's *exactly* what she'd wanted from her stay at the cabin. Maybe her weekend catastrophe hadn't been such a bad idea after all, though her ankle still hurt a bit.

She started to feel calmer and then the doorbell rang.

A swarm of internal butterflies took flight. "He's here!" Amanda clutched the phone.

"Breathe," Kate said. "And repeat after me: I can do this."

"I can do this," Amanda said, sounding decidedly less confident than Kate. She swallowed more wine. "But *why* am I doing this?"

"So you can get back to your old, fabulous self," Kate said, her tone pure Alabama steel, which made it clear she'd entertain no more weakness. "Now, suck it up and go!"

She hung up. Old, fabulous self, she thought, with the emphasis on old. Turning thirty sucked.

Amanda had long forgotten the deal she'd made with her maker while at the cabin and was back to her constant complaints and obsessions about her thirtieth birthday. Only twenty-four dismal days left before she'd have to accept the fact that she'd achieved very few items on her By Thirty List. On the bright side, her total lack of accomplishment made the development of her By Forty List quite easy. She'd just change the header.

The doorbell buzzed again. "Just a minute," she shouted. Then she drained her glass, set it on the counter and wiped her sweaty palms on her black wool pencil skirt as she walked to the door, repeating *I can do this,* over and over again.

She paused for a moment to gather her nerve, then threw her shoulders back and plastered a fake smile on her face as she opened the door. "Come in," she said, trying to exude a confidence she didn't feel.

Jake stepped inside. "Just get home?"

She nodded.

"Nice place," he said, as he glanced around. "When did you buy it?"

"Eight months ago."

He smiled. "It looks like you."

Her gaze followed his. She recalled the minimalist design of his townhouse and figured his comment meant her decor looked fussy and girly. "Thank you, I think," she said. "Kate helped me."

"It was a compliment." He pointed to his briefcase. "Where do you want to do this?"

Amanda gestured toward the sofa. "We'll be more comfortable in there. Wine?"

"Sure, unless you have something stronger."

"Sorry, all I have is Chardonnay."

"Then make it a double."

She poured Jake his double, fixed herself a fresh glass and carried them into the living room. As she leaned over to hand Jake his wine, his spicy, woodsy scent enveloped her in man and memories. She backed away and settled on the loveseat across from him, which was as far away as she could get and still be in the same room.

Jake removed a stack of papers from the briefcase, set them on the table and tapped them. "Why don't you take a few minutes to read through these?"

She slid the papers toward her as Jake tipped his glass back and swallowed a good amount of wine. She smiled. "Nervous?"

"As any sane person would be," he drawled.

"Good to know I'm sane." She looked at the first sheet and then leafed through a few other pages but the words blurred together. She laid the papers on the table and picked up her wine. "Can you just cover the high points?"

"Sure." He cleared his throat. "Most importantly, the agreement has no expiration date. Our engagement will continue for three months *after* I get access to the trust fund. Then, we'll stage a break-up. But I warn you; I don't know how long it'll take for this charade to play out. Hopefully, for both our sakes, it'll be quick."

"Why do we have to wait for three months before we break up?"

"So my grandfather won't get suspicious. It would look bad if I got the money and we broke up the next day."

"True. What else?"

He pulled an envelope out of his briefcase and tossed it on the table.

"What's that?"

"An advance," he leaned back and watched her. "You'll get the rest after the break-up."

Her eyes shifted from Jake to the envelope and her pulse raced. It was all she could do not to snatch the envelope off the table and rip it open. Instead, she calmly reached for it, but her finger trembled ever so slightly as she slid it the under the flap. When she saw the amount, she couldn't stop her sharp intake of breath and her free hand flew to her throat as she said, "This is a hundred thousand dollars!"

"Fifty percent upfront seemed fair," he said, looking like he was fighting the urge to smile.

It was all she could do not to leap onto the coffee table and dance a little victory jig. Instead, she maintained her boardroom-cool façade and slid the check back into the envelope. But her voice sounded a little shaky as she said, "Thank you, Jake."

"You'll earn it, trust me. You have to deal with me and my grand-father for God only knows how long and that's something I wouldn't wish on anyone," he said with a grimace.

She smiled and inclined her head.

"Finally, there's the confidentiality agreement. Sam and Kate are in the loop but I don't want anyone else to know. If word gets out, you'll have to repay me in full."

"I promise." She wasn't worried about the confidentiality clause. She didn't want anyone to know about their deal either.

"That's it. As soon as you sign, our agreement is official."

She pulled the papers toward her. Jake handed her a pen and then leaned back to watch. Amanda initialed the bottom of each sheet, signed the last page and then pushed the stack toward Jake. He initialed and signed on the lines next to her. When he finished, he slid the agreement back into the manila envelope, placed it in his briefcase and snapped the clasps closed.

He finished the last of his wine and stood. "Are you available for dinner tomorrow? I'll call Max in the morning to break the news. I'm sure he'll want to see you."

"Of course," she said, trying to sound composed as a sense of dread settled over her. Their agreement had just started and it was already getting a little too real.

"Good. I'll pick you up at seven."

She closed the door behind him and collapsed against it, her eyes drawn to the white envelope lying on the table. The fat check nestled inside would solve all her financial problems. She'd already decided that, first thing tomorrow, she would pay off her debts. Given her money struggles, she should feel excited, exhilarated even. But instead, all she felt was a sense of impending doom which wasn't surprising considering she'd just made a deal with the devil.

Chapter Seven

Amanda studied her reflection in the mirror and smiled. She looked pretty good. Of course, she was wearing her go-to dress, the little black number she pulled out whenever she needed an extra shot of confidence. Which tonight, she could certainly use. The dress hugged her curves where it mattered and hid all the curves that didn't. Best of all, it visually shaved off a good ten pounds, even without the help of Spanx.

She smoothed her hands down the front and tugged at the hem. Then she reached into the closet and pulled out her black platform pumps, slipped her lip gloss and keys into her black evening bag and clipped on a pair of silver hoops.

The doorbell rang.

Her stomach fluttered. Still, she felt calmer than she had anticipated, but as she opened the door, her breath caught in her throat. "Hey," she said. Typically a jeans guy, tonight Jake wore a dark gray suit that looked custom-fit to his tall, athletic body. The crisp white shirt popped against his sapphire tie and the combination emphasized his bronzed skin and impossibly blue eyes.

"You look sensational." Jake's eyes slid down her body.

She blushed. "Thanks." *Remember, this isn't for real. Don't fall for him again.* This was a high stakes game of make-believe and she had been extremely well-compensated for her part. She reached for her coat and in as business-like a voice as she could muster, said, "Are we ready?"

"Hang on." Jake pulled a turquoise-colored ring box from his jacket and thrust it toward her.

Amanda froze and stared at it. She had hoped for—no *expected*—a ring the night he dumped her. The break-up had been a harsh gesture on the eve of her twenty-ninth birthday and marked the end to a year-long fantasy in which she'd allowed herself to believe her dreams could come true. She should have known better.

As she gazed at the box now, memories of the break-up rushed back. A night spent in a darkened bedroom with Kate, two bottles of wine and three boxes of Puffs Plus. She'd emerged the next morning with a massive hangover, a bright red nose and a shattered heart. And nearly a year later, she still wasn't over it.

"Take it." Jake shook the box, the look on his face made it clear he preferred to rid himself of the offending item as soon as possible.

Of course he did. A Tiffany box bearing an engagement ring would be sacrilege to a man like Jake. If the box hadn't dredged up so many bad memories, the horrified expression on his face might have spurred a fit of giggles. When she still didn't reach for the box, Jake grabbed her hand and plopped it in her palm.

Relief permeated every aspect of his being.

As Amanda's gaze moved from Jake's relieved expression to the turquoise box, she was forced to deal with the first tangible evidence of their agreement. She must have lost her mind. Seriously. Why else would she have agreed to fake an engagement with Jake? Sure, she needed the money and now she had it, but what had possessed her to think she could pretend to be engaged; pretend she no longer felt anything for the man she had hoped to marry one day.

She could still back out. Maybe. She bit her lip and tried to remember if their contract included an out clause. As her eyes drifted to his face, she swallowed hard and searched for the right words to say to him.

"Open it," he said, back to his normal cool, relaxed demeanor. He seemed completely unaware of her inner turmoil.

She looked down at the box, in part to conceal her anguish as she said, "Jake, I...do we have to—" She glanced up at him and held it out, willing him to take it as her eyes pleaded with him to understand.

"If we want this to look real, we do." His expression made it clear he'd broach no arguments. "Open it. Go on."

She drew in a long breath and opened the box to reveal the largest, most ostentatious diamond ring she'd ever seen. "Jake! This is too... too over the top for this thing we're doing."

"It's necessary," Jake said. "My grandfather will expect a ring of this magnitude. Put it on."

She lifted the cushion-cut diamond ring from its velvet perch and slipped it on her finger. Then, she turned her hand and inspected the setting from different angles. Delicate pave stones embedded in platinum surrounded the oversized center diamond which appeared to be at least four carats. She based this estimate on Kate's ring, which equaled two and a half carats and wasn't nearly as large as this. The ring looked so completely outrageous; it actually seemed the perfect symbol of their engagement sham.

"It's a little much, don't you think?" She didn't know whether to grin at his audacity or cry at such an over-the-top mockery of her former hopes and dreams. "Besides, I thought you didn't have any money."

He shrugged.

She cleared her throat and tried to pretend it didn't bother her in the least. "I hope Tiffany's has a good return policy," she declared with a toss of her hair.

"It's on loan. In instances like this, being a Lowell comes in handy. Are you ready?"

She nodded, but she didn't feel ready. The unmistakable weight of heavy platinum encircled her finger like a noose, making her feel like she was being led to the gallows. Her jitters morphed into a mild case of nausea. She pressed a palm to her queasy stomach and briefly considered a dash to the bathroom. She might need to throw up.

"Are you okay?" Jake regarded her with concern. "You're white as a sheet."

She wasn't. But she nodded, because she didn't have any other choice but to be okay. She'd signed a contract and now, to use one of Kate's favorite phrases, it was time to put on her big girl stilettos.

This deal might be hard to contend with, but it would be worth the emotional price she might pay. Worth it because their agreement had delivered a financial freedom she feared might never come—at least not for a very long time. Now she wouldn't need to repay her debts over the next ten or twenty years. As of this morning, most of her debt was—as Kate would say—gone, pfft, finito. She just needed to fulfill her end of the bargain and deliver a world class performance tonight. And for her own sanity, she needed to keep her distance and not be seduced into thinking of Jake as anything more than her fake fiancé. They weren't the couple in love they'd once been, no matter what they portrayed to others. They weren't anything but business partners and she'd do well to remember that.

As they walked outside, Jake hailed a cab and a nearly-silent fifteen minutes later; the car pulled up in front of Max's Gold Coast condominium. They strolled across the lobby and into the elevator where Jake punched a code into the keypad. It whisked them to the sixtieth floor, where the bell sounded and the doors opened and they stepped into the travertine-tiled foyer of Maxwell Chesterfield Lowell's penthouse.

A butler took their coats and ushered them into the living room where a fire blazed and the soothing strains of classical music surrounded them. Beige silk draperies framed floor to ceiling windows that showcased the twinkling skyline of downtown Chicago.

"Nice digs, huh?" Jake spoke in an exaggerated whisper.

She elbowed him in the ribs. "*Behave* yourself."

Jake gestured broadly. "Believe it or not, I'd much rather be in a barracks in Iraq."

She expelled a long sigh. "Let's not start—"

"Amanda my dear, it's wonderful to see you." Maxwell Lowell's scotch and cigar-honed rasp preceded him into the room.

Here we go. Amanda smiled stiffly, hating to have to lie to him. "Hello Max."

Max reached for her hands and squeezed. "It's been far too long." He kissed each cheek and then stood back and beamed. "You look lovely." He cast a glance at Jake and then turned back to Amanda, his blue eyes twinkling. "I'm absolutely delighted my grandson finally came to his senses. I knew it would only be a matter of time. Lowell men never let the right woman slip from their grasp."

She laughed. But even to her own ears, it sounded forced. She hoped he didn't notice or if he did, chalked it up to nerves.

"Please make yourselves comfortable; dinner isn't quite ready." He tapped the sofa next to him. "Amanda, please sit near me."

She obliged.

A member of Max's staff took their drink order.

Max reached for her ring finger. "It's exquisite." His smile didn't quite reach his eyes as he turned to Jake. "I hoped...*thought*...you'd choose one of your grandmother's pieces."

Jake shook his head. "This ring is more Amanda's style."

It wasn't, but she kept the sentiment to herself. She would have chosen a classic, vintage style instead of the contemporary ring he'd selected and she would have absolutely adored wearing a piece from his grandmother's collection had their engagement been the real thing.

"Have you set a date?" Max's bright blue eyes danced.

Amanda glanced at Jake and then back at Max. "We haven't decided yet."

Max squeezed her hand. "Well don't let the decision linger, dear. In my experience, long engagements don't tend to work out very well."

The butler returned with their drinks.

"Actually, we do plan to have a long engagement," Jake said as he unbuttoned his jacket and settled into the chair across from them. "I need to get my business off the ground first."

Max shifted his gaze to Jake. "Since you're out of the Navy, I hoped you'd consider joining Lowell Media. I plan to retire soon and I'd like to pass leadership to you."

Amanda sipped her wine and noticed Jake tense. She tensed as well and hoped he wouldn't start an argument.

"I'm sure Uncle Leonard will handle the responsibility just fine." He tipped back his glass and swallowed a third of his scotch and soda.

"Your grandmother's brother isn't CEO material. Your father could have been if he'd put his mind to it. Unfortunately there were too many other distractions. You're different. I'd like to leave the company in your hands, Jacob."

Jake's jaw tightened. "We've discussed this more times than I can count."

Max sniffed. "You enjoyed your post as Naval Commander. This level of corporate leadership is really no different."

Jake swished his drink and the ice tinkled as it knocked against the leaded crystal. "I guess. Except it's not the Navy and it wouldn't be doing anything that matters."

Max lifted his chin. "Technology matters. It changes people's lives."

"Cable television does not change lives."

"We do more than cable TV. There's the Internet division, phone and we purchased a wireless company a few months ago. Communications is the future. If you took control, there's no telling where you could take the business. Our longer-term plans involve a satellite division and if you chose, you could even develop some military contracts."

Jake scoffed. "Lowell Media is about entertainment. My business is going to transform lives, families. It's going to make a difference. That's far more important; to me anyway."

Silence stretched between them as Max leaned back in his chair, steepled his fingers and tapped them as he regarded Jake. "Please, share your business plans."

"My business will help veterans rebuild their lives. VA benefits only go so far and actually, after the wars in Iraq and Afghanistan, they come up woefully short as it relates to mental health concerns. My business plan will reach well beyond veteran's programs so they can move forward."

Max inclined his head as considered Jake's words.

Amanda looked from one to the other. She wished she could kick off her shoes, curl her legs up and watch the two men work through their differences. So alike, they had the same erect posture and proud manner. And, on the downside, the same stubborn attitudes. Jake imagined himself nothing like his grandfather, when in reality he seemed cut from exactly the same cloth.

"Lowell Media has a foundation," Max said. "Perhaps we could fund—"

"No!" Jake jumped up, his fists clenched. He stormed halfway to the wall of windows before he calmed down. A few moments later, he returned to the sofa, once again in control, but his set jaw indicated he'd barely reigned in his emotions. "Thanks, but I plan to use outside investors. I have a meeting with the Rand Connelly's investment group on Monday. You know Rand. Sam's brother."

"Of course," Max said. And after a brief pause, he added, "You weren't planning to ask me." Regret and disappointment looked etched into his features.

Amanda glared at Jake. If he'd been closer, she would have whacked him in the shin so hard he wouldn't have walked for a week. Instead, her eyes locked on him like lasers, trying to wordlessly shame him into a more pleasant demeanor.

Jake glanced at her, his expression hard and unreadable. He looked about to speak when the butler came in and announced dinner.

They all stood and made their way to the dining room. Jake caught up with Amanda and offered his arm. She looped her arm through his, but her pleasant demeanor hid a seething anger. "Behave yourself," she hissed. To emphasize the extent of her displeasure, she pinched his forearm as hard as she could.

"Ouch."

"Next time, I'll kick you," she whispered. "Or stomp your foot with my stiletto."

"Thanks for the warning," Jake whispered into her ear as he pulled out her chair. His arm brushed against her, sending a shiver down her spine. She surreptitiously rubbed her arm to stop the tingling and refused to look at him for the rest of the meal.

The trio ate in near silence. At first, Amanda tried to make small talk, but neither man seemed keen to participate so after a few awkward attempts, she gave up. After dinner, they moved back to the living room where Max lit a cigar and took a seat near the fire. Amanda and Jake settled in across from him.

After a long, uncomfortable silence, Jake said, "There is something you can do to help."

Max flicked his ashes into a crystal tray. "I'd be delighted. What can I do?"

"Since Amanda and I are engaged, you could help cut through the legal red tape on the trust. If we leave it to the lawyers, it might take a while."

Max frowned. "What does your engagement have to do with your trust fund?"

"Well, your lawyer called last Thursday and told me the terms of the trust had been changed; that I have to get engaged before I get access." Jake cast a nervous smile at Amanda as he rested a hand on her knee. But it wasn't resting. It now gripped her thigh so hard she feared it would leave a bruise.

Amanda pasted on an overly bright smile and placed her hand over his in what she hoped would appear a show of solidarity, but she was really trying to pry his fingers loose.

"Jacob, there's been a misunderstanding. You get access to the trust when you marry, not when you get engaged."

Amanda drew in a sharp breath and nearly dropped her wine glass as her head snapped around to Jake.

"Married?" Jake's eyes bugged out and it sounded like he was being strangled.

Married? Holy crap! Amanda chugged down half her wine.

To Jake's credit, he rallied fast. "But it...it's going to be awhile before we marry, given the new business and all. Can't you do something to release the funds now? I planned to use some of my trust to start the business."

Max appeared to consider Jake's request as he slowly expelled a stream of fragrant smoke. "I designed the stipulation to be irreversible," he said, inspecting his cigar. "If you need the money now, I suggest you rethink the long engagement."

Jake's eyes grew dark. "So you won't help me."

Max's gaze shifted briefly from Amanda to Jake and she thought she detected a gleam in Max's eye as he said, "You don't need my help, Jacob. All you have to do is say I do."

* * *

She folded her arms across her chest and spoke in as stern a tone as she could muster. "For the third and last time, I'm not marrying you."

Jake stopped pacing and spread his arms wide, a wild look in his eye as he shouted, "Hey, I don't want to get married either!"

"Good. It's settled." For the last hour, she feared he might seriously consider the idea. "And by the way, you don't need to yell. I'm sitting right here."

He started pacing again. "Nothing is settled and we're in this thing together, so I suggest *you*"—he pointed at her for emphasis—"start helping me figure a way out of this mess."

"Might I remind you this mess was *your* genius idea?" She shook her head, amazed to be the calm one in this scenario. "From where I sit, the solution is simple. We'll just call off the deal."

"That won't help. We'd be right back where we started three days ago."

"Not true. Max offered to invest in your business before you rudely dismissed the idea." She shot him a reproachful look. "And you *were* rude, by the way."

"I don't want anything from that man. And I wasn't rude. I'd call it being direct."

"*That man* is your grandfather and—direct or not—you need to show him respect."

Jake thrust his thumb in the general direction of Max's condo. "*That man* tried to control every moment of my father's life until he drank himself into oblivion and wrapped his Ferrari around a tree."

"Max isn't to blame for the way your father's life turned out. At some point, we all have to take responsibility for our own actions."

"Oh, and those words mean so much when they come from the girl who's given her brother a hundred grand she doesn't have and who spends every moment bailing his ass out of bad decisions."

Amanda drew in a sharp breath. "How did you. . . ?" She stopped short and expelled a long breath. *Don't let him get to you. Who cares what he thinks he knows about my reasons for doing this.* She folded her arms and said, "Don't try to change the subject. This isn't about my family; it's about yours."

"Well please spare me the pop psychology BS." Jake loosened his tie and raked a hand through hair already mad professor disheveled. "You haven't spent enough time with Max. Once you do, you'll understand."

"You need to calm down. You're not thinking clearly," she said "Also, your hair is sticking up." She pointed at the top of his head.

"Who gives a rat's ass about my hair? We're in an unholy mess here in case it's escaped you." He glared at her. "And as it relates to my grandfather, I decided long ago that I want nothing from him."

She tried to ignore his mania. "But you *do* want something from him. You want your trust fund, which bulges—by the way—with the money *he's* made the last several decades. What's the difference if you get the money from your trust or if you just let him invest through his foundation the way he wants to do?"

"There's all the difference in the world." He pointed his thumb at his chest. "The trust fund is *my* money. I'm entitled to it."

"Actually, it's *his* money," she pointed out. "So he gets to decide the terms by which you can access it and in this case, it's after you marry. Which brings us back to my original point; I won't marry you."

Jake scowled. "You aren't helping."

"You don't need my help. There's a simple solution and you're so blinded by emotion, you've missed it."

Jake flopped down next to her. "How do you figure?"

Amanda leaned forward to emphasize her point. "Max basically offered to invest in your business." She shrugged. "Let him. We can stay engaged for a while after you get the money to maintain appearances."

"I'm not groveling for dollars the way my father always did."

Amanda threw her hands high. "Again, I don't get it. Why would an investment in your business be any different from the money in your trust?"

"Payments from the trust happen automatically—a very different thing than having to grovel to Max. He'd give me the money to feed his need for control, but it would be humiliating. I watched my father do it too many times and long ago, I promised myself I'd never stoop to that behavior."

"Jake, your reasoning makes no—"

"When I say I want nothing from him, I mean it." His elbows rested on his knees. "I plan to use just enough of my trust fund to get the business started and as soon as it starts bringing in revenue, the first thing I'll do is pay it all back. And then, I'll never touch the trust again; ever."

"So I guess it's out of the question to suggest you go to work for him—just for a few years until you either save or raise enough money to start your business."

"No way," Jake said. "I won't spend one second of my life hawking cable to a bunch of potato-chip-eating, beer-swilling couch potatoes."

She arched a brow. "I'd be careful with labels of that sort. I've seen your fifty-inch flat screen, remember?"

"You know what I mean. I like football and beer as much as the next guy. But I won't earn my living that way."

"That's a tad hypocritical."

He shrugged. "Not really. The cable industry is fine, but it means nothing to me. I want to make a difference; to help people who are truly in need and deserve it."

"Before you can make a difference, you have to get your business funded," she reminded him. "And you might find you need a little infusion of cash from the cable industry in order to do so."

He crossed his arms. "Are you always this reasonable? It's really irritating, in case you wondered."

She choked back an urge to laugh. He reminded her of an angry little boy, pouting because he hadn't gotten his way—especially with the sprig of hair bobbing about every time he moved his head.

He leaned forward and continued. "The way I see it, we have to get married. We're out of options."

"We have options." She hadn't thought of any yet, but she knew she could come up with something.

"Since I won't grovel to my grandfather, I'd love to know the other choices you believe we have."

She could think of several things and a fake real marriage to him wouldn't even make the list. "You could postpone the plan to start your own business."

Jake shook his head. "No. I have buddies who've sacrificed *every-thing*. They need the help my company can give them today, not a few years from now."

Amanda pursed her lips. She couldn't believe this whole mess had started with a simple weekend getaway. More specifically, it had started six months ago with her decision to loan her brother money because if she hadn't done that, she wouldn't be in debt and if she wasn't in debt, she would never have agreed to fake an engagement with him

"We need to comply with the terms of the trust and take our deal to the next level." He laid a hand on her knee and turned to face her. "This is my only option. I need your help."

She shifted away in an attempt to dislodge his hand, but it remained maddeningly in place which was incredibly distracting at a time when she needed to concentrate. "Get married." She lifted his hand and placed it on the sofa. "You're *serious*."

Jake nodded.

"I can't. Jake, I just *can't*. I felt low enough pretending to be engaged and lying to Max. To fake a real marriage—followed by a real divorce—well..." She tipped her chin down as she shook her head. "It would just be taking this whole thing too far."

He watched her intently. "What would it take to get you to agree?"

"You can't afford it."

"Try me. Money isn't the obstacle here. I've got plenty; I just have to play my grandfather's game in order to get my hands on it."

She shook her head more vehemently. She wasn't marrying anyone she didn't intend to stay married to for the rest of her life—especially when it came to the only man she'd ever loved. "We've already gone down that path and look where it got us," she said. "I won't screw up my future trying to fix problems from my past."

"I believe your past may be the way to your future," he said.

She frowned. "That makes no sense."

"Think," he said. "You could have a ton of money in the bank, live your Paris dream and—"

"But I'd have to fake a marriage and then get a real divorce. Meantime, I'll have lost a few years of my life. Why would I do that? I turn *thirty* in a matter of days. I want a family, kids. If I do as you suggest I'll be headed in the wrong direction."

He leaned forward. "If you do it my way, you'll get what you want much sooner. You'll have financial freedom, you'll be divorced. You'll be able to move on with your life, free and clear. If you do it your way, you won't be able to help you brother and you may never get that year in Paris."

Her gaze locked with his and a long silence stretched between them as she considered his words.

"If you do it my way, you can have it all. You can get everything you want—just like that." He snapped his fingers to emphasize the last word.

"I don't know if I can do it," she whispered.

He stood. "I know it's messed up, but from where I sit, my approach is the only option." He strode toward the door.

"What if I want out?"

Jake shrugged into his jacket. "If you say no, I'll respect your decision and we'll cancel the agreement. We'll devise a break-up story, you'll give me back the advance and we'll consider it done."

She drew in a sharp breath. The money; shit! How the hell had she forgotten about the money. She'd paid off most of her bills that morning. If she backed out now, she owed that same huge sum to Jake Lowell. Cold tentacles of fear slithered around her as she followed him to the door and for the first time that evening, the solution to their problem suddenly didn't seem so clear.

Jake reached for the doorknob and then turned back to face her. "This option is our best alternative. But if you still haven't accepted that fact, I'll give you a day to consider it." He held up his index finger. "One day. Let me know your decision tomorrow."

Amanda closed the door behind him and leaned against it as she replayed Jake's words. She could have everything she wanted just like that.

My ass.

She turned the deadbolt and it clicked into place. But instead of feeling safe and secure, she'd never felt more vulnerable or petrified in her entire life.

Maxwell Lowell's trap had been brilliantly set and she and Jake had walked right into it.

Chapter Eight

hat's such a big emergency it couldn't wait until after yoga?" Kate didn't bother to hide her irritation as she struggled into the booth; her baby bump making the maneuver difficult.

"A peace offering," Amanda said, as she pushed a coffee cup and a paper plate across the table. "Grande skinny decaf latte with a sprinkle of mocha and a slice of fat free cinnamon cake, as ordered."

"I didn't order cake."

"You'll want a slice after this chat, trust me."

"What's up?" Kate popped the lid off her latte and took a sip.

Amanda drew a deep breath and leaned back in the booth. "We have to get married."

"You're pregnant?" Kate squealed. "I didn't even know you guys *did it*!"

Amanda's cheeks burned and she slouched down in the booth in an attempt to hide. Several people seated nearby whispered; more than a few were laughing. She leaned forward held a hand up to shield her face and said, "A little *louder* next time. I don't think your two sisters back home in Birmingham heard you."

Undeterred, Kate's eyes danced. "I'm *so* excited. I hope our kids—"

"Before you get carried away and start planning the wedding of my nonexistent child and yours, I'm *not* pregnant and we *didn't* do it."

Kate's ear-to-ear grin fell so fast she looked deflated.

"Jake misunderstood," Amanda said. "The trust fund thing was never about an engagement. We have to get *married* before he gets access."

Kate flipped her golden hair over a shoulder and lifted a well-groomed brow. "Married like, for real?"

"For real."

Kate's French-tipped fingers pulled the plate closer. "You're right. I do need this cake."

"Told you," Amanda said. "I've already eaten two slices."

"Two slices? Come to the nine o'clock class with me. They take walk-ins."

"It's a prenatal class and as we've already established, I'm not pregnant."

"Anybody can go. It's like beginner's yoga." Kate cut a bite of cake. "When did this happen?"

"Last night at dinner with Max." Amanda blew on her coffee and took a sip.

"What are you going to do?"

"I don't know. We talked for two hours last night. Jake thinks we need to get married."

"No, no, no." Kate shook her head so hard, her hair fanned out. "There has to be another way. Don't get me wrong; I think you two belong together but I don't want you to walk down the aisle if the marriage isn't for real. You know?"

"We don't belong together. Not anymore." Amanda plucked at her napkin. "And now I have to deal with this"—she gestured at the over-sized ring on her left hand—"as a constant reminder of what we'll never have; what we'll never be." She cleared her throat and added a quick clarification. "Not that I want that with him anymore."

"Of course you do. Let me see." Kate eyes bugged out and she yanked Amanda's hand so hard it bent her over the table. "Now that's some serious bling. Damn girl!" Kate squeezed her hand and smiled. "Totally gorge."

"I really don't want something with him. I mean, of course I did at one time, but now I know it would never work between us."

Kate tilted her head to the side and regarded her with interest. "What makes you say that?"

"He's afraid of commitment," Amanda said.

Kate waved a hand dismissively. "Please. What man isn't afraid of commitment? Most of them get over it eventually."

Amanda shook her head, her voice laced with regret. "I don't know. When he ended things between us, he said we were just too different; that our values were too far apart." She shrugged. "At the time, I didn't agree. But now I'm not so sure. After seeing him again with Max and all, I wonder. Maybe he's right."

"I don't believe that," Kate said. "You're just saying that because seeing him again has been harder than you expected." She reached across and squeezed Amanda's hand. "You know, we *all* thought he'd propose on your birthday last year—Sam included. It made his heartless breakup the night before all the more deplorable. I still haven't forgiven him."

"Me neither."

After a few moments of silence, Kate cleared her throat and said, "Anyway, one way or another, now that he's back we'll know for sure. You'll either find your way back to each other or you'll get over him."

"I'm almost over him," Amanda said. "I mean, I did fine when he was in Iraq."

Kate scoffed. "You didn't do fine."

The look in Kate's eyes said it all. Amanda could insist she didn't care; try to put off her best who-gives-a-crap vibe, but she wasn't fooling anyone. The realization made her even more upset. She gave Kate the evil eye and said, "I did when you weren't fixing me up with losers."

"They weren't *all* losers."

Amanda pursed her lips. "Name me a winner, any winner," she said. "Just pick *one*."

Kate glared at her as she stirred her coffee.

"Don't get me started," Amanda said. "You know I'll win *this* argument."

"Whatever." Kate tucked her blonde locks behind an ear and lifted her chin. "My mother says it's a game of numbers. You have to kiss a lot of toads before you get your cushion cut diamond."

"I've kissed more than my fair share, thanks to you," she said.

Kate made a face and then changed the subject, "Anyway, Sam says Jake's not over you either."

Amanda's laughter held a heavy dose of bitterness. "Sam's wrong. Jake is about as over me as he could get, which is what makes this situation so depressing. I thought I'd moved on, but clearly I haven't." Not yet anyway. But she would; she absolutely would. She was sure of it.

"I wouldn't be so sure." Kate studied Amanda's face as she said, "A few days ago, Jake stopped by and asked Sam to prepare the contract. While there, Sam told him you loaned your brother the money; now he knows the real reason you agreed to the deal."

Amanda smacked her leg as a light bulb went on. "Jake mentioned that last night. I wondered how he knew." She paused for a beat and then eyed Kate with disapproval as she said, "Is there anything you don't tell your husband?"

Kate sniffed. "It's not good to keep secrets in a marriage."

"I'd love to know how gossiping about *me* helps strengthen your marriage."

Kate ignored her and circled back to her original point. "A few days after Sam told him that, Jake gave you a hundred thousand dollar advance. Just a tad coincidental that it's precisely the amount you loaned your brother." She arched a brow. "Don't you think?"

"It doesn't mean he cares about me," Amanda said. "If he did, he wouldn't have dumped me."

"Like I said, none of us anticipated the breakup, not even Sam.

Personally, I think Jake got scared. And...you know... his dad died and he was about to ship out." Kate tapped her finger on the rim of her mug. "Still, I think his actions now say something else. He didn't have to pick *you* for this little scam. And he *definitely* didn't need to give you an advance which just happens to be the exact amount you owe. Why do you think he did that?"

Amanda shrugged. Jake chose her because of her strong connection with Max. He'd said as much. With her, his deception stood the best chance for success. She wasn't naïve enough to believe it to be related to any feelings she might wish he still harbored for her. Unlike Kate, she preferred to live in reality. Life tended to be less of a disappointment that way.

"Regardless, you can't go through with it. Jake's wrong." Kate shook her head. "It would be taking this whole ridiculous plan too far."

"That's what I said." Amanda shook another packet of sugar substitute into her coffee. If ever a situation called for a sweetener—artificial or not—this would be it. Maybe it would help neutralize the bitter aftertaste of their breakup.

"Did Jake give you an out?"

Amanda nodded. "He gave me a day to think about it. He wants to know my decision tonight."

Kate looked relieved. "Good. And you'll be telling him no, right?"

Amanda chewed the inside of her lip and tapped the coffee stirrer on the table. "I don't know if I can."

"Why?"

"I'd have to pay back the advance."

"So pay him back." Kate shrugged. "I know you need the cash, but no matter how badly you need it, the money wouldn't compensate for the downside of a fake marriage."

Amanda shifted in her seat. "No. . . I mean. . . I *can't.*"

Kate frowned. "What do you mean you can't?"

"It's gone."

Kate threw her fork down and it bounced onto the floor. "You spent *a hundred thousand dollars* in the last *two days?*" Her bellow reverberated through the crowded Starbucks. Dozens of heads snapped in their direction.

Amanda turned her head away from the crowd and spoke to Kate out of the corner of her mouth, "Could you use your inside voice please? Geez! I finally understand why you beat me out for Rush Chair our senior year."

"What the hell, Amanda...*a hundred grand?*" Kate lowered her voice, but it dripped with disapproval.

Amanda knew she didn't owe her friend any explanations, but couldn't help herself. "I paid off my second mortgage, most of my credit cards and gave Rob twenty thousand. I have a little left, but not much."

Kate opened her mouth, but Amanda held up a hand to cut her off. "Before you start shrieking again, I'd just like to say...*I know,*" she said. "I *know* I shouldn't have given Rob the twenty thousand extra he asked for. I get it, I *do*. I couldn't help it."

Kate leaned forward and shook a finger under her nose. "You *can* help it. Now Amanda Wilson, you march yourself over to Rob's house and get that money back right this second."

"There you go with the full name thing again. I hate it when you get bossy."

"I'm *always* bossy, so if you didn't want to hear it, you shouldn't have called me." Kate sat back and her folded arms rested on her bump. "You knew what I'd say."

She had known. So why had she asked? Unsatisfied with her artificially-sweetened coffee, Amanda picked up her fork and reached across the table to cut off a bite of Kate's cake.

Kate swatted her hand away, pulled the plate closer and cut another bite. "Take the amount Rob gives you back plus whatever you have left and offer it to Jake as a down payment," she said. "Then tell him you'll repay the rest later." She popped the cake in her mouth and a smile of supreme satisfaction spread across her features.

"I don't know if Jake will go for it."

Kate swallowed and fixed Amanda with her most hardcore steel magnolia gaze. "Oh he will, or he'll have *me* to contend with."

As Amanda knew from personal experience, hell hath no fury like Kate thwarted. In their circle she was referred to as Hurricane Kate, because things were never quite the same after she had passed through.

"Okay, I'll head to my brother's place as soon as we're done here. You're right. I need to get the money and back out of this deal." She didn't know if it would work, but she needed to give it a try. Her entire future depended on it.

"Yeah, this whole thing was a bad idea."

Amanda's mouth twisted. "It was *your* idea, remember?"

"You're right." Kate pushed the cake plate toward Amanda. "Here, you can have the last bite to make up for it."

Amanda scooped up the cake. "Mmm," she cooed as the sweet bite melted in her mouth. "It's *so* good. I think I'll get a slice to go."

Kate frowned. "You don't need any more cake."

"Kill joy," Amanda said as she licked her lips.

"Your thighs will thank me later."

"My mouth is thanking me now." Amanda rolled her eyes and rubbed her belly in an exaggerated show of ecstasy.

"Amanda, promise you'll stop this brother thing."

"What thing?"

"You enable him."

It seemed too easy an observation for Kate to make—especially when she lacked any common frame of reference. She didn't get it.

"You'd have a different perspective if you were me. I'm all he's had since they died. What did *I* know about parenting a thirteen year-old?"

Kate squeezed her hand. "It's tragic. But you aren't responsible for their deaths and you can't over-compensate for their loss the rest of your life. Their deaths happened to both of you, remember? Not just him. It affected you, too and yet never got a chance to work through it because you've always been focused on him. How he feels.

What he wants. Plus, you won't do Rob any favors if you continue to give in to him."

"I'm doing my best," Amanda said.

"I know you *think* you are. But you need to get the money back, get out of this deal and give Rob a dose of tough love. He's twenty-three. It's time to man up."

Amanda twirled a strand of dark hair and considered Kate's advice. It might be partially true, but Kate couldn't possibly know how she'd respond to a situation she'd never experienced herself.

"You'll be firm with him, right?" Kate arched a brow.

In an attempt to put a kibosh on the lecture, Amanda said what her friend wanted to hear. "Absolutely."

"Okay, I'll back off. But you better stand your ground."

The girls gathered their purses, slipped on their coats and headed to the door. Amanda tried to ignore the grins from customers that followed them outside.

Show's over folks.

Out on the sidewalk, Kate pointed a leather-gloved finger at Amanda. "Call me later. And I don't want to hear any excuses."

* * *

Rob lived nearby and it wasn't too cold outside, so Amanda decided to walk. At the first intersection, the light turned red. She stopped and turned back in time to see Kate waddle around the corner, headed toward the yoga studio. She shook her head. Kate meant well, but she didn't get it. And how could she? Her parents were still around.

The light changed and Amanda crossed the street with the crowd, while she practiced her approach to confronting Rob. She had no idea what to say to him and with each step closer to his apartment, the knot in her stomach grew tighter and larger. Before she knew it, she stood in front of his door—still absolutely clueless as to what she'd say. So she stood there for a full five minutes before she summoned the courage to knock.

She rapped on the door three times.

Take control early. That's the key.

She stood there for several minutes and when he didn't open the door, she knocked again, louder this time. When he still didn't answer, Amanda checked her watch. Nine-thirty. Maybe he had already left for the restaurant. Yeah, that was it. She'd come back later.

She turned away, so relieved to be off the hook, she felt weak in the knees. Thank God he wasn't home because she had no earthly idea what tough love even looked like. She'd have to Google it as soon as she got home so she'd be better prepared when she actually had to do it.

The door opened. Amanda stopped in her tracks and turned to see Rob in the doorway. Her stomach dropped. Not even Google could help her now.

"Hey, sis," Rob said as he opened the door wider. "What're you doing here?"

She stepped inside and after surveying his rumpled appearance and equally messy apartment, she shook her head in disapproval. "It's nine-thirty. Please tell me you weren't still in bed."

You enable him, Kate's voice whispered.

Pipe down. She wasn't in the mood to hear it from Kate's evil twin right now. She needed to concentrate.

Rob yawned and mussed his hair as he shuffled into the living room. He scratched his chest and said, "I was out late."

She trailed behind him. "Working at the restaurant?"

"A couple of us went to a club."

Irritation simmered and her jaw felt tight as she said, "You'd get farther faster with your business if you put less emphasis on your social life."

Rob raised his brows and glanced over his shoulder. "You're pissed because I went out last night?"

Irritation turned to a low boil. He didn't get it. "I'm somewhere between disappointed and pissed." She studied his face. "You're not being responsible."

Rob plopped down on the sofa and gazed up at her. "What do you mean?"

"You stay out late and party. You sleep in when you should be at work. You constantly ask for money you *know* I don't have."

"So you're really mad about the money."

She didn't miss his blasé attitude. "It's partly about the money, partly about your actions. You've yet to demonstrate that you're ready to own a business." He didn't even take accountability for himself. Amanda wished she could express the sentiment aloud, but she couldn't make herself do it. The words would sound too harsh and once said, she'd never be able to take them back.

"I'm ready. It just takes longer to get a business off the ground than you'd think."

"Yes"—she cast a pointed glance—"it does; especially when your social life comes first."

"I went out last night; it's not something I do all the time."

She was quiet for a long while and then said, "I think you need to work for someone else awhile longer."

"You don't get ahead when you manage a restaurant; you get ahead when you own one."

Amanda perched on the edge of the sofa and crossed her legs. "You can get ahead later. You're only twenty-three."

His brow creased. "What are you saying?"

She drew in a fortifying breath and forced the words out. "I need the twenty thousand back."

His eyes grew round as saucers. "But I don't have it anymore."

"What do you mean you don't have it?" Her voice sounded sharper than she'd intended and she willed herself to calm down as she said, "I just gave it to you a day and a half ago. You couldn't possibly have spent it yet."

He shrugged as if he hadn't a care in the world. "We owed the construction company money and used it to pay them so we could get the interior finish work done."

Stay calm. The money's probably still in their bank account.

She looked down at the tips of her shoes and counted to ten. One of her favorite business books recommended the tactic to avoid making unfortunate outbursts when in stressful situations. She combined that with the deep breathing she'd learned from the yoga class she attended occasionally. Breathe...

Kate's advice from earlier drifted back; it was time for some tough love.

Amanda assembled every scrap of courage she possessed and dove in. "Rob, go to your partners and get that money back." She internally congratulated herself on how effectively she'd channeled Kate's miss-bossy-pants tone. Then again, it should have been easy; she'd been the recipient of it more times than she cared to count.

Rob looked unfazed. "I can't. They don't have the cash either."

"You need to ask." She fixed him with her best intimidating look.

He appeared unmoved. "I'm telling you; they don't *have* it."

Amanda chewed the inside of her lip. Now what? Kate's way hadn't worked. What came after tough love?

She glanced at Rob and noted he appeared completely unfazed by the conversation, which only added to her consternation. She watched him lounge on the sofa, totally relaxed and indifferent to her panic. While she didn't agree with Kate's perspective, in this instance she could understand why her friend considered Rob a taker and, occasionally, a brat. In that moment, Amanda was inclined to agree with her. She needed to leave before she said a bunch of things she'd regret later.

She stood and headed for the door.

Rob followed, his bare feet slapping the floor like a child and his voice approached a whine as he said, "Why did you give me the money if you just planned to ask for it back?"

He didn't attempt to hide his peevish tone or mask his total lack of concern for her needs. He hadn't even bothered to probe her reasons for needing the money back, just as he'd never truly thanked her for the amount she'd given him already. Or anything else she'd done for him the past ten years.

She studied his face. Looking past the brooding expression and mussed appearance, she saw the reminders of their parents. They were there in the slant of Rob's eyes and the line of his jaw and it caused her tone to soften as she said, "I'm sorry I gave you the money, because I didn't have it to give." Rob frowned and opened his mouth to respond, but she shook her head and said, "Save it. We're done for now. I'll call you later when I'm not so pissed."

Amanda closed the door behind her and Amanda felt numb as she trudged down the hall and into the elevator. When she walked outside, it was like someone had hit the mute button on Chicago. The cars, the El, horns and people—Amanda heard none of it as she made her way home. By the time she arrived, a little cloud of doom had settled over her.

She dropped her coat, purse and keys onto a chair and plodded down the hall to the bedroom. Months of sleepless nights caught up and she didn't even attempt to fight the fatigue. She shut the blinds, stripped down to her underwear, unplugged the phone and then crawled into bed, yanked up the covers and fell into a deep, dreamless sleep.

* * *

"You're drunk," George declared as the elevator doors opened.

Amanda giggled and handed him the keys to her apartment as she swayed from side to side. "So are you."

George fiddled with the keys but finally got the door unlocked. He held it open and followed her inside. "Not as drunk as you," he said. "You girls can't hold your liquor."

"Yes we can."

"Uh-huh," he said. "I still can't believe you're taking a leave of absence. All night, I've been wondering what we'll do without you at the office. You're the miracle-worker; the one everyone depends on. We'll sure miss you."

"I'll missh you guys too."

"You're slurring your words."

"Who caresh? I don't have to get up in the morning." She kicked off a shoe with all the grace of an NFL Hall of Fame punter. The black patent leather pump whizzed by George's dark head, missing his cheek by little more than an inch.

"Hey, watch it!" George glanced over his shoulder as one shoe landed on the coffee table. She kicked off the other and it flew over his head, crashing onto the sofa, where it dangled precipitously off the edge.

Amanda threw her head back and laughed.

George raised a dark brow. "You're drunker than I thought. This leave of absence thing may not be such a good idea. When will you be back?"

She shrugged and weaved into the kitchen. "Dunno."

"This isn't like you, Amanda. What's going on?"

Her head snapped up. "Nothing." Nothing she wanted to talk about with him, anyway. While she didn't believe George would spread gossip at the office, she still couldn't bring herself to confide in him. Plus, she'd signed the damned confidentiality agreement, so legally she couldn't do so anyway.

"You need coffee."

She waved him away. "I don't want coffee. I want wine."

"You don't need more wine. And I have to go to work tomorrow, so I don't either."

"I'm having *wi-i-ne*," she sang as she pulled a bottle of Chardonnay from the refrigerator.

"So, you're as hard-headed out of the office as you are while there. I wondered..." He shook his head and watched her pour. "You need to take some aspirin or you'll have a massive hangover in the morning. Where's your bathroom."

Amanda pointed toward the hall and then shoved the cork back in the bottle. George followed her finger and disappeared around the corner.

She picked up her glass and swallowed a large portion of wine just as someone knocked on the door; loudly. "Come in," Amanda called, also loudly—too busy with her wine to answer the door and far too busy to wonder who might be stopping by so late.

"Why are you ignoring my calls? I need an answer, Amanda."

She spun round and some wine sloshed onto the floor. "What're you doing here?"

Jake's eyes narrowed as they focused first on her glass and then shifted to the bottle. "Are you drunk?"

"Nope," she lied, as she took a sip.

George walked through the other doorway. "Here's your aspir..." His voice trailed off when he saw Jake.

Furious blue eyes locked with curious brown ones as the two men spoke in unison. "Who are you?"

Chapter Nine

Jake had the guy sized up inside a minute and he didn't like his conclusion. "Who are you," he repeated, fixing the other man with his most intimidating glare.

"George." The man locked eyes with Jake as he slapped an aspirin bottle on the counter. "You?"

"Her fiancé," Jake said, deciding the guy didn't need to know anything more.

"Fiancé. Really?" George raised a brow and shot a pointed glance at Amanda. "I didn't know you had one of those."

Amanda cleared her throat and said, "George this is my uh, my um"—she flung her hand awkwardly in Jake's direction—"my fiancé, Jake Lowell."

"Really," George said as his gaze moved back to Jake.

Amanda chewed a fingernail and her brows knit together as her gaze shifted between the two men.

"Sorry to disappoint you," Jake said. If he thought he could make a move on Amanda while Jake just stood around and watched; *he'd* be the one sorry.

"George and I are friends from work. He wanted to make sure I got home okay." Amanda regarded him warily—as if trying to decipher what he'd do next.

Jake decided to let her stew awhile. It served her right since she'd brought another guy home, which wasn't exactly part of their deal. To be fair, he hadn't outlined that clause in their contract. Still, the level to which it bothered him went way beyond their business deal and he wasn't sure what grated on him more; that she'd brought the guy home or his own reaction to it.

"I'm sure he did." Jake didn't bother to mask the hint of menace in his tone.

George swept a dismissive gaze over Jake. "So the ex-boyfriend is now the fiancé. Nice. And to think it only took you a year to figure it out."

Jake's jaw tightened as he bit back a retort.

George leaned over and kissed Amanda's cheek. "Take two aspirin before you go to bed so you don't get a headache."

Jake's jaw clenched harder and he mustered every ounce of self-restraint to avoid grabbing the guy by the collar and shoving him out the door.

"Thanks for seeing me home." Amanda's smile lit her face.

Jake flinched at the sudden stab of jealousy. He couldn't remember the last time she'd smiled at him that way.

"Anytime," George said. He smirked at Jake as he ambled by, clearly not in a hurry. "I'll let myself out."

The door closed and a long, uncomfortable silence stretched between them. Jake rubbed his jaw, sore from all the clenching, and told himself to get a grip. A few moments later, a little more in control, he jerked a thumb toward the door and said, "Who is he?"

"I told you. He's a friend from work." Her voice held a hint of amusement.

"Define *friend*."

"I think you know the definition." Amanda tilted her head to the side. "But I'd love to know why you think my relationship with George is any of your business." Her blue eyes issued a challenge as they peered at him over the top of her wine glass.

"We're engaged." In his view, her non-answer sealed the deal. Now he knew something was up. "Are you two involved?"

Her laughter seemed to mock him as she said, "Careful. You sound like a jealous fiancé and we're not really engaged, remember?"

"Given our contract, this engagement is about as real as it gets, baby." He looked down at her left hand and frowned. "Where's your ring?"

She tossed her hair over her shoulder. "I decided not to wear it."

"You decided..." He kept his tone calm, but inside, steam rose.

She jutted out her chin. "I wanted to pretend I still had a normal life; just for one more night." She gazed broodingly into her glass as she swished the wine around.

"Normal as in, you brought cabana boy home for a last little fling."

Her brows knit together. "For God's sake, George isn't my boyfriend or my cabana boy. He's a friend. And I don't like the implication I'm in the habit of bringing guys home for a romp in the sack."

"That's not what I implied."

She placed a hand on her hip and said, "That's *exactly* what you implied."

Jake's gaze slid over her. "You're dressed for a date." She looked smoking hot, too. "And it's clear the guy has a thing for you."

She tottered into the living room, unsteady on her feet. "That's ridiculous. I don't date co-workers. And I'm dressed for happy hour, not a date," she said. "If you must know, I had a bad day and when I went to the office to arrange my leave of absence, I decided to organize a happy hour." She flopped onto the sofa. "You've made my day even worse, by the way, and I didn't think that was possible."

Jake settled on the opposite end of the couch. "You've had enough to drink tonight. You can't even walk straight."

Amanda tucked her legs under her, causing her skirt to ride up. "A few minutes ago, I might've agreed with you, but you've killed my buzz and now I plan to finish every drop."

He reached for her glass. "You'll get sick if you don't slow down."

She snatched her hand away which caused a few droplets to slosh onto the couch. She brushed them off and glared at him. "Much as I love this Chardonnay, I won't hesitate to toss the whole glass in your face if you don't let me drink in peace."

He gave up trying to reason with her and leaned back. She'd pay the consequences tomorrow. "What happened to upset you?"

Amanda's eyes bugged out. "You mean beyond the insanity of the past week."

Jake inclined his head. "Fair enough; but from what you said, it sounded like something in particular happened today."

She heaved a dramatic sigh. "Well, let's see." She held up her index finger. "First, I took a leave of absence from work, which will probably ruin my career." She raised a second and third finger as she continued. "Then I realized I had to marry my ex for money *and* I've already legally agreed it will end in divorce." She held up a fourth finger. "Oh, and last but not least, I'll turn thirty in twenty-three days." She eyed her glass pointedly. "This would be the reason for the large quantities of wine." She tipped her glass and a good amount slid down her throat.

"It won't hurt to take a few months off. Your career will be fine." He shook his head, long familiar with her drama queen routine. "As I recall, your branding job is demanding. I doubt you could deal with the realities of our agreement and *still* cope with your crazy job— especially since we have a real wedding to plan. I think the time off will do you good."

Amanda pursed her lips. "You assume I care what you think, why?"

"Listen, I didn't make any of those decisions, you did. Yesterday, I merely suggested a leave of absence might be a good idea. Clearly you agreed, because you went through with it. And as far as marriage goes, I didn't force the idea on you. We both heard the news from Max at the same time last night. I gave you an out. You thought everything through and decided to do it." He jabbed a finger at her. "You decided that, not me."

She tipped her head down and plucked a piece of lint from her skirt and then brushed it away. "I need the money. I don't have a choice."

"Regardless of your reasons, you have to accept responsibility for your decision. I won't be the guy who forced you into something you didn't want to do."

She pushed her lower lip out and her pout reminded him of a sullen teenager.

He took a deep breath and steered the conversation in a more positive direction. "Look, I know this situation isn't ideal, but there's an upside for both of us. And since the stakes are higher, you should get paid more. How much will it take?"

She twirled a wayward curl. "I haven't thought it through yet."

"You said you're doing it for the money, so you must have an amount in mind. Let's hear it."

Amanda tapped a fingernail on her glass. After a brief pause, she locked eyes with Jake. "Half a million in cash—"

He rubbed his chin as he considered the amount. Half a million dollars was a large sum, but given the magnitude of his trust, he could swing it. He supposed it's what she should get since her life would be on hold for potentially a very long while. After all, he stood to gain the most from their deal. He'd get his new business—his future—off the ground. All she'd get is whatever cash he paid her. "That sounds fair."

"I wasn't finished." She eyed him sternly. "That amount is on top of my original terms."

Jake frowned as he did the math in his head. Seven hundred grand? "Hey wait a—"

"And I *keep* the Paris apartment." Amanda tossed back the last of her wine and set the empty glass on the table as a look of supreme satisfaction spread across her features.

Jake jumped up. "You want seven hundred grand *and* a two-million-dollar Paris apartment my family has owned for generations?" Granted, the cash would come from his trust, but since he'd vowed to pay it all back, he didn't intend to give her a penny more than he needed to. He wanted to be fair but his generosity had limits.

She shrugged and he detected more than a hint of cockiness in her tone as she said, "You asked what it would take and I told you. My terms are—"

"Extortion!" He glared at her.

"Fair." She sounded infuriatingly calm. "You're just mad because I'm a good negotiator."

"I'm *mad* because you're trying to take advantage"—he jabbed a thumb at his chest—"of me!"

"Stop shouting," she sniffed. "If I have to enter a marriage that I've already agreed will end in divorce, then I deserve to get paid." She lifted her chin. "You have to admit this deal isn't how either of us should spend the next year. Our agreement is duplicitous, immoral and just plain stupid."

He couldn't argue with that. But trapped and desperate people tended to do stupid things. "It's too much. I never pegged you as a gold-digger." He didn't really believe it; he just wanted to jolt her a little.

She sat up ramrod straight and squared her shoulders. "If you don't like the price, then don't buy the product. It shouldn't be too hard to find another girl. I'm sure *Bethany* would do it for free." Her eyes issued a challenge. "Of course, it could prove difficult to get a divorce given the way she's always stalked you. My guess is her rich daddy would tie you up in divorce court for years."

Jake tamped down his frustration and looked away. Amanda Wilson may be the poster child for stubborn, but she wasn't a gold-digger. He'd known his fair share and she wasn't among them. Bethany on the other hand, his former next door neighbor who he'd had the misfortune to date once or twice before he discovered she was loony tunes, still inspired Fatal Attraction type nightmares.

By contrast, everything about Amanda screamed independence. In fact, her complete inability to ask for or accept help from anyone irritated him beyond measure. She'd let herself die of starvation rather than tell anyone she was hungry. Hell, when she grew old and gray, she'd be far likelier to whack some poor Good Samaritan on the head with her purse than to allow him to help her across the street.

Her out-of-character behavior this evening revealed more than she'd ever confess. She felt trapped into the deal; into needing Jake's money and so she'd over indulged. He knew from long experience; Amanda didn't like to *need* anyone and as a result, she refused to be open to the possibility she couldn't do everything herself. On the other hand, her behavior could have a much simpler motivation; it could be an attempt to piss him off. If so, her strategy had worked.

Amanda brushed the black pump off the pillow and it fell to the carpet. Then she shifted her body so she could lie down. "My head hurts." She stretched out her legs and her toes just grazed Jake's thigh. She closed her eyes and sighed. As her skirt rode up, she tugged it back down and then folded her hands on her tummy.

Jake tried not to stare at her legs. "Amanda, we're not done talking. We haven't agreed to terms yet."

She opened an eye and peered at him. "We're done for tonight. You asked for my demands; now you have them." She closed her eye again. "You decide whether to accept them or not."

A lock of hair fell across her cheek and Jake fought the urge to brush it away.

How one woman could inspire such a wide spectrum of emotion in such a short timeframe was beyond him. She could incite a red hot anger as easily as she could inspire searing, soul-baring passion. His emotions tended to the extreme with her, there wasn't much in between and that emotional rollercoaster had been a big reason he'd ended their relationship. Everything between them felt too intense; too infused with emotion and Jake preferred things clean and rational. He'd chalked it up to their differences. But he knew the real reasons ran deeper. He didn't think straight when he was around her.

Amanda emitted a delicate wheeze and her head fell to the side.

Jake shook her legs. "Wake up. We're not done talking. I have some demands of my own and we need to get things between us settled tonight."

She opened her eyes and sighed, her voice pure steel as she said, "We're *definitely* done for tonight."

"Where are you going?"

"To bed," she said. "You've killed my buzz and now I'm exhausted. Plus, it's pretty obvious I won't get any sleep if I stay out here."

Jake watched Amanda carry her glass to the kitchen, his thoughts a confused mixture of self-recrimination and desire. He should've never gone to the cabin. She'd been hard enough to get out of his head while in Iraq. And now, he wasn't just haunted by thoughts of her, he had to deal with the *real* Amanda. He didn't understand why he couldn't get her out of his head. They didn't make sense together. They'd proven this time and again. It's why he'd been so sure about the break-up. He'd thought through the facts countless times in the past year and was convinced he'd been right to end it.

But he couldn't rationalize away his fantasies of her. It had to be a sex thing. She bent over to pick up a shoe and his eyes drifted to her perky bottom. Yeah, it was definitely a sex thing. They were wrong for each other in every way but one and it all came down to chemistry. His attraction to her just hadn't burned out yet and until it did, she would drive him crazy.

Amanda picked up the other shoe and strutted by, her chin in the air. Jake's fingers closed around her wrist. "Wait."

She tossed her hair over a shoulder and looked up at him. "I've done everything you've asked. What more could you possibly want?"

His arm snaked around her waist and he tugged her close. She came willingly, but her eyes widened and in them, he saw fear, confusion, hurt. But he also detected a glimmer of desire. And that was all he needed. He drew her closer. She came willingly, nestling into his chest and his hand skimmed up her arm and then came to rest under her chin. He tipped it up and his gaze drifted to her slightly parted lips. "I want this," he whispered.

His lips captured hers. Their kiss started whisper soft but a heartbeat later, passion ignited. Blood roared through his veins and blocked out whatever coherent thought he still possessed. As he molded her body to his, he no longer cared whether they made sense together or not. He wanted her. Jake deepened the kiss. Amanda dropped her shoes and her lips parted as she wrapped her arms around his neck. But it still wasn't enough. Jake wanted more. After a long, empty year without her, he needed more.

He laced their fingers and dropped to the sofa. She sank into his lap and melted into him. She threw her mussed, dark tresses over a shoulder, exposing the graceful creamy arc of her neck.

"I missed this," he whispered. He'd missed *her*, but he couldn't bring himself to say those words; didn't want her to know the truth. He didn't want to feel more vulnerable than he already felt. "You're a very good negotiator," he said as he planted a trail of kisses down her neck.

She moaned—a throaty, feral sound—and threw her head back, her thick tangle of curls spilling over his hands. He buried his fingers in her hair and nibbled at the delicate skin of her earlobe. "If this is part of our deal, where do I sign?"

Amanda stiffened and pulled away. "What did you say?" The pliant, passionate softness was gone, replaced by a cold, steely glare.

"What's wrong?" Jake tried to pull her close again, but she pushed against his chest and stood.

"Sex isn't part of the deal."

"You know that's not what I meant. But clearly, it's what we both want."

She yanked down her skirt and bent to pick up her shoes, tossing her hair as she flounced away. "Speak for yourself."

He couldn't hide his frustration as he said, "Where are you going?"

"To bed," she said, pausing at the hallway to cast a frosty glance over her shoulder. "*Alone*. I agreed to fake a marriage, but sex isn't on the menu. Oh, and you can let yourself out."

She disappeared and a moment later, the bedroom door slammed and Jake heard the unmistakable click of the lock.

Like she needed to lock him out. He'd never had to break down doors for sex and he wasn't about to start now. He growled in frustration. She held top spot as the most stubborn; the most *irritating* woman he'd ever met. Of course, this wasn't a new revelation.

So naturally he'd asked her to marry him. He shook his head, alarmed by his recent behavior. Imagining they could casually fake an engagement free of consequences had been nothing short of insanity. Clearly, he was losing it.

Jake rested his head on the back of the sofa and stared up at the ceiling. His plan had sounded so easy. Fake an engagement and get the big financial payoff. He'd convinced himself—and to some degree her—that their deal would be light on risk and heavy on reward, for both of them. Then again, he hadn't counted on the real marriage twist, followed by a real divorce. But that's what it would be now, thanks to his grandfather. And he definitely hadn't counted on their sexual chemistry. He had assumed it was all behind them; had imagined his lingering thoughts of her had more to do with a long year spent in a war zone.

He sighed. Their deal hadn't even started yet—no one besides his grandfather, Sam and Kate even knew of their engagement—and it was already far more complicated than he'd ever thought possible. And every time he was around her, he grew more and more confused.

Sam was right. Their deal had started to look a little like a car crash.

Chapter Ten

Amanda awoke to the mother of all hangovers. She pressed two fingers to each temple and uttered a soft moan as she crawled out of bed. With her eyes still half-closed, she dragged herself to the bathroom and opened the medicine cabinet, where she fumbled through the rows of face cream, toothpaste and band aids, causing several items to clatter into the sink as she rifled through.

She scowled and scratched her head. Where in God's name had she put the aspirin? A fuzzy image of George drifted back. She remembered him setting the bottle on the kitchen counter, but couldn't recall why.

So she plodded down the hall, aggravated to have to go so far, snatched up the aspirin bottle and struggled with the childproof cap. When she finally wrestled the cap loose, she shook out two pills and chased them down with several gulps of cold water. Then she placed a hand on her stomach and tried to determine if she needed to throw up and whether, if by doing so, she'd feel better.

Well done. Just twelve hours after she declared her brother irresponsible, she'd gone out and gotten absolutely hammered. Nice. No wonder Rob had problems.

She needed caffeine.

Amanda shuffled to the refrigerator and pulled out a Diet Coke. She popped the top and guzzled nearly half the can as she tried to figure out what had gotten into her. She was responsible. That was her thing. She was square, uptight and sort of un-cool. She never got drunk. She hadn't been drunk since college—in the last carefree days that had ended the night her parents died. She was always too busy worrying about life or work or her brother to let herself go in that way. But the night before, responsibility had flown the coop and she'd acted all kinds of crazy. For the second time in the past week, she wondered if she was having a nervous breakdown.

Amanda glanced down at her tank top and panties and realized she probably looked as bad as she felt. She couldn't remember taking the time to remove last night's makeup, which meant it was probably smeared all over her face. Hell, her false eyelashes must still be on. She didn't have the courage to look in the mirror or the energy to find one.

Her cell buzzed.

She glanced at the display and groaned. For a brief moment, she considered ignoring it, but knew it would just delay the inevitable, so she hit the button to connect.

"Hullo," she mumbled and then took a big swig of Diet Coke.

"You sound terrible," Kate said. "What's wrong?"

"I'm hung way over." Amanda pulled out a barstool and covered her mouth to muffle a delicate belch. Then, she propped her head up with one hand.

"Since you chose to over-indulge last night, I assume the conversation with your brother didn't go well."

Amanda sighed. "He doesn't have the money. It's gone."

A long silence followed and then Kate said, "Well then we'll just have to find another way to pay Jake back. Sam and I could—"

"Don't even say it." Amanda's tone sounded harsher than intended. "I'm not borrowing money from you guys. This isn't your problem." Amanda swallowed more Diet Coke and tried to determine if she needed a third aspirin.

"Why can't you ever let anyone help?" Kate sounded annoyed.

Why did everyone keep saying that? She would ask for help if she needed it. But she didn't. She could handle this on her own.

Instead of saying as much, Amanda changed the subject. "Also, it's too late. I'm out of options. I agreed to marry Jake."

"Amanda, you *can't!*"

She pulled the phone away until Kate was done bellowing and then returned it to her ear. "Please. No yelling. My head is killing me."

"You can't go through with a fake marriage. You need to back out."

"I don't have a choice."

"Don't go there," Kate scolded. "You have a choice and you know it."

"That's easy for you to say. You're married to Mr. Perfect Perfington with one perfect little mini-me on the way." Her voice trailed off as she recognized the sullen, jealous tenor of her words. But she couldn't stop herself from adding, "Your life's perfect."

"My life isn't perfect," Kate said. "Nobody's is."

"Yours is pretty damned close." She felt a stab of guilt. It wasn't fair to make Kate feel badly just because all her dreams had come true. Amanda was happy for her; truly happy. But Amanda's hot mess of a life situation, made Kate's real-life fairytale pretty hard to swallow. "I'm sorry," she sighed and pressed her forehead against the cool fridge. "I'm just hung over and cranky." And sick to her stomach.

"It's okay." Kate's southern drawl took on a gentle, nurturing tone—something Amanda didn't get to experience too often and it soothed her prickly nerves. "You know"—Kate paused in that way she had when she considered herself about to say something profound—"daddy always says making two left turns doesn't compensate for not turning right when you should have."

Amanda frowned and pinched the bridge of her nose. The pressure didn't relieve her headache or her general irritation. "Maybe it's the wine fog, but your dad's words of wisdom make no sense."

"It *means* you need to do what's right; now, not later. Say no to Jake's deal. Figure the rest out later."

"I can't. I spent the money and so did my brother. I'm out of options."

Kate heaved a great sigh which made Amanda feel like a lost cause. "How much did you drink?"

"I lost count."

"Getting drunk won't help."

"Says the girl who's seven month's pregnant, and therefore, unable to drink," she said. "If you weren't pregnant, you would've been right beside me having sympathy cocktails and this morning you'd be in exactly the same condition as me."

"I would've made you stop at two," Kate sniffed. "You need to spend your time dreaming up a real solution to this problem, *not* drowning your sorrows."

Amanda rolled her eyes. "I find it fascinating I'm getting the lecture when *you're* the one who first suggested this—what did you call it?—a left turn?" She shook her head which only make it hurt worse and wished she'd let Kate's call roll to voicemail. "I should've known better than to listen to you."

"That's not fair." Kate sounded wounded.

"Oh, and that's not even the best part. I went out with some work friends last night and George brought me home. Jake walked in right before he left."

"Jake ran into *Gorgeous George*?"

"Yes, Jake ran into Gorgeous George." Her memory wasn't great, but she recalled how the two men had stared each other down. "As I recall, there was a whole lot of testosterone flying around."

Kate giggled. "Oh, wow. If I knew George would show up, it would've been worth getting dressed up and sipping Shirley Temples all night. I'm sorry I missed it."

Amanda stood and reached for the third aspirin. "Why is this funny?"

"I just think it's a good thing Jake saw you with another guy," Kate said, a hint of laughter lingered in her tone. "I can just picture the look on his face. It doesn't hurt that George is such a hottie." She snickered.

Amanda envisioned Kate rubbing her hands together like some twisted love fairy. "You're evil."

"I'm realistic—at least as it relates to men," Kate said. "It's good for Jake to think he's got a little competition."

"He doesn't," Amanda said. "Believe me, I wish he did."

She popped aspirin number three and washed it down with more Diet Coke. Then she leaned over and placed her elbows on the counter. "If you owned a gun, I'd beg you to shoot me right now."

"I do own a gun. It's got a pink and white handle," Kate said, a twinge of pride in her voice.

Of course she did. "So are you always packing heat?" It was a sobering thought.

"Sometimes. Anyway, tell me what happened," Kate said, her voice laced with excitement. "And you have to tell me *everything*!" Her drawl stretched the last word into five syllables.

"As I recall, they just gave each other the snake eye for a while, then George left. And then, I agreed to marry Jake."

"Which is a huge mistake," Kate said.

"You think? Of *course* it's a mistake." Amanda tossed the empty Diet Coke can into the recycle bin and opened the fridge to grab another. "But you'll be happy to learn, I negotiated a payment just shy of—" she paused and tried to recall the exact figure—"three million dollars." She popped the top and slouched back over the counter as Kate gasped. "I know," Amanda said. "It's ridiculous, but Jake pressed me for a dollar amount and I didn't have time to think about it, so I blurted out the first thing that came to me."

"How'd you come up with three million?"

"I asked for five hundred thousand on top of our original agreement, plus the apartment in Paris."

"Good lord," Kate whispered.

"I was pissed. He shouldn't have pushed me the way he did," Amanda said, recognizing the defensiveness in her tone. "Anyway, how was I supposed to know the apartment was worth two million? I haven't even seen it yet."

"I don't know what to say."

"Oh...and I kissed him. Or technically, he kissed me, I guess."

Kate remained quiet for so long, Amanda pulled the phone away and peered at the display to see if she still had a signal. She put the phone back to her ear and said, "Tell me what you're thinking."

"I was just thinking that I'm really enjoying this view," Jake drawled.

Amanda nearly jumped out of her skin.

She spun around, knocking her Diet Coke over in the process, to find Jake at the other end of the kitchen island watching her, the corners of his lips twitching. She snatched up a kitchen towel and threw it on top of the growing puddle of Diet Coke. She grabbed another and held it in front of her scantily clad body. "Kate, I have to go. I'll call you later."

"But I want to hear—"

Amanda disconnected the call and set the phone on the counter. She eyed the front door. Noting the locked deadbolt, she looked back at Jake and said, "How'd you get in?"

"I never left." He leaned against the wall and pointed his thumb toward the living room. "I slept on your couch last night. By the way, it's as uncomfortable as it looks, in case you wondered. My back is killing me."

"How long have you been standing there?"

"Long enough," he said with a grin. "And in case you don't remember, you kissed me back."

Her cheeks grew warm and her massive headache faded in importance as her first order of business shifted to putting on some clothes. She inched around the kitchen island in the direction of her bedroom. "Can you at least pretend to be a gentleman and close your eyes so I can get to the bedroom?"

He closed his eyes and chuckled. "As long as you're headed that way, you might want to comb your hair and wash your face."

She threw the towels on the counter and sprinted down the hall. Ten minutes ago, she wouldn't have guessed herself capable of moving that fast. Her former trainer would've loved to see that much hustle.

Then again, the trainer was history along with most other luxuries. If she really went through with this fake wedding, she'd have to give him a call again.

Amanda closed the bedroom door and headed to the closet where she pulled on faded black sweatpants and added a powder blue Northwestern University tank top over the black one she already wore. Then she strolled into the bathroom and flipped on the light. She stopped short as she caught her reflection in the mirror. Morning-After Barbie stared back.

Amanda groaned and ran her fingers through her tangled hair, which was smashed flat on one side. Mascara had smudged under her eyes and onto her cheeks. And only one false eyelash remained in place, though it was partially detached. No telling what had happened to the other one. For all she knew, she'd guzzled it down along with the Diet Coke and aspirin.

She turned on the faucet and scrubbed her face. Then she brushed her teeth and scraped her hair back into a ponytail. Several minutes later, a much more presentable Amanda trod back into the kitchen. She inhaled the heavenly scent of coffee and felt the first stirrings of life inside. "Mmm, you read my mind."

Jake turned and his eyes skimmed over her as he said, "I think I prefer the last outfit, in case you wondered." He pushed a steaming coffee mug toward her.

"Hilarious." She eyed him sternly as she reached for the cream and sugar and doctored her drink in record time. "You know, I don't recall inviting you to stay last night."

He shrugged. "Maybe I wanted to be sure you were okay." He opened the refrigerator and pulled out a carton of eggs. She sipped her coffee and tried to mask her surprise. "What're you doing?"

He glanced over his shoulder. "You need to eat. You'll feel better." Jake cracked two eggs into a glass bowl.

Her mouth dropped open. In the entire year they'd dated, he'd only cooked for her *once*—and he'd been in love then or so he'd said. Why bother now? He didn't need to butter her up. She'd already agreed to go through with the marriage. She kept those thoughts to herself and instead, asked, "Seriously, why did you stay?" And why are you being so nice?

He turned toward her as he whisked the eggs. "We haven't finished negotiating."

She groaned and her voice sounded dangerously close to a whine as she said, "Can't we finish negotiating later? I'm not in the mood. I need a nap."

"You just woke up," Jake pointed out as he dumped the egg mixture into the pan. The butter and eggs sizzled as he wiped his hands on a towel and then started to scrape the pan. "We need to finish what we started last night. Do you want toast?"

Not everything they started. She planned to stay away from him. No more kissing or anything else. The tantalizing mix of aromas finally got to her and Amanda surrendered. "I'd love some toast." Maybe it would absorb some of the alcohol.

Five minutes later, Jake set a plate of steaming eggs and toast in front of her. *"Eat."*

Her stomach growled. She broke off a piece of toast and buttered it while Jake pulled up a barstool.

"I've considered your demands and now I have a few of my own."

She stopped buttering and regarded him with narrowed eyes. "Okay." She popped a generous bite of toast into her mouth and chewed.

"After last night, I decided our new terms need to include a few things."

Every muscle in her body tensed and she dropped the toast and picked up the napkin to dab at her mouth. "Such as..."

"I need your help with marketing," he said. "My meeting with the investment group is on Monday. I'm meeting with Sam's brother's group. You know Rand, right? Anyway, I only have four days to get my pitch in shape and it needs serious help."

"That's easy enough." She hoped everything else he asked would be as easy. Cautiously optimistic, she speared some eggs and said, "Is that it?" She popped the eggs into her mouth.

"No. We need to make this deal official as soon as possible."

She coughed and a few bits of egg flew out. She picked up her napkin and wiped her mouth. Then she took a sip of coffee. After she swallowed, she said, "By official, you mean *get married* as soon as possible?"

He nodded.

Her stomach churned and she slowly pushed her plate away. "What's the rush?"

"I need access to the money and since we've agreed to do it, we need to just get on with it. Besides, the sooner we get started, the sooner it'll be over. We should get busy planning the wedding, too."

Her eyes bugged out. "Wedding!" She shook her head so vigorously, her hair tossed side to side. "No." Her stomach lurched and she told herself to calm down or she really would throw up. "I mean, can't we just do it at the courthouse? You know...no fuss?"

Jake shook his head. "Only if you plan to cause a major scandal. Lowell's don't get married at Cook County Courthouse. It might be a fake marriage, but it has to come with a real ceremony. We can keep it small, but Max will expect something nice. Remember, you're the blushing bride and of course he'll assume you'll want a fabulous wedding. Anything less would raise his suspicions."

Think fast.

She pursed her lips and tried to sound convincing as she said, "You know, I've always wanted a destination wedding. What do you think about Cabo?"

Jake shot her a pointed look. "Nice try. No courthouse, no running away to Mexico. We'll get married in Chicago."

She glared at him. "You know, I never realized how bossy you are."

"I've never had this much at stake before. Neither have you. So let's just play it safe and do what we have to do."

Her shoulders slumped in defeat as she said, "How soon?"

"I don't want to wait longer than a month or two at most. We'll pick a date in the next week or so and then we can start planning the details."

"I take it by *we* you mean *me*."

He nodded. "I'm definitely not doing it. I'll be busy getting the business funded."

Her mouth twisted. No wonder he'd pushed her to take the leave of absence. And she'd fallen for it. In truth, it had been her decision and one she'd made because she was just so damn tired and stressed out. But still, she hadn't counted on planning a wedding.

A light bulb flashed. "Wait a minute. You said the pitch happens in four days, right?"

"Monday morning."

"Maybe Rand will fund the whole thing. Then we can just forget this crazy marriage idea." Hope stirred inside and she sat up a little straighter as the idea took hold. "Maybe you won't need your trust at all." Then she could negotiate some easy payment terms and repay the hundred grand she owed him over the course of the next decade or two...or four.

"No. I wish, believe me. But these sorts of things generally take several months and numerous meetings. Plus, my pitch looks stronger to other investors if I partially fund the business myself."

"Come on...its Rand. Do you really think he's going to turn you down or drag out the decision-making process? I'll bet he forks over everything you're looking for on Monday." She sat back and folded her arms, feeling supremely pleased with herself.

"Rand is a venture capitalist. He's in the business of making money and no matter how much he likes me, he won't give me funding unless he's sure it'll generate a good return. My relationship with Sam got me the meeting, but my business idea will have to do the rest. And I don't expect him to do me any favors or short change the process due to our relationship."

She expelled a long sigh of resignation. "Fine. What else."

He turned to face her. "You need to move in with me; tomorrow."

Her eyes grew round. "Move in...tomorrow? No! I mean, can't it wait until after the wedding?"

"We probably could if you understood that being engaged means you can't date."

"Don't be ridiculous. I told you; George is a *friend*."

"Friend or not, what do you think people will think if other guys bring you home at night? And you don't wear your engagement ring."

"What if I promise not to do it again?"

He shook his head. "No dice. I need to keep an eye on you. I can't risk you blowing our business deal."

She tucked her hair behind her ear and pulled her plate closer again. She speared a huge forkful of eggs and said, "Fair enough. I'll move in and I'll keep that monstrosity of a ring on. But we'll need to define some boundaries." She shoved the eggs into her mouth and her cheeks bulged out as she chewed, eyeing him with a look of irritation.

"Like what?" He looked somewhat amused as he watched her chew. "Enjoying those eggs?"

She ignored his last comment. After she swallowed, she said, "Like no more repeats of last night; that kiss...what happened," she shook her head and dabbed her mouth with her napkin. "Not going to happen again."

His blue eyes locked with hers. "The way I remember it, you enjoyed last night as much as I did."

"I beg to differ," she said. "Last night was a bad idea."

"Last night was a great idea." His gaze never wavered as he said, "Its okay to let go every now and again, Amanda. You don't always have to be so in control."

Of course he'd say that. His heart never got involved. From her perspective, last night had been the furthest thing from a great idea she could imagine. And she couldn't afford to be anything less than totally in control around him. If she let her guard down one iota, if she allowed old feelings for him to resurface, it would only lead to heartbreak. "Thanks for the advice."

He shrugged. "This thing between us just hasn't run its course. I can't see any harm in letting it play out."

She dropped her fork on the plate. "Letting it play out."

"Yes. While we're going through the motions of faking a marriage, we could use the opportunity to get each other out of our systems."

What an ass.

"Wow. You know, when you put it like that, I'm not sure how I could resist." She summoned her sternest tone, the one she needed to start using with Rob, as she said, "I told you; sex isn't part of the package and if you don't drop it, the deal is off." They might be over, but agreeing to his idea would be tantamount to playing with fire and she was pretty sure she'd be the only one who got burned.

Jake raised his hands in mock surrender. "Okay, okay. We can keep it all business if you want."

"Oh, I definitely want. Remember that."

"You know, our agreement could take a long time to work through. You might decide you need a little fun."

She lifted her chin. "If I need fun, I'll have no trouble finding it."

"Listen. While this agreement is underway, our options for fun are limited. I can't afford for my grandfather to get suspicious. So while we're in it, we're both committed—like it or not."

She didn't like it. Not one little bit.

"But we'll play it your way. We'll see how long your resolution lasts."

"Oh, it'll last." She felt a pang of disappointment, but ignored it. The no hanky panky clause was the first good decision she'd made since they'd left the cabin. Had it really only been five days? It seemed like five years.

She took a last bite of toast. He'd been right about the food. She felt almost human again. She picked up her plate and headed toward the sink, but Jake took it from her.

"I'll clean up."

"Thanks." She sat back down. "Is there anything else we need to discuss? I am seriously going back to bed."

"Just one," he said as he carried the plate to the sink and rinsed it off. He placed it in the dishwasher and then turned and locked eyes with her as he leaned back against the counter. "I think three million is a little steep, don't you?"

She tipped her chin down and mumbled, "I didn't know how much the Paris apartment was worth." Her outlandish demands, which had seemed so smart last night, made her feel like a greedy little conniver now. But it was his fault. He shouldn't have pushed her to come up with a figure on the fly. And while drunk.

"How does half a million in cash plus the year in Paris sound? It will include the hundred thousand dollar advance plus another four hundred thousand payable when this thing is over," he said. "You can still stay in the Paris apartment, but when the year is up you have to move out. You can't keep the apartment. It's been in our family too long."

"I didn't expect to keep the apartment. I don't know why I said that last night."

"Maybe the wine made you do it." He grinned.

She drew a long breath and gazed up at him. "Half a million is very generous Jake."

"It's fair. I know how much you're giving up. Your life will be on hold. You should at least get a measure of long-term security in return." He cleared his throat. "The movers will come by in the morning and you'll be settled in by tomorrow night." He stood and walked to the door. "And if you change your mind on the fun front, just remember; my bedroom door is always open."

"Don't hold your breath."

"Oh, one more thing." The gleam in his eyes matched his wicked grin as he said, "Try to steer clear of Gorgeous George." He winked and ducked his head, slamming the door shut just before the wooden spoon she threw bounced against it.

Chapter Eleven

Jake entered the fifteenth floor law office suite Sam shared with his younger brother and waved at the receptionist talking on the phone. She smiled and pointed down the hall. Jake nodded and headed toward Sam's corner office, rapped his knuckles twice and then walked in.

"Hey bud." Sam stood and gestured to the seating area in the corner, lifted a folder from his desk and handed it to Jake. "This contains two copies of the revised agreement. As soon as you both sign this new addendum, the revised terms go into effect." Sam dropped into a wing chair and watched Jake leaf through the papers.

After a few minutes, Jake tossed the folder onto the table. "Thanks."

Sam tapped his index finger on the arm of the chair and regarded his friend thoughtfully. "It's not too late to rethink this bone-headed plan, bro."

"Don't start." Jake's tone warned his friend to back off. "I've made up my mind."

Sam grinned. "You're harder-headed than she is, if that's possible."

Jake changed the subject. "I ran into some guy named George at Amanda's last night," Jake said. "Ring a bell?"

"They work together. I've met him a few times," Sam said. "Kate says the girls love him."

Jake scoffed. "Yeah, I heard; *Gorgeous* George."

Sam chuckled. "Sounds like something my wife would've come up with." He shrugged. "He seems like an okay guy—"

"Who's got a thing for Amanda?"

Sam smirked. "What do you care? You're over her, remember?"

"She's going to be my wife."

Sam pointed to the folder and raised a brow. "Your wife for hire. Big difference."

"So my wife for hire should be able to date."

"Not what I said. Besides, I don't think Amanda wants to date him. If she did, she would've done so while you were over in Iraq."

Jake wanted to push Sam for more details, but didn't because if he did, Sam would jump all over it. He'd have to do his own research on George.

"If you ask me, you should just marry Amanda for real," Sam continued. "I never understood why you broke up—"

Jake shot to his feet and glared at Sam as he said, "I didn't ask you." His tone sounded harsher than intended and he waved his hands in silent apology before striding to the window where he gazed out at the noonday traffic. After several minutes, he turned to face Sam and said, "What do I know about making a relationship work."

Sam pushed back in his chair and cross his ankle over his knee. "What does anyone know? You do your best."

Jake bit back a harsh laugh. "Unfortunately, when it comes to relationships, my family's best can be pretty damned bad."

"Max did okay. Look how long he and Winnie were married before she died."

"Forty-five years." Jake shoved his hands in his jeans pocket. "But my father's relationship failures overshadowed my grandfather's success."

"So you broke up with Amanda because of your father."

Jake spread his arms wide. "My father divorced four times. *Four!*

And in between those catastrophes, he paraded around enough girl-friends—or whatever you want to call them—to populate a small city."

"You're not your father. You can't let his mistakes control your life."

Anger erupted inside and Jake shouted, "Why does everyone keep spewing out pop psychology garbage whenever my father is mentioned!"

Sam frowned, but didn't back down. Sam never backed down. "You and Cal couldn't be more different. I always liked your father—"

Jake choked back a bitter laugh. "Cal was a great guy to have a *drink* with. But as a parent or husband, he sucked."

"You're not Cal," Sam said, regarding Jake intently. "So you're telling me you broke up with Amanda because you consider yourself bad husband material."

"It's not the only reason, but it's a reason—and a good one, in my book."

Sam shook his head a few times, then shrugged and looked down. A few moments later, he raised his head and opened his mouth as if to speak, but then closed it and shook his head again. His mouth twisted as he looked away. "Well, this is a new one."

Jake folded his arms. "What."

Sam looked him straight in the eye. "We've been friends since we were five and this is the first time..." He paused, then lifted his chin and said, "I didn't know you were such a chicken-shit."

Jake scowled. "I'd call it being honest with myself."

"Dude, your reason for breaking up with Amanda was a cop out, and you *know* it."

Jake fought a wave of embarrassment as he skulked back to his chair. "I had other reasons," he grumbled.

Sam folded his arms across his chest and appeared to be enjoying himself as he said, "Let's hear 'em."

Jake sat up straight and tried to regain his dignity. "For one thing, I hate how she is with her brother. When I looked into the future, I saw a never-ending stream of issues with that kid. And given her current situation, it appears I nailed that one."

"Rob is immature and sometimes, he takes advantage of Amanda, but he's not a bad kid. If you ask me, you could've done him a world of good."

Jake's voice cracked as he said, "Me?"

"Yes you. Rob needs a stable male influence. Remember, he lost his parents at the age of thirteen so he missed out on a male figure at probably the most critical age. Since then, he's had only Amanda. And besides, he idolizes you."

"I never had a positive male influence either."

"You've enjoyed plenty while in the Navy." Sam regarded Jake with interest. "I always believed it to be a primary reason you went the military route instead of following the expected Lowell path into the Ivy League and then a career in the family business."

Sam was right. His Navy career had given him the foundation he'd missed from his father, but instead of admitting as much to Sam, he changed the subject. "Anyway, my family provides enough problems to keep me busy for a lifetime. The last thing I'd do is sign up for all that trouble with someone else's."

Sam's jaw went slack and he regarded Jake with disbelief, as though he had just proposed a pissing contest right then and there. "Well, if you play your cards right, maybe you can manage to go your whole life without ever *really* caring for anyone but yourself."

Jake tapped his thumb on the arm of his chair and told himself to cool off. He hadn't come here to get into it with Sam. When he felt more in control, he said, "I know Rob's not all bad, but he needs a firm hand."

"Which you could've been," Sam said—clearly not ready to concede his point. "You *still* could, regardless of what happens with you and Amanda. He'd listen to you."

Jake shook his head. "I don't want to get in the middle of it. Between my father's death and the stuff with Rob, everything became too difficult between Amanda and me. We have differing views on family and her brother and a slew of other things. Eventually, those differences would have torn us apart anyway. Plus, I was about to ship out for a year, so I decided to cut my losses."

Sam leaned forward and braced his elbows on his knees. "But see, you haven't cut your losses. You're right in the thick of it, bro. And you put yourself there. For the past week, I've begged you to forget this phony engagement idea and to not run, but *sprint*, in the other direction. But you refuse to listen." Sam jabbed a finger at the folder and his voice cracked as he said, "And now, you're going to go through with an actual marriage. You call that staying out of it?"

Jake thumb tapped the chair harder and he wished he'd asked Sam to email the contract. The last thing he needed was a lecture. But since Sam's diatribe showed no signs of stopping, Jake had little choice but to sit there and listen.

"If you didn't want to be with Amanda, you would've found some other girl for this deal—like Bethany. Your relationship with her ended long before you got involved with Amanda and you didn't care for her in the same way. So it would've been far less complicated to do this deal with her. With Amanda..." Sam shook his head as if to say Jake had been crazy to think the idea could work.

"Bethany? No way. That girl is all *kinds* of crazy. She'd be the last one I'd ask. I still have nightmares just thinking about all the crazy shit she did." Jake grimaced.

"Well, you could've asked someone else. But you didn't. You asked Amanda. You were only back for what—a day?—when you proposed." He leaned back in his chair again, looking supremely satisfied to have made his point.

Jake fixed Sam with a steely-eyed stare. He'd heard enough. "Back to Rob," he said. "Did you find anything out?"

Sam relaxed. "Yeah...well a little, I guess. I need to ask around a bit more."

"Let's hear it."

"I'm not sure which part is true and which is rumor." Sam shook his head. "But from what I've gathered, Rob is definitely involved in starting a restaurant, so he told the truth there. But what really bothers me is the gossip about his partners."

Jake frowned. "What about his partners?"

"Supposedly, there are some questionable types involved. A few partners have rumored ties to organized crime and supposedly, two or three nights a week, they host high stakes poker games at the half-finished restaurant—*illegal*, high stakes poker games."

Jake fell back in the chair. "No wonder the restaurant is experiencing construction delays. Do your sources think Rob knows the truth about his partners?"

"They didn't say, but I'd guess not," Sam said. "The kid's only twenty-three and as you know all too well, he's clueless about three quarters of the time. And, the questionable folks seem to have come in through a minority partner Rob doesn't know well."

Jake groaned. "What a mess."

"That it is," Sam said. "So what are we going to do about it?"

Jake stood and picked up the folder as he headed to the door. "I'll guess I'll pay Rob a visit."

* * *

When Amanda stepped out of the shower, the apartment phone was ringing. No one ever called her landline phone. Probably a telemarketer. She decided to let the answering machine pick up.

She didn't subscribe to the voicemail service provided by the phone company. She used one of those old school answering machines from the nineties—the kind that required a cassette tape of the sort they didn't even sell anymore; the kind that displayed red digital numbers. It had been her parent's machine and she couldn't bear to part with it. It made her feel closer to them somehow.

As she dried off, she heard a male voice leaving a message. A raspy male voice. Max.

Amanda dropped the towel, grabbed her robe off the hook and pulled it on. Then she raced down the hall, arriving just as the message ended. Elbows resting on the counter, she pressed the message button and listened intently.

"Hello Amanda, this is Max. I'd like you to swing by today after four, if you can. I'll be out at the Barrington house. I think you have the address." He paused and then said, "If you could keep our visit private, I'd be very grateful."

Private. She bit her lip and rewound the message. She listened three times. Private as in, don't tell Jake. Private as in, more lies. Would the lying never end?

She sighed. He wouldn't ask for privacy unless it was something important.

Amanda picked up the phone and punched in the number to Max's office. His assistant said Max was on a call, so she left a message confirming that she'd meet him at the Barrington house at four.

After she hung up, she yanked a paper towel off the roll and sopped up the puddle of water she'd created on her wood floor. Then she scurried down the hall to finish drying off and getting ready. Kate would kill her if she was late.

Ten minutes later, she was about the flip on the dryer when someone knocked on the door. Amanda trotted down the hall and peered through the peephole.

Jake.

She opened the door and leaned against it. "You seem to have a knack for knowing when I've just gotten out of the shower," she said. "Did you forget something?"

"Can I come in?"

"I'm sort of in a hurry," she said. "I have to help Kate with the cake tasting for Sam's party on Saturday."

"This will only take a minute." Jake walked in, a manila folder tucked under his arm.

She rolled her eyes. "By all means, come in. It's not like I'm in a rush or anything."

"You look perkier than you did a few hours ago," he said.

"The shower helped as did the three hour nap," she said, glancing at the clock on the stove. "Listen, I don't have time for chit chat. Was there something you needed?"

Jake strode into the living room, set the folder on the table and pulled out a stack of papers. "After I left this morning, I asked Sam to update our agreement and I thought we should get the formalities out of the way as soon as possible." He handed her a pen and clicked the tip.

She sat down, took the pen and pulled the papers toward her.

"Don't you want to review the terms?"

"No." She scribbled her name with a flourish and initialed in all the appropriate spaces, then held the pen out. Jake took it, signed and initialed as well and then slid the papers back into the folder.

She stood and started for the door, expecting him to follow, but he remained seated. She stopped and turned around. "Was there something else?"

"Amanda, we'll be spending a lot of time together over the next several months."

She folded her arms. "Yes."

"I've been thinking..." He glanced at her and then looked away, clearly uncomfortable. He shifted in his seat and then said, "I wanted you to know. . ." He sighed as he faltered again.

Amanda's arms dropped to her side and she took a half step forward. He always said those words in her dreams, just before he begged her for a second chance; before he asked if they could give their relationship another try. A real one. She stopped breathing for a moment as her eyes searched his face. She had convinced herself she was over him, but she was just kidding herself. If there'd been even a shred of doubt about that fact, her behavior last night had cleared it up. She'd been dancing very close to the flame and, if not for his cold, calculated mention of their deal, she definitely would have done something she regretted. Thank God she hadn't. But she knew that if Jake indicated, even hinted he wanted to give their relationship another try, she'd chuck the just business idea and pounce on him.

"I just wanted to tell you..." His lips twisted into a lop-sided grin, the one he only made when he was uncomfortable. That's all it took to convince her he'd finally come to his senses. Her pulse raced as she moved toward him. "I wanted you to know; if you need help with your brother, well, I'm here for you."

She felt like he'd dumped a bucket of cold water over her. She stopped in her tracks, her voice flat and emotionless. "My brother. You want to help with my brother," she said, kicking her volume up a notch. Anger simmered inside. She felt stupid and slightly embarrassed for what she'd been thinking. She should've known better. Jake was clearly incapable of making a commitment.

"Yes." He studied her intently as if trying to determine the reason behind her sudden change in mood. "I know you agreed to this deal because of Rob. You know...with the debt and all. I'd like to help with him, you know, to guide him or whatever." He shifted his weight, the expression on his face made his discomfort obvious.

"You want to help me with Rob." She shook her head in bewilderment. "Might I remind you that I didn't ask for your help with my brother?"

He frowned. "I know you didn't. I'm offering it. As a friend. It seems the least I can do after everything you're doing to help me get access to my trust fund."

A friend. Nice. Her hands balled into fists and she fantasized briefly about cracking him across the jaw as memories of their countless fights about her brother drifted back. She must be out of her mind. And she definitely needed to stop pinning fleeting hopes and dreams to a man she knew would only hurt her. No wonder her life was in such sorry shape. But instead of saying as much, she drew in a long breath and tried to exude a composure she didn't feel as she said, "Thanks, but I'll take a pass."

"It's okay to let friends lend a hand, Amanda." He blew out a long breath and shook his head. "It doesn't mean you're weak."

"I don't have a problem accepting help from friends," she bit out the words, still trying to hang onto whatever self-composure she could muster. "But we're not friends. We're business partners. And you can't stand my brother. You've always had it in for him." She jammed a fist onto her hip. "I haven't forgotten a single nasty, mean-spirited thing you said about him so you'd be pretty much the last person I'd come to for help—assuming I needed any help, that is."

Jake stood, his jaw clenched. "Wake up, Amanda. That kid's been without a father figure for some time."

"Let me get this straight. You want to be a father figure to my brother. You." She threw her head back and barked out a bitter laugh. "That is the most *ridiculous* thing I've ever heard."

"I just—"

"Actually, it's hysterical," she said, continuing her rant. "The last time I looked, you couldn't make a commitment to anyone. In fact, the only thing you've ever cared about or *really* committed to—besides *yourself* of course—was your Navy career. And I guess now, maybe this business you want to start. But people?" She folded her arms across her chest and tilted her head as she eyed him with disdain. "Well, people aren't really your strong suit, now are they?"

His voice sounded dangerously soft as he said, "I can't commit."

"Everyone knows this. And also, if you believe I'd *ever* ask you for help with my brother—or anything else, for that matter—then you are insane."

His eyes narrowed as he bit out, "Are you finished?"

She lifted her chin. "No, *we're* finished." She spun on her heel, but Jake stepped in front of her.

"We're definitely not finished." Jake's gazed down at her. "That much was glaringly obvious to both of us last night—no matter how much you're trying to deny it now. And continuing to pretend we can keep this deal all business is the most ridiculous thing *I've* ever heard."

He moved closer and she took a half step back. Every instinct warned her to run, but then he touched her. His hand slid up her arm and every nerve ending, every fiber of her being came alive.

"How long are we going to pretend this thing between us is over?" His lips descended and as much as her head screamed run, her body, her soul had different ideas. His arms drew her close and the second his lips touched hers, the internal warring was over. Her arms wound around his neck as their kisses grew more intense, more passionate and for the first time in as long as she could remember, desire won out over responsibility and good judgment as she finally surrendered to the urge of the moment; to her heart.

Jake pulled away and gazed down at her, the deep longing in his eyes telling her more than he would ever say to her. And it was enough. It had to be. She knew he'd never give her anything more and in that moment, she didn't care. She wanted him. She'd deal with the consequences later.

Jake reached for her hand, raised it to his lips and planted a gentle kiss. Then he flashed a devastatingly sexy smile and led her down the hall to her bedroom.

Chapter Twelve

Amanda pulled into the tree-lined drive and, as she rounded a bend, the Lowell estate came into view. She gaped at the enormity of the stone and brick structure. She'd never seen the place in the daytime and the word magnificent didn't even begin to describe it.

She parked in the alcove next to the front entrance and got out, gazing up at the two story castle-like front door as she climbed the wide stone steps. She rang the bell and waited, pulling her coat more tightly around her to protect herself from the blustery November wind.

A butler opened the door and took her coat.

Amanda gawked as she entered the palatial foyer. It had been a year and a half since she'd visited Max at the house and she'd forgotten its old world grandeur.

The butler motioned for her to follow and she tugged her skirt down and ran a hand over her hair as she followed him into the living room. She tried to compose herself—tried not to look awestruck—even though she felt like a field mouse that had accidentally wandered into the country manor.

Max sat in front of the fire and looked up as she entered. He stood, his smile crinkling the corners of his eyes. "Thank you for coming."

She kissed his cheek. "It's wonderful to see you." She settled into the chair across from him.

"Jake called this morning to tell me you've decided to have the wedding soon."

She nodded. "We haven't set an exact date yet, but it'll be sometime in the next few months."

Max reached over and patted her hand. "I'm so glad you're not waiting." He stood. "I'd like to show you something."

They strolled down a wide wood-paneled hallway in the back of the house until he stopped in front of two ornately carved doors. He opened them and stepped inside to switch on the lights. Then he turned to watch Amanda's reaction.

As she gazed about, she couldn't imagine a room more exquisite existed anywhere, even at the finest of luxury hotels. The room soared three stories and the entire front wall was floor to ceiling windows. Cream silk draperies framed the view of a charming flagstone-tiled courtyard with a fountain in the center, surrounded by lush gardens that looked absolutely lovely, even in November. Overhead, a pair of enormous chandeliers dripping with crystals cast a warm glow on the rich, caramel-colored walls.

The room screamed old world elegance and grandeur but at the same time, was so inviting. "It's incredible," she said, unable to mask the hint of reverence in tone. Kate would die.

"Winnie and I hosted all our business and charity events here, but since she passed three years ago, it hasn't been used. I couldn't bear it." He turned to face her. "Jake's parents married here. You're under no obligation, of course, but I thought you might consider this room for your wedding."

Her smile froze as she scrambled for an appropriate response. If their wedding had been the real thing, she couldn't imagine a more perfect, more meaningful setting. But she liked Max too much to stage their fake wedding at his home. She felt badly enough lying to him about their relationship and refused to take it further. Still, in order to avoid the bigger deception, she had to tell a little fib.

"That would be wonderful." Her smile felt stiff. "I can't wait to mention it to Jake." She had zero intention of mentioning it to Jake.

"Wonderful." Max looked pleased. "Gigi Malone is my personal event planner. She runs Exquisite Events and does all the occasions for Lowell Media. She's more than capable of handling the preparations for your wedding if you'd like. I hope you don't mind, but I gave her your number. She'll call you tonight."

"I've heard of her," Amanda said. Who hadn't? Gigi Malone was the hottest event planner in Chicago and a fixture on the social circuit. Every event she touched consisted of a veritable who's who of Chicago society. If this had been a real wedding, working with Gigi Malone would have been like a fantasy come to life.

"She's quite talented," Max said. "She'll make it easy and you'll get exactly what you want. I've already paid her fee as my gift to you."

"Thank you," she squeezed his arm. "I could certainly use the help." But inside, her stomach clinched. This whole thing was starting to get out of control.

Max closed the doors and they strolled back to the living room where they settled in front of the fire. He reached for a cigar and held it up. "Do you mind if I smoke, dear?"

She shook her head. "It's fine."

He lit the cigar, took a few quick pulls and then sank back in the chair, slowly expelling a long plume of smoke. "I'm sure you're curious about my reasons for asking you to come." His bright blue gaze locked with hers. "And why I asked you not to tell anyone."

"I am a little curious," she admitted. And given her afternoon with Jake, she felt more than a little guilty for the deception. She still couldn't believe what she'd done and still wasn't sure how she felt about it. She knew how she should feel about it. She should be deep in self-recrimination mode, vowing not to ever repeat the mistake—especially since Jake had made it all too clear their encounter meant nothing to him but a little unfinished business. He had kissed her forehead, mumbled something about seeing her soon and bolted out of her apartment as if the devil himself was in pursuit.

She'd expected as much, but still.

Amanda shook her head and forced her attention back to Max as he said, "It's no secret Jake and I have a difficult relationship. I wanted to explain why."

"You don't owe me any explanations." She definitely didn't need to get further wedged between the two men.

"I want to." He paused and drew another long pull on his cigar. After he exhaled, he said, "What do you know of Cal?"

Amanda thought back to what she'd heard about Jake's father. "I only met him a few times. All I really know is what Jake told me," she said. "As I recall, Jake's father"—she searched for the right words— "had a challenging personal life."

Max's smile didn't quite reach his eyes. "A very delicate way of putting it," he said. "Cal married four times and had several regrettable relationships with women who weren't...his match, shall we say?"

"Jake doesn't speak of his father very much, but I think it's sad," she said. "It doesn't sound like he lived a happy life."

It's always sad when someone neglects to live up to their true potential. But despite the way things turned out, Cal was once extremely happy. Unfortunately, his first wife, Emily—Jake's mother—passed away shortly after Jake turned three."

Amanda tilted her head and regarded Max thoughtfully. "Jake never mentions his mother. I knew she passed away, but he's never spoken of her."

"That's because he doesn't know much about her. Calvin and Emily met and married young. She exerted a tremendously positive influence on his life; she calmed his wild streak. They were very happy. She inspired the best in him."

Amanda frowned. "So why wouldn't his father ever speak of her? I would think it would be important to him to keep her memory alive."

"Cal wouldn't allow anyone to discuss her. He considered her loss too heartbreaking. You see, the accident occurred with Cal behind the wheel. He survived. She didn't."

In an instant, the fuzzy picture of Cal's troubled life came into sharp focus. "He blamed himself for her loss."

Max nodded slowly. "Cal buried her along with his heart, his hopes and dreams for the future. He spent the next thirty years running away from the memories, and especially from Jake, who was a constant reminder of what could have been," he said. "I thought his pain would fade in time, but he never got over it. He never forgave himself. Her death haunted him every single moment until the day another accident claimed his."

Amanda shook her head sadly. She didn't know what to say; couldn't think of the appropriate words to express what she felt. She didn't want to sound judgmental, but in her view, hiding the truth about his mother from Jake only made a heartbreaking tragedy even worse.

"Jake only sees what he experienced with his father—a man who drank too much, never made time for him and couldn't make a commitment to anyone, including himself. He never saw the man buried beneath the pain, the one with so much potential." Max raked a hand through his thick silver hair, reminding her of Jake.

"When I saw Cal going astray, I tried to get him on track. I kept him busy with work, limited access to his trust. I tried everything I could think of to protect him."

Amanda reached over and squeezed his hand. "I'm sure you did. But you can't make someone move forward. They have to want to. And it sounds like he couldn't find the strength."

At the same time, she wondered why he couldn't see himself repeating the very same mistake, but this time with Jake. Had she known him better, not feared overstepping her bounds, she would have said as much. But she didn't.

"For the past year, ever since Cal died, I've been concerned Jake would suffer the same fate. I had planned to spend time with Jake after the funeral to try to repair the relationship between us, but he shipped out a few weeks later."

"Jake couldn't be more different than Cal."

A ghost of a smile touched Max's lips. "The one trait the three of us share is that we're all risk-takers. I channeled my risk-taking into business. Jake chose the Navy and his fearlessness made him perfect for the SEALs. I'm so proud of his accomplishments there. Cal had tremendous promise in business, but he lost his north star when he lost Emily and his tendency for taking risks became focused on the wrong things. That's when I, we all, lost him and it happened long before his actual death."

Amanda grew quiet as she took it all in. But from the look on Max's face, it was clear the conversation had taken a toll on him. In an attempt to reassure him, she said, "Jake would never follow the same destructive path."

"Given his family background and without the structure of the Navy, I've been concerned Jake would lose his center." He flicked ashes into a crystal tray.

She couldn't envision Jake in the role of hard-drinking, serial-marrying playboy. He only drank socially and, given his status as poster child for commitment-phobic men, serial-marriages didn't seem too likely a scenario either. Heck, she couldn't even get him to spoon for fifteen minutes.

"You have nothing to worry about. The playboy lifestyle isn't his thing."

"I couldn't have envisioned Cal doing so either, but look how his life turned out." Max expelled a long sigh and said, "Jake witnessed a very troubled relationship between Cal and me for most of his life. He didn't understand the complexity of what really went on so he made his own interpretations and now, he views me as the enemy." She could see the regret etched into his features. "He blames me for how Cal's life turned out."

Max was right, but she wasn't about to acknowledge it and so instead said, "Talk to Jake. Tell him what you've just told me."

"The direct approach won't work. He won't listen."

"Honesty is always the best approach." Even before she'd finished the sentence, she felt like a fraud. After all, she'd just said them to the man she was contractually obligated to lie to. Nice.

Hypocrite.

She looked down and brushed a piece of imaginary lint from her skirt, afraid Max would be able to see the deceit in her eyes.

"There's one other way the three of us are alike. We all have one great love," Max said. "It devastated me when your relationship ended last year. When I first saw you together, I knew you had something special."

Amanda's stomach twisted. She had believed that once as well. But whatever they used to have was gone. In its place was a business relationship and, given the events of the afternoon, she guessed it could be a business relationship with benefits if she chose to let it continue. She lifted her chin and gazed into the fire and decided then and there. She wouldn't repeat this afternoon's mistake. It had meant nothing to Jake Lowell; nothing but a little unfinished business.

* * *

Amanda strolled into Jake's study and flopped into a chair. "I'm so exhausted; I need a new word for exhausted."

Jake pushed back from the computer screen and grinned. "You can't be finished unpacking. The movers just left. I was going to come up and help."

"I'm done. I've packed and unpacked more godforsaken boxes in the past year than in my entire life. Remember, I just moved into my condo a few months ago and while it looks neat and organized, you should check behind the closet doors and under my bed. It's like something exploded." She sighed. "I hate being disorganized, but I hate unpacking more so I've learned to unpack strategically."

He raised a brow. "Strategically."

"You know...just the things I need most."

"Would any of those things be lacy or black?"

She changed the subject, waving the stack of papers she'd brought with her. "With your pitch happening in three days, I thought we should discuss this."

He stood and gestured to the seating area across the room. "We'll be more comfortable over there. Have you had a chance to read through it?"

Amanda strolled to the sofa, kicked off her shoes and tucked her legs underneath her. "I scanned through and made some notes. Where do you want to focus?"

Jake settled on the opposite end of the sofa. "I think the content is good, but it's boring as hell."

She smiled. "I wouldn't call it boring, but it's definitely lacking emotion. But I think it'll be relatively easy to punch up the content. After all, your business is all about helping people."

"So what's missing?" He gestured to the papers. "I've read that damned presentation a thousand times and I'm stumped. It has everything. All the services and products we'll offer." He shook his head and pushed back into the sofa cushions. "I can't figure it out."

She flipped through, glancing at her notes. "I agree the content is there, but you're missing the brand. Your business idea is fascinating, but the proposal focuses too much on products and services. It's missing the heart. And it's the heart that will transform your proposal from good to killer."

"Where do we start?"

"First, we need to define what your business stands for. It's brand essence." She leaned forward. "The inspiration for your company came from somewhere. There's a burning reason driving you. Once we get clear on how to articulate it, we'll have found your brand essence. From there, it's relatively easy to put the details around it. We won't have time to develop a great logo or visual identity in time for the pitch, but we can mention in your pitch that the first wave of funding will help pay for that."

"I have no idea what any of that means. You're talking to a Navy guy, remember?"

She tapped the proposal. "It's easy to see the good your business will do for veterans, but it's not enough. You need the brand to paint a vivid picture for investors. Forget the services you'll provide. When you strip everything away, *why* is your business important? What's its true purpose?"

"I want to help wounded vets change their lives."

"So if you needed to articulate it in two words, what would they be?
He shrugged. "Changing lives?"

"It's not big enough. I mean, those words capture the end result, but it's too rational; too descriptive. The words you choose should inspire passion." She looked at him intently. "Try harder."

He steepled his fingers and tapped them as he considered her question.

She recalled Max gesturing in much the same way and was once again struck by how alike they actually were.

He thought for a long while and then shook his head in resignation. "I need your help."

"Okay. Let's look at it from your future client's perspective. They're seriously injured. They've gone through experiences most people can't fathom. Some may have realized dreams before being injured. Others had just begun to learn who they are, who they want to be, what the world holds for them. From my perspective, your essence has to be something about renewal, reinvention. Or maybe hope or possibilities."

Jake's head snapped up. "Second chances," he said, as his face broke into a huge grin. "My business will be about second chances."

"What about that phrase speaks to you?"

"I like the implication that it's never too late—no matter what you've been through. It captures the belief we all have inside ourselves that we matter; that our lives are supposed to mean something. That it's never too late for a fresh start."

"I love it. That's the passion that's missing here." She tapped the proposal.

"What's next?"

"Let me spend some time on it. I'll try to get a good draft by tomorrow afternoon. Then on Sunday, we can finalize it and do a few practice runs." She smiled. "You're going to kill it on Monday."

Chapter Thirteen

I can't believe you got an appointment with *her,*" Kate said, her voice laced with reverence as she gazed through the storefront window of Exquisite Events.

"Max arranged it. She handles all of his corporate and charitable events. Otherwise, she wouldn't give me and my fake wedding the time of day."

"No one knows it's a fake wedding," Kate said, her green eyes dancing. "I can't *wait* to see her ideas. Maybe I can get some inspiration for my business."

"You're a gifted interior designer." She playfully punched Kate's shoulder. "You don't need inspiration."

"Everyone needs inspiration from time to time and I've heard no one dresses an event better than Gigi. I wish she was helping with Sam's birthday." She cast a sideways glance at Amanda. "By the way, thanks for blowing off the cake testing yesterday. You know how stressed I am about the party tomorrow night."

"I didn't blow it off. Something came up. I told you."

"You told me this morning. But yesterday, you left me all alone at the cake place when I needed you there. I don't have a fancy event planner to fall back on." She gestured to the storefront. "You didn't even bother to call with an excuse."

"But this morning, I left two apology messages and four sucking-up-to-you texts. So which do I get credit for, the one blow off or the six apologies? Do I have to get down on my knees?"

Kate pursed her lips as if considering the idea. "You could have called me. I bet I gained ten pounds tasting all of that cake."

"The baby probably enjoyed it. And for the last time, I'm sorry. Seriously," Amanda said. "Besides, you said you wanted chocolate. How hard can it be to select an attractive-looking, decent-tasting chocolate cake?"

Kate cocked her head. "Do you realize how many different flavors of chocolate there are?

"Apparently not. Now I'm sorry I missed it." Amanda grabbed the door and started pulling it open, but Kate stopped her.

Her eyes narrowed. "Something's going on. Let's hear it," Kate said. "Why didn't you come? Or *call*? It's not like you to stand me up."

"No," Amanda said. "It actually sounds like you. I believe you stood me up last week when we were supposed to meet for spa pedicures. Remember?"

"That isn't the same thing. This is much more serious." She jammed a balled fist onto her Burberry-clad hip. "And just so you know, the only acceptable answer will involve something dramatic, like a hit and run."

In an attempt to distract her, Amanda fixed her gaze above Kate's head, squinted and pointed at a black-and-white striped awning down the street. "I've heard that place has amazing stuff. Want to swing by after we're done? I could use a new something cute for Sam's party tomorrow night."

"Amanda Wilson, don't even *try* to change the subject. Besides, you can't tempt me with cute clothes when I'm as big as a house."

"Buy some earrings," Amanda said. "Also, you know I *hate it* when you use my full name. It's so condescending."

Kate tapped her foot on the pavement and folded her arms. "Well?" Kate's eyes skimmed over her. "I don't see any cuts or bruises."

That's because the cuts and bruises were on her heart. Amanda's mouth twisted. She'd wanted to avoid this confession—for a while at least—but she found it impossible to keep secrets from Kate. "Actually I *was* involved in a hit and run yesterday; sort of."

Kate's green eyes grew round as saucers and she opened her mouth, then closed it again.

Amanda sighed. "Jake stopped by with the revised agreement yesterday. One thing led to another and..."

"You *did it!*" Kate squealed and clapped her hands.

Amanda glanced up and down the block, relieved to see the sparse afternoon crowd. At least they'd only entertained a few random strangers instead of the regular morning crowd at her neighborhood Starbucks.

"Is that true?" Kate's eyes narrowed. "Scouts honor?"

"Get real. You were *never* a girl scout. You didn't like the uniform, remember?"

"I liked the uniform—especially that cute little beret and the sash with all the bling," Kate said. "But my mother said green washes me out. Plus, the group involved too many sweaty outdoor activities and you know how I feel about that sort of thing."

Amanda rolled her eyes. "You hate outdoor sweaty activities, but you'll do Bikram Yoga for an hour in a studio heated to a hundred degrees."

"I prefer planned indoor sweating," Kate sniffed. "Besides, Mom was right. Green isn't my color." Amanda opened the door and nudged Kate inside as she prattled on. "My sisters and I organized our own group we called the Explorettes. My mom designed a special uniform—a really cute little two-piece outfit in powder blue. We didn't have a beret, though, or a sash."

Undoubtedly, the only thing they'd explored were the shopping malls in the greater Birmingham metro area. "I'm convinced Alabama is located on a different planet."

"We're not finished with this conversation," Kate hissed as she poked Amanda in the side.

"I'm not sure I need to hear any more about the Explorettes." Amanda swatted Kate's hand away. "Even after all these years, the stories never cease to amaze me."

"I've told you all this before, you just didn't listen," she said. "Just like now. I know you're trying to get me to talk about the Explorettes to distract me from the news that you slept with Jake. But it won't work. I'm not going to rest until you spill all the details."

"Forget it. I've already said too much and if you don't back off; you're wearing green at the wedding."

A tall glamorous redhead approached and glanced from one to the other as she said, "I'm Gigi Malone. Which one of you is Amanda?"

Amanda extended her hand. "Amanda Wilson. It's nice to meet you Gigi. This is my maid of honor, Kate Connelly."

They shook hands and then the girls followed Gigi through her posh showroom toward a seating area in the back.

"Who did your décor? It's amazing," Kate said.

"I did." Gigi smiled and gestured to the beige-and-chocolate striped sofa. "That means a lot, coming from you. I'm a huge fan. I'm hoping to work with you on my new condo." She winked. "We'll talk."

Kate beamed and pinched Amanda's arm when Gigi wasn't looking.

An assistant appeared and handed them each a bottle of sparkling water while Gigi perched gracefully on a zebra striped chair across from them. She looked up expectantly and said, "So the wedding is in the next few months."

"Yes. No date yet. We definitely want a small, intimate ceremony."

"But *super* elegant," Kate added.

Be quiet, Amanda mouthed, as Gigi bent her head to scribble some things on her pad.

"Are you using the Barrington estate," Gigi asked.

"I, uh…we're not sure yet."

"The ballroom is lovely. That might be the perfect setting," Gigi said.

"It is beautiful, but I'm not sure Jake will want to hold the event there," Amanda said. "If we don't choose the house, will it be hard to find another place in such a tight timeframe?"

"There are hundreds of possibilities in this city. It won't be hard to find a venue exactly suited to your preferences." She picked up a notebook and pen, flipped it open and looked up. "Let's talk style and theme. We need some design inspiration so we know where to start with the dress and flowers. We won't worry about a theme yet. First I want to hone in on your personal style." Gigi's green eyes scanned Amanda from head to toe. "Given your look, I would guess classic with a contemporary twist?"

Both girls nodded in unison.

Gigi stood. "I brought in some items from a bridal boutique down the street. Let me go and get those and we'll take a look."

"We need a bridesmaid dress to hide this." Kate rubbed her ever-expanding baby bump.

Gigi laughed. "Don't worry, we'll find the perfect dress. We can tackle your dress in our next session." Gigi disappeared through the chocolate-colored silk curtain that led to the back room.

"Don't you just *love* her? She'd be perfect for Sam's brother. I even love her name."

Obviously, Kate had developed a girl crush. "Which brother?"

"Who cares," Kate said. "They're both adorable. I'd *love* her as a sister-in-law."

"She is fabulous," Amanda agreed. "But I'm sure she already has a boyfriend."

Kate waved a hand dismissively. "Most fabulous girls are single because men are either intimidated or mistakenly convinced they already have a boyfriend," Kate said. "Besides, I didn't see a ring, which makes her fair game."

It was impossible to repress Kate's matrimonial instincts once she'd set her sights on a fix-up, so Amanda didn't even try.

"One of Sam's brothers would be good," she agreed. "Just make sure you don't start picking up stray guys at the grocery store. That wasn't your shining hour and I'm sure she'd be less tolerant of your experiments in matchmaking than I."

Kate ran a hand over the lush fabric of the sofa. "This fabric is *uh-mazing.* Planning this wedding is going to be so much fun. She has impeccable taste."

"This isn't a real wedding, remember? Actually, it's a little depressing."

Kate gazed around. "Depressing? This is a dream come true."

"A dream come true." Amanda glared at her. "How would you have liked to plan a fake wedding to Sam?"

"I wouldn't have because *I* wouldn't sit around waiting for Sam to figure out he can't live without me. I'd make sure he knew that and therefore, it wouldn't be a fake wedding."

"So you think I'm just sitting around waiting for Jake to figure out he can't live without me."

Kate's arched brow and tilted head said it all. "After what happened between you two yesterday, it wouldn't have to be a fake wedding." She shot Amanda a pointed look. "*If* you played your cards right, that is, which you probably won't."

"What cards?"

Kate rolled her eyes. "If I have to explain it, then you're a lost cause."

"No, I just mean, we have a business deal, that's all. I have the signed contract to prove it. Yesterday changes nothing. Except now, if I let it continue which I probably won't, we would be business partners with benefits."

"There's more to what happened yesterday than that. I'm sure of it. But you'll have to give him some time. He just got home from Iraq a week ago."

"Please. He's had two years. We dated for a year and have been broken up almost a year. In that time I didn't hear a peep out of him, which proves how much he cares. How much more time could he possibly need?"

Kate glanced sideways through her curtain of blonde hair. "You can't rush him. Some men need space."

"*Clearly,*" Amanda said. "All I'm saying is you can't put too much emphasis on yesterday. Granted, it happened. But it's not like he declared his undying love afterward."

"What *did* he do?" Kate's eyes searched her face. "Did you talk or...anything?"

"Afterward he just kissed me on the forehead and then bolted. I told you; hit and run." Amanda picked a piece of lint off the couch.

Kate groaned. "He didn't. Not the forehead kiss."

"Oh yes. The kind you give your kid sister."

Kate pursed her lips, looking decidedly displeased. "Well, he didn't waste any time proposing the second he got back in town. That has to mean something. If I'd agreed to fake marry the man of my dreams, I'd just go for it."

"Define *go for it.*"

"Make him fall in love with you again," she said. "Seriously, when did you become so clueless about men? This is not the time to go with the flow. It's time to go for what you want."

"What do I want?"

"Jake."

"I'm not so sure about that," Amanda said. "I mean, I'd never be able to trust him not to bolt. He'd probably leave me standing at the altar if it were a real wedding." Yesterday afternoon had scared the crap out of her and had hurt far more than she cared to admit. "I mean, sure, I still have feelings for him, but yesterday raised more questions than it answered. Maybe I just need closure."

"Or maybe you really *do* want to marry him," Kate said.

"I don't know." Amanda bit her lip. The only thing she knew for sure was she didn't want to get hurt.

"You want Jake, trust me. You're just scared and I don't blame you. But you have to push through the fear in order to get what you want. Those were your words to me when Sam and I were going through all our pre-wedding drama, remember?"

"Yes, well, Sam never ran away from you. You actually ran away from him because you didn't know if you should buck your parent's wishes and your loser of a fiancé, so you could marry the man of your dreams. That's very different."

Kate reached over and squeezed Amanda's arm. "Hon let *go*. Let yourself believe. Sometimes dreams really do come true."

"Kate—" Amanda stopped short as she heard the tip tap of designer stilettos which signaled Gigi's approach.

The glamorous redhead popped through the curtain, pulling a rack of bridal gowns behind her.

"I love it!" Kate clapped, chortling with glee. "This reminds me of my pageant days."

Gigi laughed, while Amanda shook her head ruefully.

The trio spent the next hour immersed in bridal gowns, flower arrangements and invitations. For a long while, Amanda managed to stay above the excitement. But by the time Kate zipped her into the third gown—a Vera Wang and by far her favorite—the internal warnings and cautionary voices had gone silent. She gazed into the mirror, seduced by the fantasy she saw reflected there. On some level, she knew it was dangerous. She realized that if she let herself believe she could have a happily-ever-after with Jake, her already chaotic world could come crashing down around her in a spectacularly horrific way. But as she gazed at the beautiful, form-fitting designer creation which just happened to be featured on this month's issue of Elegant Bride, she gave in to the fantasy and let go.

Kate was right. She needed to let herself dream. After all, they actually came true for some people. Why not for her?

Chapter Fourteen

Amanda shrugged off her coat and laid her gloves and purse on a chair in the foyer. Then she strolled into Jake's office. "Hey." Still on her wedding planning high, she perched on the edge of his desk and watched him type.

He stopped and peered at the computer screen. Then he looked down and began typing again, using an awkward hunt and peck method. After he finished his note, he pushed away from the computer and looked up at her with a grin. "How'd it go?"

"Awesome. I'll fill you in later." She twisted around to peer at the screen. "What are you working on?"

"My presentation," he said. "I'm trying to get it ready for you to work your brand voodoo on it."

She smiled. "Brand voodoo. I like it." Her stomach emitted a loud, prolonged grumble.

Jake's brows shot up and his grin split his face ear to ear. "Hungry much?"

She giggled. "Sorry. I haven't eaten since breakfast and I'm starved."

Jake checked his watch. "What about Luigi's? It's early so we shouldn't need reservations. Not that you'd ever need them."

She tilted her head. "What's that supposed to mean?"

"Seeing you always sent Luigi into a frenzy of activity. He'd cook a special entree; send over champagne, trip all over oozing compliments." Jake laughed and shook his head. "I figured eventually I'd have to challenge him to a dual at dawn or risk him wooing you away."

"Please. He's old enough to be my father."

"Don't be fooled by his age. He's a smoothie," Jake said. "Besides, given the way he can cook, that's one dude I wouldn't even try to compete with."

"I'd *love* to go to Luigi's. Let's go."

They strolled down the tree-lined streets of Jake's Lincoln Park neighborhood. It oozed a warm, cozy charm and ranked among her favorite neighborhoods in Chicago—consisting of a mix of young, urban professionals and families. And with Sam and Kate's place just a few blocks away, the location seemed even more perfect. The girls had dreamed of mornings at the yoga studio or Starbucks and future afternoon kids play dates in the park. Several times a month, the foursome had met at Luigi's. The corners of her lips curved up as memories of long, laughter-filled dinners drifted back and her smile blossomed into a full-blown grin when she glimpsed the familiar red and green restaurant sign.

Jake held open the door and then followed her inside. They checked their coats at the front and headed toward the hostess stand. The touch of Jake's hand at the small of her back brought a sense of comfort, reminding her of how much she'd missed his touch, his strength.

Luigi glanced up as they approached and when he spotted Jake and Amanda, his cherub-like face transformed into huge smile, displaying a generous set of unevenly-spaced teeth.

"Jake. It's good to see you, my friend," Luigi said in his accented English. He grasped Jake's hand with both of his and pumped heartily. His eyes danced as he turned to Amanda and kissed each cheek. Then he pressed a hand to his heart and his velvet brown eyes bore into hers as he said, "Amanda, I will pretend I'm not heartbroken that you've stayed away so long."

She smiled and squeezed his hand, while carefully avoiding Jake's I-told-you-so gaze. "I promise I won't let so much time pass again."

Luigi seemed satisfied with her response and as the hostess approached; he waved her away and led the couple to their favorite semi-private booth in the back. Once there, he lit the candles in the center of the table and then announced, "I cook something special. No menu."

Jake winked at Amanda as he said, "Anything you make will be great."

Luigi grinned and hurried toward the kitchen.

"I hate to say I told you so," Jake said, his blue eyes dancing. "But I told you so."

Amanda giggled. "I never noticed before."

"I don't know how you could've missed it."

"He's a charmer," she said. "He probably does that same routine with all the ladies."

"He seems to have a special thing for you." Jake said.

The U-shaped booth had been built to accommodate intimate dinners for two and she found it impossible to ignore Jake's hard, muscular thigh as it pressed against her. Even through the thick fabric of her jeans, his touch made her skin tingle. She shifted away slightly.

The waitress arrived with two glasses of champagne and a plate of calamari. After she left, Jake lifted his flute and turned to Amanda. "My new brand platform deserves a toast, as does its architect." He smiled. "Here's to Second Chances."

"You came up with it. But I agree; definitely toast-worthy." Her leaded crystal flute clinked against his. Then she tipped her glass and took a sip. "It's a great brand idea, Jake." She set her glass down and transferred some calamari to her plate.

"It definitely captures the core reason for starting the business. I can't wait to see how you weave it into the presentation for Monday."

"I'd love to hear why the phrase resonates so much. I mean—besides the obvious." She speared a calamari and popped it into her mouth.

"I've known a lot of injured men and I've seen the different ways the wounded handle the situation." He paused and appeared to consider his next words carefully. "Some dig in and go at it—charge right into—the process of moving on. They don't hesitate to change course and continue making plans for their life." His mouth twisted. "Others struggle to even see the possibilities. That's hard to watch and when it's someone you really care for, it makes you feel damned helpless."

"I can't imagine what it would be like to watch someone you love struggle through those injuries. Especially on top of how much they've already given; how much they've sacrificed." She found his dedication and passion admirable. It made her career in brand strategy seem all the more hollow by comparison. "So will your company get involved in the physical aspects of their recovery?"

"Not really. I want to structure programs and services to cover what the VA misses. Right now, the government has significant issues as it relates to diagnosing the invisible wounds. Things like PTSD and even the effect of concussive injuries on the brain."

She tilted her head to the side. "But the VA covers those things, don't they?"

He shrugged. "Yes and no. They cover it, but the truth is a lot of guys get misdiagnosed—especially as it relates to depression or PTSD or traumatic brain injuries caused by IEDs. And if they're misdiagnosed, they tend to fall through the cracks."

"That's horrible. I never realized."

He glanced at her sideways. "I know. It's shocking and it can ruin lives." He turned toward her. "Some of these injuries, if unaddressed, can lead to suicide. Did you know more veterans commit suicide in a year than have been killed in the wars of Iraq and Afghanistan combined? My business will combine treatment of those invisible wounds with post-military work programs. The military was something they believed in. Now that they're out, beyond the healing, it's important they find something else they can be as passionate about."

"I can't believe the difference your business is going to make." It actually made her feel better about how they were deceiving everyone. It made it seem worth it.

"It feels good to do something that can make a difference." His grin crinkled the corners of his eyes as he leaned forward and gazed at her intently.

Her breath caught in her throat and she snatched up her glass and sipped, trying to ignore the devastating effect of his smile.

"Anyway, the next step is to get the business funded," he said. "The private sector has to help because who knows how long it will take the government to solve the problem for those that do slip through the cracks," he said, as he raked a hand through his hair. "Even if they heal physically, if there are sustained psychological or traumatic brain injury or if the men can't envision a future where they're as fulfilled, maybe even more so, than they were before, then what's the point?" He pushed against the back of the booth and pounded his fist on the table. "They just need some help; some direction and they'll find their hope again."

She'd never seen this side of Jake before. Not really. She'd only had glimpses. It was a side of him he hid from her, from everyone— the side disguised behind a grin, a kiss or a change of subject. And it only made her fall harder.

"So what made you think of taking this on?" she asked.

The waitress appeared at the table and uncorked a bottle of Chianti. Jake did a quick tasting and nodded his approval. She poured two glasses and disappeared again.

"I saw good buddies struggle. Strong men, you know? And I wanted them to know it's never too late to change your life. Everyone deserves a second chance." He popped another bite of calamari into his mouth, no doubt to keep himself from saying more. His face, what Amanda could see of it in the shadows, appeared tinged with pink.

She bit back a smile. Her warrior faced man-made weapons and crazed terrorists without fear, but his own emotions made him squirm.

"You won't have a problem getting your business funded. I just *know* it." His perspective inspired her and surprised her, given his unforgiving views on members of his own family. This prompted her to say, "It's such an optimistic viewpoint."

He cast a lopsided grin as he picked up his wine glass. "What. You mean coming from me?"

But before she had a chance to answer, the waitress returned with a basket of warm rolls. By the time the waitress left, she rethought her answer. She didn't want to do anything, say anything to spoil the mood. He had opened up to her more in the last half hour than ever before and she just wanted to enjoy the moment. Who knew when it might come again, if ever.

She shook her head ruefully. "I forgot what I was going to say. The bread distracted me." She leaned over and closed her eyes as she breathed in the fragrant aroma. Then she reached into the basket and pulled out a piping hot roll. "I think I'm in love..." Jake regarded her with barely-concealed amusement as she slathered a generous amount of butter onto the warm bread. "This means a double workout tomorrow, but right now, I simply *do not* care." She bit into the bread, closed her eyes and moaned.

"I think I'm jealous," he said. "You never looked at me that way."

She laughed. "That's because I can't butter you."

His mouth spread into wicked grin and he winked as he said, "You never asked."

Her stomach fluttered. "Aren't you going to have any?"

He patted his mid-section. "I don't need bread. I've only been back a week and—at the rate I've been shoveling in food—I'll turn into one of those couch potatoes I despise so much within a matter of months."

"Please." She buttered another bite. "No one *needs* bread. The best things in life are not what we need; they're about what we *want*." She popped the bread into her mouth and picked up her wine glass, peering at him over the rim.

Kate was right. It wasn't over for her. Relaxed and emboldened by the wine, she buttered another piece and leaned over, teasing the warm bread to Jake's lips. He opened his mouth and his eyes never left hers as she popped it in. "Well?"

Jake nodded and after he swallowed, he gestured to the basket and said, "Hit me up."

She giggled and handed him a roll just as the waitress appeared with their entrees.

Jake looked down at his plate and eyed his entrée with lust. "Is this what I think it is?"

The waitress smiled and nodded. "Lobster ravioli; Luigi said it was your favorite."

"Oh no," Amanda gazed at her plate with a mixture of anticipation and dread. "Cream sauce." She reached over and touched his arm. "I'm going to try to find the strength to stop when I'm halfway done. If I can't, pull the plate away. Rescue me from the Lobster Ravioli or I might have to buy a whole new wardrobe."

Jake took a bite and chewed. "Live a little. Eat it all."

She scowled. "Easy for you to say. You don't have to fit into skinny jeans."

He grinned at her. "I think you look great in your skinny jeans."

They sipped at their wine and fell into silence. A few moments later, the waitress reappeared to clear the table and Luigi followed with a plate of tiramisu and two forks—a big plate of tiramisu.

Amanda's mouth—the one she'd thought completely satisfied for the night—if not the week, began to water. "*Luigi…*"

"The dessert looks perfect, Luigi, just like the meal. We'll enjoy every crumb."

"And I'll leave you to it, my friends."

As he disappeared, Amanda eyed the decadent concoction in horror. "Please don't let me eat any dessert. After that dinner, I don't need any.

"But you said it's not about needing, it's about *wanting*, remember?" Jake dug into the luscious-looking sweet and danced the mounded fork toward her mouth. "Open up."

Her gaze moved from the fork to his eyes as she said, "Are you trying to tempt me?"

"Maybe." His voice was a husky whisper. "Is it working?"

It was working alright. She looked deep into his ocean blue gaze and felt lost, gone. She dragged her eyes from his and turned her attention to the dessert. It was safer for her heart, if not her waist-line. She dug her fork into the creamy tiramisu and popped it in her mouth. "Yummy," she cooed, as she closed her eyes. She savored the taste and then ran her tongue around her lips and said, "There are no words."

"I agree." He regarded her with a burning intensity and then his gaze shifted lower. He brushed a finger at the side of her lips and said, "You forgot something."

She looked from his finger to his face and, emboldened by the wine and the man, she closed her lips around his warm skin and licked off the sweet remnants of the dessert.

"Amanda," Jake whispered as his lips touched hers.

Her heart thumped madly in response and to steady herself, she rested a hand on his thigh. With the other, she traced a finger along his strong jaw and then tenderly cupped his cheek.

"You enjoy the tiramisu?" Luigi appeared delighted to have caught them mid kiss.

They sprang apart like guilty teenagers, caught necking.

She cleared her throat. "Luigi, dinner...everything...tasted amazing."

Luigi beamed. "Then you will not wait as long next time. No?" He shifted his gaze to Jake who smiled and patted his belly.

"No chance. Now that I'm back, we'll be regulars." He turned to Amanda. "Are you ready?"

She slid out of the booth, kissed Luigi on both cheeks and then headed toward the front of the restaurant. Jake settled their bill and followed a few moments later after he'd collected their coats. He helped Amanda into hers before they stepped outside.

"Jake. That was a wonderful dinner. Thank you."

"I agree. I haven't eaten so well in a year."

Unable to resist, she jabbed him playfully in the ribs. "You didn't like my steak dinner at the cabin?"

"Okay, so it's my *second* best meal in a year." He threw his hands high.

"You're a very bad liar." Amanda snickered. But as her laughter faded, her thoughts drifted back to her meeting with Max yesterday and her mood sobered. She had felt guilty about it all day, but after dinner, she felt closer to him than ever and hated keeping it from him. It felt like her whole week had become a lie and she couldn't bear to tell another. She wanted to be honest with Jake. Before she had time to think through the consequences, she said, "Jake, I've been thinking about your brand. Something you said about why your business appealed to you."

She paused and he glanced down at her and smiled. "What."

She took a deep breath. "Do you really believe everyone deserves a second chance?"

He appeared to consider her question and then said, "I do."

"I want to tell you something." She mustered her courage and then plunged in. "Your grandfather invited me over yesterday. He shared some things—important things I think you should know—about your father."

Jake stopped short and his head snapped around, his voice sounding dangerously soft as he said, "You went to see my grandfather yesterday."

She stopped as well and pivoted to face him as she said, "Yes."

The set of his jaw hinted at the anger burning beneath the surface of his still relatively calm exterior.

She opened her mouth to speak and then faltered, instantly regretting her decision to come clean. But it was too late now. She had no choice but to keep going, so she lifted her chin and cleared her throat, trying her best to sound calm as she said, "Max asked me to drop by."

Jake's mouth set in a hard line. "And you're just telling me about this now—even though it happened yesterday."

"He asked me not to." It was true, though it sounded like a feeble excuse now.

Jake glared at her. "Oh, well if he asked you not to." His tone dripped sarcasm. "So tell me...what made you keep a meeting with my *grandfather*—the man who ruined my father's life and who seems determined to do the same with me—a secret?"

"For someone who prides himself on being calm and rational, you're completely the opposite when it comes to your grandfather. You should go see him; ask him what we discussed. It concerns your father and since that's what's driven the wedge between you, I think learning the truth could go a long way toward healing your relationship."

Jake stepped closer, his eyes glittering. "You have one private conversation with my grandfather and suddenly you're the expert on my father," he said, nearly shouting the last word.

The sweet afterglow of their dinner had vanished. Max had called it. Apparently the direct approach didn't work best when it came to Jake.

Still, she couldn't let it rest and she held her ground, refusing to budge as she said, "I think I know more than *you* do, mostly because I bother to listen. I only mention it because I thought you meant what you said earlier about everyone deserving a second chance. Clearly you didn't."

"I meant it. I *do* believe in second chances—for people who actually *deserve* them."

"Oh and you're the judge and jury on who's deserving," she said, hands on hips. "Is that right?"

"As it relates to my grandfather, yes, I am," he shouted. "You think you know him so well, but you have no idea who he really is."

Suddenly aware of the spectacle they must be creating; Amanda glanced around and noticed several interested onlookers hovering nearby. "Stop *yelling*," she commanded through clenched teeth.

"I'm not. . ." He halted and glanced around too, then took a deep breath and lowered his voice as he said, "I'm not yelling."

"Well you were speaking too loudly for a public sidewalk and I'm done having this argument in the middle of the street." She spun around and marched the last few yards toward his townhouse with Jake right on her heels and the cluster of interested neighbors following their every move.

Who could blame them? It must be like watching live theatre.

"What did you expect? You were the one who brought up the subject of my grandfather while walking down the sidewalk."

She stomped up the stairs and tapped her foot impatiently as she waited for Jake to unlock the front door. "I thought you could control yourself." Once inside, she shrugged off her coat and started for the stairs.

"Where are you going?"

She drew a long, calming breath and glanced over her shoulder. "I'm done arguing with you. I have a brand platform to work on." She muttered under her breath. "I just didn't realize it was all a lie."

"I heard that."

"I meant you to," she said. "At work, I have a steadfast rule that the brands I work on have to be authentic, which means they have to walk the talk. And that's exactly what you're *not* doing."

He glared at her. "What are you talking about?"

She met his gaze unflinchingly. "Your belief in everyone deserving a second chance; it's all a lie."

He closed the distance between them, stopping at the base of the stairs as he said, "It's not a lie. And you don't know anything about my family."

"I understand more than you would imagine."

"Really." Jake folded his arms and his entire being oozed arrogance as he said, "I can't wait to hear it."

"I know that where your family is concerned, you only see what you choose to see." She jammed a fist onto her hip. "I know you draw conclusions based on surface observations and never even bother looking deeper to see what's *really* going on."

He glared at her. "One private meeting with my grandfather doesn't make you an expert on him or my family."

"Apparently spending a *lifetime* as a Lowell hasn't made *you* one either." She turned and intended to start up the stairs, but Jake reached for her arm. She yanked it out of his grasp.

"That's pretty interesting coming from you, especially considering what's going on with your brother." Jake's face settled into a smug half smirk. "Maybe if you were less concerned with my family and paying more attention to yours, you'd be aware of what he's up to."

Anger erupted inside. "Don't even *try* to drag my brother into this. You don't know anything about him."

He held her gaze, looking unfazed by her outburst. "I know more than you do—at least based on everything I've heard."

"What do you mean *everything you've heard?*"

His entire being oozed arrogance and it took everything she had to keep from slapping him.

"I know about his questionable business partners and I know where the money for the restaurant really comes from," he said. "I know about the illegal high stakes poker games he and his partners host at his half-finished place twice a week."

Amanda couldn't stop her sharp intake of breath.

Jake didn't miss a beat as he continued. "I—and apparently everyone else in town—know the brother you're so focused on helping has played you for a fool."

The blood pounded in her ears and her knees felt weak. "What are you talking about? Why are you making up lies?"

"They're not lies. And from what I hear, Rob's escapades aren't that big a secret," he said. "It certainly wasn't too hard for me to find out the details."

Tears welled and she blinked rapidly, trying to hold them back. "I don't believe you." Her voice shook. "I think you're so jaded and messed up about family; you're just looking for things to pin on my brother."

Jake appeared to make an effort to calm himself. "Why would I do that?"

He'd do it to hurt her; that's why. A wayward tear trickled down her checks and she brushed it away as she continued. "Rob's not perfect, but I have news for you, Jake. Nobody is—not me, not your grandfather,"—she spread her arms wide—"hey, not even *you.*" She thrust a finger at his chest to punctuate the word. She whirled around and started up the stairs, unable to believe their beautiful, romantic evening had gone so far off the rails.

"Amanda, wait."

She stopped, but didn't turn back. "We're through for the night."

"Let's talk about this," he said. "I don't want tonight to end this way."

She turned and her eyes narrowed. "What...did you think it would end in your bedroom?" Earlier she'd thought so; hoped so. But now, that was the last thing she wanted and her anger fueled her words as she said, "I told you sex wasn't part of our deal."

"You know that's not what I meant." His jaw tightened.

She glared at him and then tried to calm herself before she said, "I didn't bring up the subject of your grandfather to upset you and I didn't go there yesterday to make you angry. I only brought it up because I think you need to reach out to him."

Jake's mouth set in a hard line. "I'll take it under advisement."

He was, without a doubt the most hard-headed man she'd ever met. Max's advice drifted back and she finally understood what he'd tried to tell her. The word stubborn was an understatement. No wonder Max had resorted to blackmail in order to get him to listen. She decided to try the rational approach, which always worked so well in business when disagreements got a little heated. She drew a long, fortifying breath and then said, "It isn't logical to blame your grandfather for everything that went wrong in your father's life. He was an adult. He made his own decisions. And blaming Max won't change how his life turned out."

"True." Jake's voice sounded calm, but the hardness in his eyes told a different story. "And coddling your brother as you do will only ensure he never grows up." Jake paused, but as she glared at him, she could tell he wasn't finished.

Amanda willed herself to walk away; to leave before he could say more. Before they passed the point of no return, which she sensed they might be about to do, but she remained rooted to the spot and her hand tightened on the stair rail as she braced herself for his next words.

"No matter what you do for Rob; regardless of how much money you give him or how much of your life you continue to sacrifice trying to make everything perfect for him, someday you'll have to accept the fact that you can't fix everything. Your parents died, Amanda.

They're gone. And nothing you do can bring them back." He folded his arms and his eyes locked with hers.

She tried to look away, but couldn't.

He continued. "And that's the real problem, isn't it? Losing your parents is the one thing in your life—and your brother's—you can't control, can't fix. And you've spent the past ten years torturing yourself because of it."

Chapter Fifteen

manda pressed the doorbell twice in quick succession and—when Kate didn't instantly appear—she pushed it again, holding it down for a count of five. The three block walk in the crisp November evening had calmed her a little, but it hadn't done a thing to improve her mood; or her patience.

She tapped her foot and peered at her watch. What the hell was taking Kate so long? Unable to stand it a millisecond longer, Amanda balled her fist and pounded on the door three times.

The porch light flipped on.

"Dear God. Are you trying to wake the dead?" Kate's hair was scraped back into a ponytail and her burgeoning belly poked through the front folds of her pink robe. "Give a pregnant girl time to waddle to the door." She stepped aside to let Amanda enter and her frown deepened when she spotted Amanda's overnight bag. Her eyes drifted from the bag to Amanda's face as she said, "What's wrong?"

"Take a wild guess. Can I stay here tonight?"

"Of course," Kate said. "Just a few hours ago at Gigi's, everything seemed perfect. What happened?"

Amanda tucked her curls behind an ear and looked down at her shoes. "What usually happens? We had a fight." Sensing a lecture headed her way, she went on the offensive. "And before you start in on me, I think you should know the argument was mostly his fault."

Kate locked the door and turned around, her expression stern as she said, "What do you mean *mostly*?" She folded her arms and looked at Amanda in a way that made her feel like a fifth grader about to be scolded for not completing her homework. "You were supposed to seduce him, not fight with him. Remember?"

Amanda held up a hand as Kate waltzed by, headed to the kitchen. "Don't start with the seduction lessons. I'm not in the mood." She fell in behind her, plopping onto a barstool while Kate shuffled around the kitchen preparing a pot of coffee.

"All I have is decaf. I'm off the hard stuff until the little one arrives." Kate rubbed her belly.

"I don't need caffeine. I'm high on anger."

Kate arched a brow. "Okay, out with it. What did you fight about?"

"Take a wild guess. Since we only ever fight about two things, there's a fifty percent chance you'll be right."

Kate stopped her coffee preparations and shot a sideways glance at Amanda. "Rob."

"We eventually went there, of course, but the fight started with Max." Amanda paused for a moment, dreading the confession she was about to make. Or more specifically, she dreaded Kate's inevitable reaction to it. "I told Jake I went to see his grandfather yesterday and he flipped out."

Kate dropped the coffee filter and smacked her palms on the black flecked granite, her steely-eyed gaze making Amanda wish she could shrink down under the counter. "You went to see Max yesterday and you didn't tell Jake?" Kate yelled.

"Man, you've got a set of lungs on you. There's no need to bellow. I'm sitting right here," Amanda said. "And I didn't tell you because Max asked me not to."

Kate's eyes bugged out. "And you *listened* to him."

"Of course I listened to him. He asked me to keep the meeting private and I wanted to honor his wishes."

Kate tilted her head and shot her the look Amanda knew meant she was about to receive a tongue-lashing, Alabama-style. "Are you *insane*? You know Jake's feelings about Max. You never should have agreed to go, let alone, go, keep it a secret and then spill it later. That's just plain stupid. But since you decided to do it without telling him, you should've just kept it a secret. In this case, two wrongs *do not* make a right. You had to know Jake would be upset."

"I wasn't going to tell him. But I started to feel guilty, you know"—Amanda tucked a few brunette curls behind her ear—"after what happened between us yesterday and all."

Kate folded her arms so they rested atop her belly. "I don't blame Jake for being upset."

"Why are you all on his side?"

"Why didn't you tell Jake before you went? Or me? You kept the meeting with Max a secret from me too. Me!" She jabbed a thumb at her chest. "Your best friend. You told me you and Jake spent the afternoon in bed; blamed that for the reason you missed the cake tasting. You lied to me."

"So to be clear, you're really mad because I kept a secret from *you*. Not about my failure to tell Jake. Did I get that right?"

Kate pursed her lips and appeared to consider Amanda's words as she continued.

"I met Max right after Jake left. I didn't have time to think it all through; everything happened so fast. And I didn't have a spare second to call you." To be clear, she hadn't had the inclination either. Even now, yesterday afternoon felt like one big super-confusing swirl of emotion. And at the time, she definitely hadn't had her head screwed on right.

"I don't get you," Kate's voice took on an edge as she poured their coffee. "You shouldn't keep secrets from me. I'm on your side, remember?"

"You could've fooled me." Amanda returned Kate's disapproving glare, trying to shame her for the lack of female solidarity. "Maybe if you could keep a secret from your husband, I would have. But since you can't, I've learned to edit what I tell you because I know you'll just run home and blab everything to Sam."

Kate had the grace to look slightly embarrassed as she pushed a mug across the counter. "Fair enough. I guess I forgive you."

"What a relief." Amanda rolled her eyes and, without even bothering to taste it, she added a dash of cream and another smidgen of sugar to her brew. Kate never got the mixture quite right. "Can we get back to the reason I'm here?" Kate looked at her expectantly as Amanda stirred her coffee and said, "Look, I know I should've told Jake before I went, but it all happened so fast. Max called. Jake stopped by right after. Then, we ended up sleeping together, after which, he immediately bolted. The whole thing was too confusing, so excuse me for not living up to your expectations." Amanda sipped her coffee, made a face and then reached for more cream.

Kate sipped her own coffee and rolled her wrist to encourage Amanda to continue.

"And then during dinner tonight, everything went so great," Amanda said, placing her elbows on the counter and gazed up at the ceiling. "Actually, dinner was so amazing. It felt like the way we used to be, only better. We had this great conversation and, between the wine and the food and our kiss, I started to think..." Amanda sat up straight and tapped a fingernail on the side of her mug. "I felt guilty for keeping my visit with Max a secret and so I decided to confess."

"I guess that makes sense. But aside from the fact that you probably just blurted out your confession while strolling down the sidewalk—"

Amanda frowned. "How did you know?

Kate rolled her eyes. "How long have we known each other? You're absolutely clueless where men are concerned. As mama would say, you're like a hillbilly at a debutante ball. For someone so genius at business, you're completely dense where men are concerned."

"Gee thanks."

Kate shrugged and shook her head in a way that seemed to say *you poor thing*. "What did you expect Jake's reaction to be? You knew he'd be upset when he learned you saw Max." Kate's frown made the depth of her disapproval clear. "You should've chosen a more delicate way of coming clean instead of just blurting it out the way you did."

Amanda considered her advice and tried not to feel irritated that her friend knew her weaknesses so well. "I guess, but I thought he'd get over it. I didn't expect him to verbally attack me."

"How did he verbally attack you?"

"He spewed out a bunch of crazy ass lies about my brother, which I won't even go into because it will just piss me off all over again. But during the worst of it, he said I spent the past ten years trying to make up for the fact that my parents died because it's the one thing in my life I haven't been able to control or fix. He claimed I'm wasting my life trying to make everything perfect for Rob and as a result, all I've really done is kept him from growing up. According to Jake, that's my 'real issue'" Amanda used air quotes to emphasize the point. "Like I care what he thinks."

Kate didn't comment as she pulled out a barstool and squirmed around, trying to get comfortable.

"Don't you think that's mean?" Amanda prodded her.

Kate cast a sideways glance while she took a sip of coffee. Then she cleared her throat and said, "I think it's sort of true."

Amanda's head snapped around. "What is *with* you today? If I didn't know better, I'd think you were Jake in disguise."

"You know how I feel about your parenting skills *and* your brother."

"Are you saying you *agree* with Jake?"

"On this topic, I do." Kate sounded gentle but firm. "But we'll never see this particular subject from the same perspective, so I think it's best if we just agree to disagree."

"Hang on a minute." Amanda turned to face Kate straight on. "You're wrong about this and I want to know why you feel the way you do."

Kate heaved a theatrical sigh. "Fine, but you won't like it." She paused and took a sip of coffee. Then glanced at Amanda sideways and looked down again as she said, "Ever since your parents died, you've taken your parental responsibilities very seriously."

Amanda spread her arms wide, palms to the ceiling. "And this is a bad thing?"

"*Too* seriously," Kate said, eyeing her sternly.

"Parenting is serious business, especially when you're only nineteen and thrust into the role overnight. I had a lot to figure out and it all happened in real time."

"I'll agree that you stepped up admirably. I doubt I could've done the same. But you never shared your feelings. That thing Jake said about their deaths being the one thing you couldn't control; he nailed it. I could never quite put my finger on it, but as soon as I heard what he said, I knew it was true," Kate said.

"What are you talking about?"

"You refuse to let anyone help you—even though my parents offered hundreds of times," Kate said. "Instead, you insist on figuring the whole parent thing out for yourself so you spent all your free time reading books and blogs and listening to call-in radio shows."

Amanda bristled. "Do I get any credit for being proactive or resourceful?"

"You'd get more credit if you admitted—at least occasionally—that you might be in over your head. If you bothered to ask for help from people who have actual experience; people who care about you."

"Maybe I don't need anyone's help." Amanda found it impossible to keep the defensiveness out of her voice.

"See what I mean?" Kate's pursed lips spoke volumes. "Everyone needs help occasionally, Ms. Smarty Pants. Even *you*," Kate said. "You had no idea what you were doing." She shook her head. "I mean...you've spent the past ten years Googling parenting advice. *Googling*!" Kate circled a finger near her temple and rolled her eyes to emphasize the point. "Hello crazy."

Amanda lifted her chin and said, "You can learn a lot from Google."

"It's a great resource when you're researching some random fact. But Google practically raised your brother and since you're in the marketing biz, you should be all too aware you can't believe everything you read online." Kate shook her head sadly. "I mean, no wonder Rob has issues."

Amanda's cheeks grew warm as the words hit home. She sipped her coffee as Kate continued.

"You could've turned to dozens of people; experienced parents who would've been happy—who desperately *wanted*—to help. But instead, you relied on yourself and Google." Kate bit her lip and paused for a moment before she said, "It's like..." Her voice trailed off and she tapped a fingernail on the granite countertop.

"It's like what?" Amanda asked, though she felt pretty sure she didn't want to hear the rest.

Kate turned to face her. "Your parents always emphasized your role as big sister and I know you took it very seriously; maybe too seriously. And when they died, you took it to an extreme. I'm sure your parents would never have intended for you to go this far. You placed all kinds of pressure on yourself to know exactly what to do in every situation. You tried to be a model parent and to make life perfect for Rob."

"I don't understand why this is bad."

"The intention wasn't bad. Unfortunately you didn't know what you were doing. And being so determined to figure it out on your own, you could never see things objectively with Rob; never realized when your own actions might be adding to his issues."

"I don't see what's wrong with trying to be a parent to my brother or for trying to figure things out on my own."

"I know you don't; you're far too close to it," Kate said. "But what you don't see is the challenge it's created with Rob. Or you for that matter, but we'll get to that in a minute. You don't get that by always catering to Rob, by covering his mistakes, he avoids paying the consequences associated with them. And therefore, all you've really done is to prevent him from growing up."

Anger welled and Amanda opened her mouth to protest, but Kate held up a hand.

"And before you say it's not true, let's look at the facts." Kate arched a brow and her green eyes issued a challenge. "Rob managed to con a hundred grand from you over the course of the last six months; a hundred thousand dollars!" Kate's palm smacked the countertop, coffee sloshed from Amanda's mug onto the granite. "In order to get out from under that debt, you had to agree to a fake engagement and then a real marriage, followed by I guess a real divorce a few months from now. *You're* paying the consequences of Rob's actions, just as you always do." Kate threw her hands high. "But this time, it's even worse. Rob has partnered with a bunch of low lifes on his restaurant. He's even involved in illegal gambling—"

Amanda sprang from the barstool. "You're listening to Jake's lies?" Amanda glared at her. "I should've known he'd spread his poison to Sam. Don't tell me you *believe* him."

"I don't know for sure the rumors are true. I only know what Sam found out after he asked around."

"What *Sam* found out?" Her eye's narrowed. "So your husband helped Jake dig up dirt on my brother. You're kidding, right?"

Kate shifted on the barstool and looked uncomfortable. "He just..."

Amanda's mouth dropped open. She couldn't believe her best friends would poke around in her brother's affairs behind her back. This went way beyond Kate's typical meddling or spousal gossip. This felt like betrayal. She folded her arms and lifted her chin. "He just, *what*?"

"Amanda, Jake...*we*...just wanted to help." Kate's eyes pleaded with Amanda to understand. "Do you really believe either Sam or I would ever do anything to hurt you?"

She didn't want to believe it, but the last few minutes had shaken her to the core and she no longer knew what to believe. "Then why? Why would Rob be of any concern to either of you?" And if they'd heard some wayward gossip, why wouldn't Kate just tell her? They'd always been straight with each other before. It made no sense.

"Sit down and we'll talk," Kate said.

Amanda sat, but regarded her friend warily as she tried to assign logic to actions that seemed completely out of character with the friend she'd known, and trusted, for so long.

Kate sighed. "Okay, here's the truth. We've been worried because of everything going on with Rob. And earlier this week, Jake asked Sam to check around; to find out what your brother is up to."

"But—"

"You have to admit," Kate said. "This situation with Rob got completely out of control and Jake...*we all*...wanted to understand what might be going on."

"Why would Jake assume my brother is any of his business?"

"Maybe for the same reason you consider his relationship with Max *your* business." Kate shook more sugar into her coffee and stirred. "I swear; you're both super clueless when it comes to love."

"This isn't love. It's just some convoluted, unfinished business between two people who used to date."

Kate tilted her head and the corners of her lips turned up as she said, "No honey. This is about two people who can't stand to be apart but are too afraid to admit it. Two people who hate to see the other hurting or being hurt, so they interfere and nudge and make all kinds of mistakes in an attempt to get the other on what they believe to be the right track."

"That's not—"

"Hon, I know you'd like to believe this deal of yours is just about business and a little bit of residual chemistry, but somewhere deep inside, you know it's not true. If so, Jake's relationship with Max wouldn't concern you and it wouldn't hurt so much when he meddled in your brother's life." Her voice grew husky. "What's going on between you two is about as real and as deep and as complicated as it gets. This is *love*, sweetie."

Amanda's shoulders slumped. "But I don't want to love him," she whispered. "There's no point. It won't work. I could never trust him to make a true commitment."

"You can't choose love. It just happens. And most of the time, it doesn't make any sense." Kate shrugged. "Look at Sam and me.

Who would've ever imagined we'd end up together—especially after everything my family did to prevent us from getting together. Not to mention the fact that I had the gown on and was a mere five minutes from walking down the aisle with Mr. Wrong," she said.

"But you guys are different. You two make sense. We don't."

"Love isn't logical and it's almost always inconvenient." Kate paused to sip her coffee. "I know you like to pretend you're all tough, but you're not. You're scared. It was easy to talk all tough when Jake was half a world away, but the idea of giving it another try with him scares the crap out of you. And I don't blame you." Kate turned to face her. "Jake *is* afraid of commitment and sure, you *could* walk away when your deal ends, but I don't believe you want to." She set down her mug and squeezed Amanda's hand as she said, "Do you."

Instead of answering, Amanda countered with a question of her own. "If he loves me, why would he do this with my brother?"

Kate shrugged. "He didn't like what he heard about the money you loaned Rob, so he asked Sam to look into it. Nothing more. I know you want to believe the only thing going on with your brother is a few construction delays, but get real," Kate said as she tapped her index finger to her temple. "Use your brain. Pretend it's not your brother. You have to recognize the ring of truth in what we learned."

Amanda decided she'd heard enough about her brother. She'd also listened to enough lectures on love and Jake and everything she'd done wrong over the past ten years. She shoved her mug aside, causing some of the coffee to slosh onto the counter and stood, glaring at Kate as she said, "I don't *have* to do anything. I'm disappointed in you. After everything we've been through together; after all these years, this is how you act?" Amanda turned and strode toward the door. "I would *never* keep a secret like this from you or go behind your back like that. Ever."

Kate shimmied awkwardly off the barstool and waddled after her. "Mand...don't leave," she said. "Please. You know I'd never do anything to hurt you. You *know* that."

She cast a glance over her shoulder. The sight of her pregnant friend struggling to keep up dissipated some of her anger and Amanda stopped, expelling a long sigh as she said, "I know you wouldn't hurt me intentionally, but what everyone seems to miss is that Rob is my brother; my only family. He *needs* me." Amanda said. "And it pisses me off to know my best friends felt free to investigate him like he's some dangerous criminal."

"We—"

"I'm done. I came over tonight for some moral support. I didn't expect to find out you've been sneaking around my back. I'm just... I'm really pissed at you guys."

"I'm sorry," Kate whispered, her eyes round and glistening with tears.

"We'll talk about this later; when I've calmed down. Right now, I'm tired. Can I still stay tonight?"

"Please stay. You know where the room is."

Amanda nodded and started toward the stairs. "Thanks. I really don't want to go back to his place tonight." She stepped onto the bottom stair and then turned back to Kate. "I know you thought you were helping, but I don't believe Jake was as well-intended. As it relates to my brother, I think he's out to hurt me because of his own messed up beliefs about family."

"Actually, I think it's just the opposite," Kate said. "I believe he wants to protect you."

Amanda scoffed. "Then you're more delusional about this relationship than I've been, if that's possible."

* * *

Amanda stood at the door to Rob's apartment for a full ten minutes practicing what she'd say and gathering the courage for the conversation to come. She was running on two hours of sleep and three Venti Skinny Lattes—a deadly combination.

What little sleep she got had been punctuated by nightmares—the kind where you show up late for class and inexplicably find you aren't wearing pants. She'd experienced that one twice and in between, she'd spent hours staring mindlessly at the ceiling, replaying the conversation with Kate over and over in her head.

By the time the sun came up, she knew what she had to do. She needed to confront Rob in person. She didn't believe the gossip, but couldn't quite dismiss the prickle of doubt; the stirring of unease. Kate's words held an undeniable ring of truth and, while she wouldn't ever admit it to her, Amanda had always wondered if Rob was telling the truth about his reasons for needing the money. By challenging him in person, she'd be able to look in his eyes and see the truth. But she felt sure, hoped so deeply, that the crazy stories Jake and Kate considered fact were only vicious lies.

Amanda checked her watch again. She couldn't put it off any longer. It was time to get on with it. She smoothed sweaty palms down the front of her jeans and rang the bell.

When Rob opened the door, his unkempt hair and bleary eyes made it clear he'd just dragged himself out of bed. "Holy crap, sis," he said as he scratched his head. "What're you doing here so early?"

"We need to talk." Amanda strode purposely through the door and all the way into the living room before she stopped. She was a woman on a mission and determined to prove it.

Rob must have picked up on her mood because he instantly looked more alert as he plopped into the chair across from her. "What's going on?"

She kept her voice calm and cool as she said, "Funny, that's exactly what I'm here to find out." She eyed him with a firm, unflinching gaze—determined to catch even the slightest hint of deception. "I've heard some very disturbing rumors."

His eyes grew round and he stared at her more intently as he said, "Like what?"

"Like the real reasons for the construction delays." She folded her arms. "And I expect to hear the truth."

His brows drew together. "Why would I lie?"

She vowed not to waver—especially with the wild fabrications still bouncing around in her head. "Don't try to deflect my question with more questions. Answer me." She wouldn't prompt him. She wanted him to voluntarily tell her the truth, the *whole* truth.

"We ran into delays due to permit problems. You have no idea what a nightmare Cook County can be." His gaze never wavered. "Then the sub-contractors we hired to do the interior finish work backed out so we needed to find another crew. We're still trying to get the money back from the original guys, since we paid them before they ditched us. The twenty thousand you gave me a few days ago helped us get the new sub-contractors started and now, we're making progress again. You should stop by." He grinned. "The place is really coming along."

In the lengthening silence, she studied every aspect of Rob's demeanor, trying to discern fact from fiction. Everything about his tone and manner—even his direct eye contact—indicated he was being truthful. "So there's nothing you're not telling me."

He stood and plodded into the kitchen. "The only thing I left out is what a massive pain in the ass these delays have been. But that's my problem, not yours."

She chewed her lip. He hadn't even blinked which meant he was either a very good liar or Jake had gotten his facts wrong. She was betting on the latter. But, but couldn't resist one last test. "Who are your partners?"

Rob opened the cupboard and pulled out the coffee can and a filter. "You don't know them. *I* don't even know them all."

This jived with what Jake had said and seemed to be the basis for the wild rumors her friends seemed to believe. It gave Amanda a degree of confidence in Rob's explanations.

He poured water in the coffee machine and turned it on. Then he leaned against the refrigerator and folded his arms as he continued. "It takes serious bank to gut and rebuild a restaurant, so we've had added some new partners over the last few months to help ease expenses." He picked up a cup and lifted a brow. "Want some?"

"No." She still wasn't sure whether to believe him.

"You seem pissed," Rob filled his mug, looking completely at ease despite Amanda's obvious concern. "What's going on?"

"Last night, I heard all these crazy rumors about the restaurant and it scared me. I want to make sure you're not in over your head," Amanda said. "I hope you know, if you're worried about something, *anything*, you can tell me. We'll figure it out together."

He yawned. "Everything's fine. You know how people like to talk in this town—especially that crowd of yours. My place is going to be huge. You'll be proud of me, sis." He grinned and looked so pleased with himself, her anger and fear began to dissipate. "I promise. You have nothing to worry about."

Amanda sank onto a barstool and watched as he swigged his coffee. His version of the story was consistent enough with what she'd heard from both Kate and Jake that she felt reassured. They must have taken random bits of information and patched it together to create the wild stories they had told her. She didn't understand why, but she'd worry about it later.

"You sure you don't want some?"

Amanda relented. "I'll take half a cup and then I need to go." As she reached for the mug, the overhead light bounced off her ring and shards of light flashed in a showy display of bling.

Rob set down his mug and grabbed her hand. "Damn, sis! You're engaged?" His look of reproach shamed her. "Talk about keeping secrets."

"That's the other reason I'm here; I wanted to tell you the news in person." She pasted a sunny smile on her face. "Jake and I are engaged." She hated deceiving him—especially since she'd just accused him of lying to her.

A huge grin spread over his face as he trotted around the counter. He wrapped her in a big bear hug, picked her up and spun her around twice. "I *knew* it! I *knew* this would happen once he got home."

He dropped her with a clunk the way he used to do when they were younger. She giggled and smacked him on the arm.

"When's the big day?"

She braced her elbows on the counter and watched him reach over the counter to pick up his mug. "We haven't decided yet. You'll be the first to know."

They spent the next hour catching up and by the time she left, her fears were completely allayed. Jake and Kate had dug up a few half-truths and some outlandish rumors and threaded them together into a crazy story. Based on Rob's history of irresponsibility and bad decision-making, she couldn't really blame them. But they needed to realize people made mistakes and give Rob the opportunity to prove he'd grown up; that he'd changed. Sure, a hundred grand was a lot of money and it had caused her a ton of financial problems. But he was taking a professional risk by opening a restaurant and she was proud of him. To her, it seemed a signal he might finally be growing up.

* * *

Later that afternoon, Amanda lay on her bed pouring over US Weekly when Jake knocked on the door. "Come in." She lowered the magazine and peered at him over the top, trying to gauge his mood.

Jake leaned against the door jamb, his expression unreadable and his muscular arms folded across his chest. "Hey."

She laid the magazine on her tummy. "Hey." She'd long since decided to just apologize and move on. There was no point in rehashing their arguments of the night before. "Listen Jake, I—"

"No." He held up a hand. "Let me go first." He smiled. "Please."

"Okay."

He looked down and appeared to consider his next words carefully. "I wanted to apologize for last night." His blue eyes locked with hers. "I'm really sorry I upset you."

"It's okay."

He paused for a beat and then said, "I was worried when you didn't come home last night."

"I stayed at Kate's."

"I know," he said. "I sent her a text."

She looked down and plucked at the bedspread as she said, "I'm sorry, too. I shouldn't have kept my meeting with Max a secret. I should've known it would hurt you and I hope you know that wasn't my intention. I don't have an excuse. I guess I just wasn't thinking."

"I know how Max feels about you, so I should've expected he'd do something like this; he probably will again. He put you in an awkward position." He cleared his throat. "I apologize too, about Rob. I didn't mean to meddle."

Amanda gazed up at him through her lashes. "Yes you did."

His mouth twisted into a sheepish grin. "You're right. I did. But only because I wanted to be sure everything was okay. I'm still worried."

Amanda nodded and decided not to mention the visit with her brother. Jake wouldn't believe Rob's explanation anyway. While her brother wasn't perfect, she knew him well enough to know when he was being straight and when he wasn't. She steered the conversation to neutral territory. "I worked on your proposal earlier and made some progress. Want to take a look?"

Jake nodded. "I need some caffeine, though."

Amanda swung her legs over the side of the bed and followed him downstairs. She stopped in the office to print a fresh copy of his proposal and joined him in the kitchen. She plopped onto a barstool and spread the papers out as Jake sat beside her. They reviewed the content and chatted through some potential changes while the coffee finished brewing.

Jake stood and walked over to the coffee machine as it finished percolating. "I think we're in pretty good shape," he said as he pulled two mugs from the cupboard. "What do you think?"

"We're almost there," she said. "I have a few tweaks in mind, but I want to think about it a little more."

Jake poured the coffee.

Amanda reached across the island to grab a mug but Jake pulled it just out of her reach, grinning. "I'll bet you fifty I can doctor my brew to match yours."

She tossed her hair over a shoulder. "You like yours black."

He grinned. "For fifty bucks, I'll drink your watered down, sickeningly sweet version." His grin broadened and his gaze issued a challenge. "We on?"

She lifted her chin. "Bring it." She pulled the mug toward her as she stood, carrying it to the counter behind her and turning her back. She peered over her shoulder. "No peeking," she said as she curved her body around to block his view and dumped in just the right amount of cream, sugar and mocha.

Jake made a show of trying to peer over her shoulder as he mixed his concoction. "Ready?"

She nodded and carried her mug back to the island. They picked up the other's cup and tasted. Both made a face.

"This is terrible," he said, setting her mug down with a clunk. "How do you drink that stuff?"

She scoffed. "You're just mad because you lost. You used too much cream and not enough Splenda." She extended a palm and waggled her fingers. "Pay up."

Jake pulled his wallet from his trousers and smacked the bills on the counter. "I should have known I couldn't mix it to suit those high maintenance taste buds of yours."

"Sore loser," she said. Then she took a sip of her coffee and smiled. "Ahhhh," she sighed, drawling out the sound in an intense show of satisfaction. "Nectar of the Gods."

He tossed his mixture into the sink, rinsed his mug and poured himself another cup. This time, he left it black.

She couldn't believe it had only been a week since he'd burst in on her at the cabin. And it was even harder to believe how much had happened in the days since. In the year since their break-up, she'd almost convinced herself their relationship had meant nothing; that she was over him. And that—as far as women were concerned—Jake was the devil. Now, she wasn't so sure.

Jake leaned over and braced his forearms on the counter, grinning at her in that lop-sided way he sometimes did when nervous. "I need to ask a favor."

"Shoot."

He sighed. "I'm nervous about the pitch—especially about the marketing section."

"We'll be ready, don't worry."

"I know the content will be ready," he said. "I just mean I don't think I can present it."

She frowned. "Even though you're presenting to Rand? He's like your brother."

"I'm still totally out of my league on the marketing piece. It'll only take one or two questions and they'll have me stumped." Jake shrugged. "And while I appreciate Rand taking the meeting, I want him to invest because he believes in my business, not because he's Sam's older brother."

"He's an investment banker. Like you told me; he'll only finance it if he believes it's a good business proposal, which it is," she said. "But I get it. I'd feel the same if I had to engage in military speak in front of a bunch of experts."

"So I wondered...would you..." he cleared his throat and grinned as he continued. "Could you come with me on Monday? You know the content so well and I could really use your support." He stood up straight and shoved his hands into the pockets of his jeans. "I need your help."

His praise warmed her like sunshine and she was touched by his humility.

"Of course, I'll go with you," she said. But she had something even better up her sleeve and the thought made her smile.

Chapter Sixteen

Jake and Amanda were among the last to arrive at the party. As hosts, their primary duty consisted of corralling the troops. So they didn't waste any time getting busy. They moved about the room—over-crowded with forty of their closest friends—handing out noise-makers and confetti, cueing up the designated toast masters and topping off champagne glasses.

At exactly nine o'clock, Kate and Sam stepped through the doors, the crowd shouted *Happy Birthday* and—after a sentimental round of toasts—Sam's thirty-fifth birthday bash began in full force.

As the music went up and the lights went down, Amanda scanned the room for several minutes before she located George. He was leaning against the back bar, chatting with a few guys and observing the crowd. Her eyes locked on him like a homing beam as she made her way through the throng of dancing, slightly-inebriated well-wishers, smiling and greeting friends as she passed, but never veering off course.

She hadn't seen or spoken to George since the night of her drunken happy hour three days before. She had intended to call him—to apologize for Jake's over-the-top jealous boyfriend act—but she hadn't gotten around to it. So it could be more than a little awkward to ask him for a favor now, but she planned to do it anyway. He owed her a few and she had no problem calling in a favor. As she drew close, Amanda glanced over a shoulder and searched for Jake. A wave of relief washed over her when she located him clear on the other side of the room, deep in conversation with Sam and his younger brother.

She stood up straight and threw her shoulders back as she sidled up to George. She flashed a friendly smile and punched him playfully on the bicep. "Hey G."

He grinned. "Well, if it isn't the lady of leisure. So tell me, exactly how bad *did* your head hurt the next morning? Scale of one to ten."

She made a goofy face. "Twelve."

He threw his head back and laughed. "I tried to warn you."

"You should have tried harder. The next morning, I thought I was having an aneurism. The aspirin helped, though. Thank you." She laughed and shook her head ruefully. "Two drinks tonight and that's it."

"Good girl. Moderation is the key." George swirled his scotch around in his glass and then took a long pull. "When are you coming back to work?"

"I have no idea." She turned sideways, using George to shield her from Jake's view. She braced her elbows on the counter and said, "Thanks for coming tonight. I know you don't know Sam and Kate very well yet."

Enough small talk; get down to business before you run out of time.

"I wouldn't miss it. Sam's a nice guy. Which reminds me"— George cast a dark look over her shoulder—"where's lover boy?"

Amanda pointed a thumb over her shoulder and then stood. "Listen"—she leaned closer and pulled on his arm to coax him away from the bar, as she cast another nervous glance over her shoulder— "can I talk to you for a sec?"

George looked confused, but followed her anyway. "Sure."

Amanda headed down a hallway so they could have some privacy. George trailed after her and stopped as she turned to face him.

He leaned against the wall and swigged some of his scotch and soda as he regarded her with what appeared to be a healthy dose of curiosity. "What's up?"

"I need a favor."

"Shoot."

"Can you develop a two minute brand video in a day?"

He shrugged. "Why would I do that?"

"It's for Jake's business. He's got a pitch with an investment group on Monday morning and..." Her voice trailed off and she frowned as he vigorously shook his head. "What's wrong?"

George pushed away from the wall, his jaw set and a hard look in his eye. "I won't do anything to help that dude."

"You'd be helping *me*," she said, doings her best to sound persuasive. He owed her, but she hadn't pulled out the favor card yet. Not that she was afraid to. She just didn't want to use it if she didn't have to. "I'm doing the brand and marketing strategy for his new company and I need your help."

"No," the word sounded harsh and angry and his eyes glittered as he took a long pull of scotch and soda.

She placed her hands on her hips. "Are you going to make me beg? You're the only one who can pull off a miracle like this."

Amanda cast another nervous glance back at the crowd and her stomach flip flopped as she realized she could no longer see Jake. The last thing she needed was for him to catch her with George or—God forbid—overhearing their conversation. She wanted him to be surprised on Monday and planned to unveil the video just a few minutes before the pitch started. It would give him a nice, last-minute shot of adrenaline and the confidence he would need to pull off a flawless performance. Besides, if he knew who had developed the video, she figured he'd refuse to use it. Jake didn't appear to like George any more than George liked him.

"Just keep it simple," she said. "Title screens, a little stock video footage and the standard emotional soundtrack. You know the drill." He could produce genius creative faster than anyone she'd ever seen.

He could pull off the request without much effort at all if he wanted to. She just needed him to say yes.

George's mouth twisted. "Why should I. I don't like the way he hurt you. And he didn't make too good an impression on me the other night."

She squeezed his arm. "Please George," she said. "I need you."

Her eyes pleaded with him to agree and she was just about to throw down the *'you owe me one'* card when George's expression changed to a scowl. She felt Jake's presence before he spoke—every nerve ending in her body seemed to flip on whenever he came near.

"Am I interrupting?" His voice sounded calm, but from the set of his jaw and the icy glare, she could see he was anything but.

Amanda smiled with false brightness. "George and I were just catching up."

"Great." His gaze never wavered from George's. "Anything you care to share?"

George glared at him. "Nope." He looked back at Amanda. "Send me the information in the morning and I'll see what I can. No promises, though." He pushed away from the wall, his mouth set in a thin, hard line as he tossed back the last of his scotch. "Later." He smiled at Amanda and ignored Jake as he sauntered away.

"Thanks George," she called at his retreating back.

"What was all that about?"

"Nothing," she said. "Just work stuff."

"You aren't working right now." Jake's eyes bored into her. "I'll ask one last time: are you involved with him?"

Amanda groaned. "That question is getting a little old."

He continued as if she hadn't spoken. "Because you know there's no better way to blow our deal—to ruin the whole thing for both of us—than to have you running around with some other guy."

She glared at him, anger simmering inside. "That's what you think of me. Really?"

He looked down and didn't answer for a moment.

She felt her blood pressure rise. "I'm going back to the party," she said, whirling around and starting toward the crowded room.

"Wait." His fingers gripped her arm. He tugged her gently back toward him. "What if I asked you to stay away from him?"

She expelled a long, exaggerated sigh and looked Jake directly in the eye, her voice quiet as she said, "There's no reason to ask that. Like I said, he's a friend; nothing more."

"That didn't sound like something you'd say to a friend." He stepped closer. "I didn't like what I heard."

She swallowed hard and folded her arms as she said. "What do you think you heard?"

"You said you needed him." His voice sounded low and husky as he stepped closer. "I didn't like it."

Amanda's heart thumped. She backed away, stopping only when she encountered the rough brick wall.

Jake leaned forward and braced a hand on either side of her. His scent enveloped her like a warm, familiar embrace and every part of her body tingled as she gazed up at him. She wanted to look away; willed herself to duck underneath his arm and lose herself in the crowd, but she couldn't. In all honesty, she didn't want to. While a part of her felt compelled to run, the part that wanted to stay proved stronger.

His gaze held her captive and in his eyes, she recognized a softness she hadn't seen in more than a year. Her hand quivered as she reached up and cupped his cheek, her eyes pleading with him to understand. "That...it was nothing," she said. "I...we...we were just—" She was about to confess, to tell him the truth about the video surprise she had planned when his arms wound around her and pulled her close.

He lowered his head until his lips were a breath away from hers, his voice sounding husky as he uttered his next words. "I want you to say those words to me."

Her heart was thumping so loudly she was sure he could hear it. "Say what?" She pretended not to understand.

When their deal ended, she'd be cast aside. She knew this. Hell, they'd already legally agreed to it. All Jake wanted right now was a little fun to spice up their business deal and in the process; he could get her out of his system. He'd already said as much. And while he'd caught her in a weak moment the day before, she didn't plan to fall for his game again. The only way she'd survive this deal was if she kept her emotional distance and so that is exactly what she planned to do. The only problem was, she didn't want to keep her distance.

Lord she was in trouble.

"I'm not afraid to say it, Amanda." Jake's voice held a gruff tenderness she'd never heard before. "I fantasized about you every hour, every minute when I was in Iraq." Her breath caught in her throat and her eyes grew wide as he continued. "I tried not to. God knows I tried. I kept trying to convince myself that my obsession didn't mean anything, that I was just lonely and exhausted. But I knew it wasn't true." He traced a finger over the contours of her face. "You're so beautiful," he whispered.

A shiver ran down her spine.

"And since I've been back, it's even worse. I can't get you out of my head." His arm tightened around her waist, which was good because she feared her knees would buckle. "I need to know you feel it too; that you can forgive me for running away. That you want to give our relationship another try; a real one."

Amanda's knees wobbled and she melted against him, resting her cheek against his chest.

His arms tightened around her.

She had dreamed of him saying those words for more than a year. It was more than he'd ever said before and it was enough; more than enough. She gazed up at him and finally acknowledged to herself what she'd known deep inside all along. She needed him.

"Say it." Jake's voice was a gentle command. He bent his head closer, his lips stopping just shy of hers.

Her breath caught in her throat as she said, "I...I need you." She blinked back the moisture in her eyes and lifted her chin, refusing to acknowledge, even to herself, the fear those words induced. She hadn't let herself need anyone since the night she'd lost her parents. But God help her, she *did* need him. And even more, she wanted him.

"I never stopped needing you," Jake's lips captured hers.

She tried to push her fear aside as she dissolved into his arms. She nibbled at his lower lip. Jake groaned and pulled her close. His kiss took her breath away and when he finally lifted his head, they were both panting. He took her hand in his and squeezed as he whispered, "Let's go home."

* * *

Amanda checked her watch for the third time. Kate was always late, but thirty minutes was pushing it—even for her. She pulled her cell from her purse and checked for messages. She laid the phone on the table and looked up to see Kate headed toward the table.

She waved and smiled in greeting, but her grin faded when she caught the dour expression on Kate's face. "You look pissed," Amanda said as Kate pulled up a chair and plopped her Marc Jacobs bag on the chair beside her. "I thought you'd be deep into gloat mode given the fact that the party went off without a hitch. What's wrong?"

Kate glared at her. "Oh, I don't know. Maybe it's the fact that my two hosts—our best friends—ditched my fabulous party after only an hour and a half."

"We didn't ditch," Amanda said, raising a hand to flag the waitress. Better change the subject before she really got riled up. "By the way, today's special is spinach and goat cheese omelet."

"Don't even try to change the subject. You ditched. Own it," Kate said, pushing out her lower lip. "Some hosts you two turned out to be. You only stayed for an hour and a half before you snuck out. You better have an amazing excuse."

"Stop pouting. It's not an attractive expression on a pregnant woman."

Kate glared at her as the waitress arrived.

They ordered and after the waitress walked away, Kate eyed Amanda with expectation as she drummed her fingers on the table. "Well?"

Amanda sipped her water and then said, "I'm sorry. We didn't intend to ditch. Something came up," she said.

"You can do better than that."

Amanda leaned forward and placed her elbows on the table. "Jake found me talking to George and he jumped to all kinds of crazy conclusions. We sort of got into it. One thing led to another and...we ended up leaving."

"What were you doing with George? Did you finally decide to take my advice and try to make Jake jealous?" She leaned back in her chair, her face settling into a self-satisfied little grin. "Jealousy always works."

Amanda arched a brow. "It's not 1965, so no, I didn't." She rolled her eyes. "I swear. Alabama must be some sort of portal into a different dating era. It's like you came here through a time machine, you're so retro when it comes to love. You would've done very well in the era of Frank Sinatra and Doris Day."

Kate looked about to respond when the waitress arrived with their entrees. Instead, she tilted her head and glared at Amanda as she plucked the lemon off the side of her glass and squeezed it into her water.

The waitress left and Amanda continued.

"Actually, I cornered George and tried to convince him to create a brand video for Jake's pitch tomorrow—something that'll wow the investors," Amanda said. She wanted to tell her what had happened between her and Jake the night before, but didn't feel ready yet.

Kate studied her for a moment and then said, "And then what happened?"

"What do you mean?" Amanda feigned a look of innocence.

"You look more satisfied with yourself than you did the day you found that gently worn Zac Posen dress on the clearance rack in Sweet Repeats."

"This is *way* better than the Zac Posen."

"I knew it!" Kate's eyes danced as she playfully slapped a palm on the table. "Okay, out with it."

Amanda smiled, but it didn't quite reach her eyes. "Jake said he wanted to give our relationship a try, for real."

"O. M. G. I *knew* it," Kate said as she pushed back in the booth. Her tone oozed know-it-all superiority as she said, "Retro or not, I *told* you it would work to make Jake jealous."

"I don't think jealousy is what did it." Amanda paused to consider her next words. "I'm not sure where he came up with the idea."

"Well it doesn't matter. All that matters is that you two are back on track." Kate placed her elbows on the table and stared dreamily at Amanda. "So, are you still getting married in a few months or do you want to wait?" She clapped, her eyes dancing. "I can't wait to plan a huge, extravagant wedding with Gigi. A real one! Maybe we should do a destination—"

Amanda held up a hand. "Stop. You're getting way ahead of yourself. We haven't even discussed that yet. I think he meant he wanted to keep dating; you know, pick up where we left off before he ended it a year ago." She shook her head. "Honestly, I don't know what he meant."

Kate's eyes searched her face. "Would that make you happy?"

"Yes." Amanda sat up a little straighter as she added, "I'm thrilled."

Kate frowned. "Right. And I'm Princess Catherine." She buttered her toast as she said, "Okay, what's wrong. Out with it." She took a delicate bite and rolled her wrist signaling for Amanda to continue.

"I just don't know if I want to put myself emotionally out there with him again," she said. "He crushed me."

"I know he did. But everyone makes mistakes."

"That was a pretty big one, I'd say," Amanda said. "You know, for months after he left, I felt sure he'd call or email or something." She shook her head. "Pathetic, I know. And when he didn't, I then convinced myself it would all change when he got home. That one day, I'd come home from work and I'd walk in to find him sitting on the couch waiting for me, whistling that damn off-key key tune." She laughed. "Then in my fantasy, he'd beg me for a second chance and of course, pledge his undying love." She paused for a long moment and said quietly, "Yes, I'm an idiot. That's why I finally moved out of my old apartment and bought the condo. I needed to be someplace that Jake had never been. I needed to get away from him."

Kate squeezed her hand. "No you're not. He did come back to you. He didn't even hesitate to race up to the cabin to get you the second I asked. And then he came up with this deal, which I'm convinced was just a way to spend more time with you. I mean, last night he actually told you he wants to give it another try...for real. It's what you said you wanted."

"I only want it if he can really commit. And I don't know that he can. And even more, I'm not sure I have it in me to try again."

Kate regarded her for a long moment and then said, "Remember what you said to me when I was going through all my stuff with Sam?"

"This is not the same."

Kate continued as if she hadn't spoken. "You asked if I wanted my life to be ordinary or extraordinary."

"This is not the same," Amanda repeated.

"It *is* the same. You love Jake. You can't live your life cowering in the corner and hiding behind your brother's problems and your own fears about putting yourself out there. You had something extraordinary with Jake. And if you want to get it back, you're going to have to step out in faith and believe; in yourself and in him."

Amanda speared a huge forkful of her omelet and shoved it in her mouth. She took her time chewing. Just as she swallowed, her cell phone buzzed. Grateful for the distraction, she picked it up, frowning as she glanced at the display.

Rob. She didn't feel like talking to him, so she let the call roll to voicemail.

"Jake?" Kate winked, her eyes dancing.

Amanda shook her head. "It's Rob."

Kate stared at her expectantly and her eyes grew round as Amanda dropped the phone back in her purse. "Aren't you going to answer?"

"No. Why do you look so surprised?"

"You always drop everything when Rob calls. The house could be burning down around you and you'd still stop to take his call." Kate pushed back in her chair and tilted her head as she regarded Amanda with interest. "Well, this is a new one."

"It's no big deal. I'll just call him back later. I can't be at his beck and call all the time."

Kate's mouth dropped open and then she arched a brow as she said, "Wow. This is like something straight out of *Invasion of the Body Snatchers.*" She leaned forward and made a silly face, waggling her finger as she said, "What have you done with Amanda?"

Amanda picked up her napkin and dabbed at her mouth. "Are you ready for shopping?"

Kate shot her a look. "I was born ready."

The girls stopped at the front to pay and then strolled out into the mall, chatting and window shopping until they got to Nordstrom, where they headed straight for the make-up section, as usual.

Kate grabbed Amanda's arm and pulled her toward the Chanel counter. "I saw this new foundation advertised in this month's Elle. Supposedly it contains these little silicone spheres that let the makeup sit on top of your wrinkles." She looked at Amanda expectantly.

Amanda's mouth twisted. "Are you saying I have wrinkles?"

"No. But look at that photo of Sharon Stone." She pointed at the countertop display in front of them. "She's in her mid-50's and if it makes her skin look that good just imagine what it'll do for ours. We'll look twenty one again." She elbowed Amanda in the side. "Not bad for someone who's two weeks from their thirtieth."

"Don't remind me." Amanda rolled her eyes. "And Sharon Stone only looks that good because some world class air brush artist doctored that ad."

The saleswoman appeared and Kate said, "We're interested in this foundation. Can you help us find our color?"

Amanda waved a hand. "I'll pass."

Kate shot her a strange look as she allowed the saleswoman to test several shades on the back of her hand. After she paid, she flounced over and pressed her palm against Amanda's forehead. "Are you feeling okay?" She pretended to reach for her phone. "Do I need to call a doctor?"

"Stop," Amanda said as she playfully pushed her hand away. "I feel fine."

"Since when do you avoid your brother's calls and resist buying the latest wonder makeup?"

Amanda shrugged.

They shopped for awhile longer and then headed to the benches outside Nordstrom.

"Do you mind if we sit a minute?" Kate placed a hand on the small of her back and eased down onto the bench. "I have to head home soon, but I wanted to go back to what we were talking about earlier." She cast a sideways glance at Amanda. "I know you're scared to try again with Jake and like I said, I don't blame you. But I think it's more than that." She turned to face Amanda. "Ever since your parents died, you've lived your life expecting the worst. What if you let yourself expect—to actually believe—that it's possible for things to work out the way you want?"

"I honestly don't know what I want." Amanda said, looking out at the crowd and pretending to people watch. But the people just looked like blurry blobs as her eyes welled with tears. She blinked them away. "It's safer not to try. I've been through it once, remember? I don't think I could bear it if I let him in only to have him bolt again, which you know he'll do." She hated feeling this way, so vulnerable and exposed. She lifted her chin and shoved her emotions back into the dark little recesses of her heart where they had lived for the past year; where she didn't have to deal with them. "If I don't let him in, I won't get hurt."

"You're wrong. If he runs again, disappoints you again, it'll hurt whether you allow yourself to believe in the possibilities or not. You've already let him in." Kate chided her gently. "The only question is whether you'll let yourself experience the joy and happiness that comes with allowing yourself to hope; to believe. Or if you'll play it safe." Kate put an arm around her shoulder. "I don't think playing it safe is your style. Not really."

"Why? I think I'd be great at that." Amanda was only half joking, trying to lighten the mood.

Clearly Kate wasn't buying it.

"Just because your parents died, just because Jake left you last year, it doesn't mean everything in your life will unfold in the same way."

Leave it to Kate to cut right to the heart of the matter. Amanda's voice sounded shaky as she said, "I know."

"Yes, but are you ready to do something about it?"

She sniffled and reached into her purse for a tissue "Like what?" She blew her nose.

Kate eyed her sternly. "Like turn off that Negative Nellie soundtrack in your head and let yourself go for once. Throw yourself into this relationship with Jake if it's truly what you want. And I think it is." She smiled. "I *know* it is."

Amanda laughed through her watery eyes. "Negative Nellie, huh?"

"You've got the routine down pat. But let's see if we can't tune the dial to a different station for a while. You know, learn some new moves."

"Trusting Jake Lowell again would probably not be the wisest decision I've ever made. Maybe I need to just find someone safe."

Kate shot her a *get real* look. "Everyone makes mistakes, Amanda. Maybe the break-up was his. Forgive him. Believe in him. Believe in yourself. It's the only way to live." Kate gave Amanda's shoulders a last little squeeze and then stood. "I have to run—or more accurately waddle—back home. See you later."

Despite her melancholy mood, Amanda laughed and waved as Kate made her way slowly through the mall. She sat there for a long while until her cell buzzed again. She pulled it out of her purse. Rob again. He was nothing if not persistent.

This time she answered. "Hey."

"How'd the party go last night?"

"Great. Sorry I missed your call earlier; I was having brunch with Kate."

"No problem," he said. "Listen, can you stop by the restaurant tomorrow morning at ten?"

"I can't. I have to go to a meeting with Jake at ten thirty."

"Oh. Will this afternoon work?"

She sighed. She didn't feel like dealing with Rob's stuff right now. "No. I'm sorry Rob. It'll have to be later in the week."

A long silence followed. "Is everything all right?"

Good question. She wished she had a clue. Only time would tell, she supposed. "It's fine. I just have a lot going on. I have to help Jake tomorrow and I have to finish writing his presentation today and I just can't deal with anything else. Call me tomorrow and we'll figure out when we can meet later in the week."

"But—"

She hung up. This saying no thing was getting much easier.

Chapter Seventeen

Amanda looked up from the computer when the house phone rang. After working on revisions for the last three hours, she needed a break. She sat up straight and stretched. Then she checked her email to see if George had sent the brand video through as he'd promised. He hadn't.

Just as she was about to dive back into the presentation, Jake walked in and sat in the chair across from her. Judging from his expression and tense posture, something was wrong.

She frowned. "What's wrong?"

"My Uncle Leonard just called," he said, his expression grim. "Max got admitted to the hospital a few hours ago."

Amanda leaned forward. "What? Is it serious?"

"They thought he had a heart attack so they rushed him to the emergency room."

Amanda gasped, her hand covering her mouth.

"It wasn't, or if so, it was very mild. He's okay, but they're still running tests and plan to keep him overnight for observation."

Amanda leapt from the chair and swung into action. "I'll be ready in a flash. Just give me a minute to—"

"I'm not going to the hospital—not tonight, anyway." He looked down and away. "I'll go tomorrow after the pitch. I don't want to be distracted right now."

Amanda frowned and sank slowly into the chair. "Distracted? What are you talking about? We're going to the hospital right this minute. And if we need to reschedule the pitch tomorrow, then we'll do that to."

He looked at her; the expression in his eyes was one of pure steel. "No."

She stared at him, incredulous. He must be in shock. He wasn't thinking straight. She decided on the rational approach. "Jake, you *have* to go to the hospital. Max is your only family now, except for an uncle you never see."

He scoffed. "Whatever that means."

She stood and walked around the desk and, perching on the edge, she leaned over and touched his knee. "Jake, he *needs* you."

Jake shot out of the chair and her hand fell to her side. He strode across the room and then turned and his tone was icy as he said, "My father and I needed him too. But he wasn't there for either of us. So I'll do exactly as he would've done back in the day. I'll handle my business matters first and then I'll pay him a visit. When you're a Lowell, it's called having your priorities straight."

Her mouth fell open. "Jake—"

He turned away. "I'm going upstairs. Email the presentation when you're done. I want to run through it a few times before tomorrow morning."

She rushed after him and grabbed his arm. "Jake, wait!" He turned to look at her and the expression in his eyes chilled her to the bone. "What's *wrong* with you?"

"You don't get it," he said, his voice flat and completely devoid of emotion. "I can't pretend to have a relationship with Max that doesn't exist. I'm not going to rush to his side just because of a little health episode."

"I wouldn't exactly call it a little episode if they're keeping him overnight." She folded her arms and decided that, if ever a time called for the direct approach, this was it. "You know, you're the one who doesn't get it. You've had plenty to say about my selfish brother. But from where I'm standing, the only selfish one in the vicinity is you."

He folded his arms and his jaw clenched as he said. "I'm selfish."

She glared at him. "You are. You had so much to say about Rob, I suggest you take a long, hard look in the mirror and I'm pretty sure you won't like what you see." She stalked past him, heading for the door.

"Where are you going?" he shouted.

"I'm going to the hospital to visit your grandfather." She snatched her coat and purse off the chair and flung the door open, not bothering to look back.

* * *

The intensive care nurses finally kicked Amanda out at ten thirty and, by the time she let herself into the townhouse, it was well after eleven. Thank goodness Max was okay. But as her worry about Max dissipated, her anger at Jake had increased and it was now at a boiling point.

She trudged up the stairs and glanced down the hall. Light streamed through the crack under Jake's bedroom door. It was all she could do not to race down the hall, throw the door open and give Jake the tongue-lashing he deserved. Instead, she tiptoed into her bedroom and eased the door shut.

Once inside, she opened her laptop and checked email. Sure enough, she saw a note from George. She clicked on the attachment and played the brand video twice. Her lips curved up. He'd done it. The video was genius. But instead of feeling triumphant, all she could think about was how she'd like to throttle Jake. She certainly didn't feel like helping him at this point.

The video was poignant, emotional...perfect—exactly what she'd envisioned. A big part of her wanted to fly down the hall, thrust the laptop in front of Jake's face and watch his reaction. He'd love it. But she couldn't make herself do it. And it wasn't because she wanted to keep it a secret as she'd originally planned. It was more than that.

The truth was, at this point, the whole brand platform felt like nothing but a lie. And after all the deceptions she'd been party to in the past week, she couldn't stomach another.

She jotted off a quick, heartfelt thank you to George and turned off the laptop. Then she brushed her teeth, washed her face and crawled into bed, trying to figure out whether she would use the video tomorrow or not. She didn't feel like going at this point, but she couldn't let Jake down when he needed her.

Jake knocked on her door. She pretended not to hear, hoping he'd go away. He didn't.

The door opened. "Amanda," he said softly. "Are you awake?"

She lay there, still as a statue, breathing deeply as she tried to mimic the sound of sleep and taking care not to move a muscle. Jake stood there for a long while. She couldn't see him because her back was facing the door, but she could feel him, could sense his penetrating gaze studying her. After what seemed an eternity, he closed the door and plodded back to his bedroom.

Amanda rolled over and stared up at the silhouette of the ceiling fan. As exhausted as she felt, she knew she wouldn't get any sleep. And it wasn't pre-pitch jitters that would keep her awake. It was the selfish, emotionally-closed off man down the hall. The one who didn't even care that his last living relative was lying in the hospital.

To think that she'd actually begun to listen to Jake as it concerned her brother. Had told Rob she couldn't meet him tomorrow. Had convinced herself it was time to reevaluate her priorities so her brother didn't always top the list. It was ridiculous. Jake had no business lecturing her or anyone else about anything that actually mattered. He could serve as the poster child for messed up values.

She shouldn't have placed Jake's pitch before Rob's needs. What if he needed to talk to her about something important? She rolled onto her side, yanked the covers up to her chin and decided that, first thing tomorrow, she'd go see Rob.

And if that made her late for Jake's pitch then so be it.

* * *

Jake was still at the gym when Amanda came down the stairs wearing a black business suit and carrying a briefcase with her laptop. It was nearly nine thirty and she would have to go right from Rob's restaurant to the business meeting.

Before she left, she scribbled a note for Jake saying she'd meet him at Rand's office. Then she dashed out the door and hailed a cab. Ten minutes later, the cab pulled up in front of the restaurant. Amanda paid the driver and stepped onto the sidewalk.

She looked around, but didn't see Rob. Then she remembered. He didn't know she was coming. Yesterday, she had told him she couldn't make it. Amanda sighed and rooted around in her purse. She pulled out her cell and dashed off a quick text letting him know she was at the restaurant. Then she dropped the phone back in her purse and gazed about, taking it all in.

The place looked deserted—especially for nine thirty on a Monday morning. It certainly wasn't bustling with construction crews the way she had expected. She decided to head inside. If he wasn't here, she'd give him a call.

Amanda opened the door and walked inside, noting with satisfaction that the interior looked further along than the exterior suggested. The flooring had been installed and the drywall installed and taped. The walls looked ready to paint. And off to one side of the large dining room, tables, chairs and what looked like upholstered booths had been stacked on top of each other, still wrapped in plastic.

Voices drifted up from the back of the building. She followed the sounds, making her way through a series of dining rooms and the huge kitchen, stepping around power tools and over discarded drywall nails and piles of saw dust. The voices grew louder and seemed to be coming from behind a closed door that appeared to be a storage room. Amanda knocked once, then opened the door and stepped inside. As she crossed the threshold, she stopped short and her eyes widened in shock.

The room reeked of cigar smoke and stale beer. A bunch of filthy, bedraggled men with mussed hair and bloodshot eyes encircled a beat-up card table. Empty beer and scotch bottles littered the floor and a huge stack of cash and chips lay in the center of a table.

A few of the men glanced over their shoulders and then turned their attention back to the game. She opened her mouth to speak, but Rob materialized by her side and pushed her gently out the door, shutting it behind him.

He looked about to speak but she cut him off, her shock gone and replaced by a blistering, white hot rage. "What the *hell* is going on here!" she yelled at the top of her lungs.

"Quiet." Rob said, under his breath. "We don't want to disturb them."

"Speak for yourself. I'd love to disturb them." She lifted her chin and reached for the doorknob.

"Stop," he commanded in a voice slightly above a whisper. "These aren't people we want to mess with."

She stepped back and regarded him with disgust. "Which would be exactly why you chose to go into business with them, I guess." She folded her arms and glared at him. "You *lied* to me on Saturday. You looked me *directly* in the eye and you *lied* to me. How could you."

His eyes grew round. "Let me explain."

She wasn't about to listen to anything else from him. She slowly shook her head and her eyes searched his face. For the first time in years, she no longer saw the vulnerable, slightly awkward thirteen-year-old who'd just lost his parents. She saw what he'd grown into, what she'd helped to create—a selfish, self-absorbed young man who'd taken advantage of her, lied to her, for years.

Tears welled. She whirled around and ran blindly for the front of the restaurant. She tripped on a power tool, which sent her sprawling onto the floor, skinning her knee as the contents of her purse spilled out. She barely felt her skinned knee as she gathered herself up, brushed off her skirt and began grabbing items and shoving them back into her purse.

Rob bent down to help her.

"Get away from me." Her voice shook with rage.

"I can explain." His eyes implored her to listen.

"I'm not interested in hearing any more of your lies." She stood and started for the door. He reached for her arm but she snatched it away, pointing at him. "If you know what's good for you right now, you'll get away from me and you'll give me some space until I'm ready to talk."

"Wait," he said, his voice pleaded with her to listen. "You don't understand—"

She stopped short and whirled around. "No, *you* don't understand." She glared at him, her hands trembling as they clutched her purse and briefcase. "I've spent the last ten years trying to make everything okay for you. I felt guilty and so inadequate that I was all you had; that mom and dad were gone. So instead of spending my time grieving and making sure *I* got better, it was all about you, making everything better for *you*." Tears streamed down her cheeks and he looked about to interrupt, but she held up a hand and continued. "I know it was my choice. I know you didn't ask me to do it. But I *wanted* to."

"And I appreciate everything—"

"Stop! Stop the bullshit." She drew in a ragged breath as she continued. "And how do you repay me for everything I've tried to do for you? You lie, you take my money, you lie again, you take more money and you get involved with shady people doing illegal things to start a business you've no idea how to run in the first place." She gestured wildly toward the huge mirror leaning against the wall and said, "Take a long hard look in that and I think you'll see what I see. You're a liar." She stared at him, her chest heaving. After a few moments, an eerie calm settled over her and she said, "I'm actually glad mom and dad aren't here to see what you've become."

Rob stared at her, looking dazed. "But…"

She held up a hand to stop him. "No, I'm not finished yet. I'm *done*," she said quietly, brushing away the tears spilling down her cheeks. "I'm done making everything okay for you. I'm done trying to figure it all out while you wander through life happily causing one catastrophe after another. I'm done trying to be everything for someone who doesn't appreciate it." She drew a long, fortifying breath and then said, "From now on, *I* come first."

She threw open the door.

"Wait," Rob said. "Please."

She stopped and turned back, her gaze swept over him, trying to figure out how things had gone so wrong. "You know, you never once stopped to ask how I was doing." She arched a brow. "I lost my parents too. And actually, I finally realize I lost something even more troubling, if that's possible. I lost myself." She paused and was barely able to choke out her next words. "But you're too selfish to see that, or care, I guess. And now, I feel like I've lost you, too." She sucked in a long, shaky breath and stood up straighter. "I'm not sure I even know who you are anymore." She shrugged. "Maybe I never did."

Rob stood rooted to the spot as she turned and walked out the door. It swung closed behind her with a thud.

She stepped into the blinding sunlight of the clear November morning and lost herself in the bustling morning crowd. She plodded along in pace with the pack, numb and completely out of it for a long while. After several minutes, she glimpsed a park bench and made her way through the crowd towards it.

She flopped down and looked around her. Where the hell was she?

Amanda looked around and didn't recognize the neighborhood so she scanned the skyline, searching for a landmark to give her a point of reference. She found Willis Tower, which was right across the street from the building where Jake's pitch would happen.

She sat bolt upright.

After all the drama with Rob, she'd forgotten about Jake's meeting. She pulled up her coat sleeve and peered at her watch. Ten forty five. Jake's pitch started fifteen minutes ago. And she was on the other side of town.

Crap, crap, crap!

She sprang off the bench and raced to the curb, her laptop bag bouncing. She waved her arms wildly in an effort to hail a cab and practically had to fling herself in front of one to get it to stop. She ignored the glare of the driver, yanked the door open and scurried into the back, rattling off the address.

"Hurry please!"

Obviously irritated with her, the driver grunted and floored it; tires screeching as they peeled out. The force threw her against the back of the seat. She could feel the cabbie glaring at her in the mirror and she bit back an urge to ask him to keep his eyes on the road. Instead, she pretended not to notice and gazed out the window. At this pace, she could get there in ten to fifteen minutes. She might not be alive. But she'd get there.

No sooner had she formed the thought than they turned a corner and encountered a wall of unmoving, honking, exhaust-spewing cars.

Amanda let out a blood curdling scream and squeezed her eyes shut as they careened towards the stopped cars. The cabbie slammed on the brakes and they screeched to a halt. The sudden stop turned Amanda into a human bullet and she slammed against the front seat and then bounced back hard.

As she glared at the driver's reflection in the rear view mirror, she could have sworn she saw him smile.

They sat there, unmoving for several minutes and neither spoke. The driver just muttered and occasionally pressed on the horn.

Like that was going to solve anything.

Amanda checked her watch for the tenth time in the last five minutes. Then she rolled down a window and poked her head out, looking for a street sign or a familiar landmark, but she couldn't see anything she recognized. She leaned forward and asked, "Where are we?"

The driver pointed. "Ten blocks ahead and two to the right."

They inched forward. At this rate, she'd be there in a week. She checked her watch again. Five after eleven. She was running out of time.

"I'm going to walk. How much?" She shoved some bills at the driver and scurried out of the backseat. She adjusted the laptop and purse and then took off, racing down the sidewalk as fast as her impractical stilettos would allow.

She hit every red light. At one of them, she caught her reflection in a glass building and groaned. Her hair looked wild and frizzy and—

between the crying jag and the multi-block sprint—she could only imagine the state of her makeup. And her skinned knee was killing her. It felt like she'd gotten some dirt or sawdust in it.

She turned away from her reflection. Nothing she could do about it now.

The light turned green and she dashed off, her laptop bouncing so hard against her leg, she was sure it would leave a bruise. Eight blocks later, winded, sweaty and exhausted, she glimpsed the building. Her footsteps slowed. And her thoughts shifted to potential excuses for her tardiness. She was so intent on the task, she failed to notice the steel grate beneath her feet and she stepped right into it. The heel on her three hundred seventy five dollar shoe sank all the way in and got wedged between the steel bars. She walked right out of it. When her bare foot hit the sidewalk she looked down, confused. Then she looked behind her and down.

She groaned. She was definitely cursed. No doubt about it.

Amanda bent over and pulled, expecting it to come right out. The shoe didn't budge. She dropped her briefcase and purse on the side-walk, bent further down and pulled harder. It still didn't dislodge. So she hiked her skirt up and squatted, assuming an extremely unlady-like pose for someone dressed in a black pencil skirt and—ignoring the amused glances of passersby—she grasped the shoe with both hands, grunted and pulled with all her might. The heel cracked off and fell into the sewer. The velocity sent her sprawling backwards and she landed on her bottom with a thud, holding the heelless shoe up in one hand like a trophy.

She blinked and stared at the disfigured stiletto for a long moment. Then she shook her head and sighed as she slipped it on. *It just keeps getting better.*

Gathering what dignity she could muster, she picked up her purse and briefcase and hobbled across the street, her uneven gait making it look like one of her legs was four inches shorter than the other.

She glanced at the clock above the security desk. She had ten more minutes. She scrawled her name on the register and flashed her driver's license, grateful the security guard hadn't bothered to look up as she approached because—between the state of her shoes, hair and makeup—she was sure she would've scared the crap out of him.

The man barely glanced at Amanda as he barked out the floor number and jabbed a thumb toward the bank of elevators behind the security desk.

Amanda thanked him and limped into the elevator, where she punched in the floor number and then slumped against the wall. She looked and felt like absolute hell, but she wasn't about to let Jake down.

She still had no idea what she'd say when she got there. She knew she couldn't just burst into the meeting mid-stream. But she wasn't about to miss it, especially after the planes, trains and automobiles efforts she had undergone to get there.

The bell sounded, the doors opened and she gathered every scrap of pride as she tottered to the reception desk. She smoothed a hand over her hair and tried to tamp down her frizzy curls as she smiled nervously at the receptionist.

The mixture of horror and amusement on the perfectly-groomed woman's face gave Amanda a sense of just how frightening she looked. She drew in a long breath and feigned as dignified an air as she could manage. "Rand Connelly, please. I'm here for the ten thirty meeting."

"Would you like to use a restroom first?" The woman's lips twitched, but Amanda detected a hint of sympathy in her eyes.

She lifted her chin. "No thank you," she sniffed.

The receptionist scanned her log and then looked up at Amanda. "I'm sorry," she said. "The meeting ended five minutes ago."

It was all Amanda could do not to just fling herself on the floor. Her thin veneer of confidence cracked and she collapsed against the desk, prepared to plead her case. "But they're still back there, right?"

The receptionist shook her head. "According to this, they signed out five minutes ago, which means they just left. I'm sorry."

Amanda nodded slowly and turned away. Perfect.

She hobbled back to the elevator; her shoulders slumped in defeat as she made her way out of the building and hailed a cab. She gave the cabbie the address and then closed her eyes, replaying her disaster of a morning over and over in her head until the cab pulled up to the curb.

Amanda paid the driver and opened the door, gazing about in confusion. Crap. She'd given the driver the address to her condo instead of Jake's townhouse. She briefly considered giving the driver Jake's address and then thought better of it. After the morning she'd had, she could use a little alone time to regroup.

She limped into her building. In the elevator, she pulled off her damaged pumps and then trod barefoot down the hall toward her condo. She let herself in and pulled off her coat.

Glancing around, she felt an odd sense of comfort to be home. Still, the place seemed dismally empty and it reminded her of how she'd felt in the days after the break-up with Jake. They hadn't lived together, but had spent most of their time together. And, after Jake had ended things, it took her a very long time to get used to the silence; to be alone without feeling lonely.

She strolled over to the windows and gazed down at the noon-day traffic. She couldn't believe she'd actually missed his meeting. Especially after finding out that everything Jake and Kate had shared about her brother was true. He'd lied to her.

She needed to call Jake.

Without taking the time to plan what she'd say, she picked up her phone and punched in Jake's number. After five rings, the phone rolled to voicemail. Not a good sign.

Amanda briefly considered leaving a generic message just asking him to call her, but once she heard the beep, the words poured out of her—straight from the heart. She apologized effusively for missing his pitch, explaining about what had happened with Rob and prattling on about the pitfalls she'd encountered en route to the meeting.

Then she mustered her courage and—just before the voicemail cut off—she uttered the four hardest words she'd ever said in her life. "I need your help."

* * *

Amanda gazed at the laptop, trying to figure out if she should do it. Kate had text messaged Rand's email address an hour ago and she had written and rewritten the note a dozen times since then. She read it again.

Should she do it? Honestly, she had nothing to lose. She'd already missed the meeting and Jake must be livid, which is why he hadn't returned her call. So it really couldn't get any worse.

She positioned the email like a planned follow-up to the meeting. It was her last ditch attempt to help Jake secure the money for his business. The blinking cursor issued a dare. With every blink it seemed to say send it, send it.

Before she could second guess herself, she attached the video file, reviewed the note one last time and pressed Send.

* * *

The doorbell rang shortly after two o'clock.

Her stomach flip flopped. It had been more than two hours since she'd left the groveling, pleading, rambling voicemail for Jake and an hour since she'd sent the email. She had checked her watch every five minutes since.

It took every iota of self-control she possessed not to call him or send a text. But electronic stalking wouldn't solve anything. By this point, he must have gotten her voicemail, so he knew what had happened and knew she was at her condo. When and if he wanted to talk, she knew he'd reach out. And now he had. He was here.

The doorbell rang again. Her pulse raced as she hurried to the door. She paused to glance in the mirror. She'd long since made herself presentable. But still, she tugged her sweater down and licked her lips as she tried to figure out what to say.

'Sorry to have ditched you on the single most important day of your professional life' probably wouldn't cut it. Maybe just *'I'm sorry'* would be enough.

Amanda opened the door without looking through the peephole and her tentative smile faded instantly. Rob.

She glared at him. "I don't want to talk to you. I'm not even ready to see you, right now." She went to close the door, but he held it open and stepped inside.

"I know you don't, but you're going to."

She frowned. "No, I'm not."

"Yes, you are." Rob's voice sounded determined and he took her arm and steered her purposefully to the sofa. "I listened to you this morning and now you're going to listen to me."

She plopped onto the sofa and regarded him warily as he settled next to her. Still livid, she studied Rob. His whole demeanor seemed different. His bearing and posture exuded strength, a confidence she'd never seen before and it reminded her of their father. Rob had never reminded her of their father before now.

Still, she expected him to let loose an endless string of excuses; to try to explain away the events of the morning with a pack of lies. She folded her arms and waited for him to start. Given this, his approach caught her completely off guard.

"You were right about everything," Rob said. "And I deserved every word you said." She gaped at him as he continued. "I also came to give you this." He pulled an envelope out of his pocket and handed it to her.

She hesitated briefly before reaching for it, noting the pride evident in every aspect of his being.

"Open it."

She ran a fingertip under the flap and pulled out a check for a hundred thousand dollars. Her eyes grew wide. "Rob, where did you get this money?" She shook her head. "These people you're dealing with are—"

"Jake." Rob sat back and stretched his arm out along the top of the sofa cushions, looking extremely pleased. "I got the money from Jake."

"Jake," she repeated, staring at him blankly.

Why would Jake give Rob money? Especially given how irresponsible and clueless he thought Rob to be. And why did Rob possess the self-satisfied look of someone who knew something the other one didn't?

A huge grin spread across his features. "Jake and I are business partners."

Her brows knit together. "What are you talking about?"

"Jake got me out of the deal; he got the partners to return the money I invested, which is where that money came from." Rob pointed to the check and then leaned forward, bracing his elbows on his knees as he gazed at the floor for a long moment and then turned to her. "And he's bringing in a friend of Rand Connelly's—you know, Sam's investment banking brother—from California, who owns a national restaurant group. The group owns several high end chains and they're going to fund a place using my concept. They'll put in a management team to operate it initially and I'll start out with a ten percent stake. Over five years, I'll learn from the team and gradually gain sweat equity. I'll end up with a sixty percent stake, the restaurant group will keep twenty percent and Jake wants to keep twenty percent." Rob grinned and sat up straight, looking proud. "He believes in me."

Despite her lingering anger, Amanda smiled.

"You were right about everything," he said, glancing back at her, a look of contrition in his eyes. "Some pretty questionable people did get involved. It happened as time went on; everything just got so out of control and I didn't know how to stop it."

"You should have told me. I could've helped you."

He clasped his hands and tapped his index fingers together. "I wanted to—especially when you came by on Saturday. But I didn't want to be any more of a burden than I'd already been. He glanced at her sideways. "But Jake came by on Saturday—."

"Jake came by to see you?"

Rob nodded. "Right after you left."

She flopped back in the sofa cushions.

"I told him the truth," he glanced at her apologetically. "I'm sorry, sis. When you came by on Saturday, I couldn't tell you what was really going on. I didn't want you to worry." He turned to face her.

"But when Jake stopped by, we sorted it all through. Then we went by the restaurant and Jake convinced them to let me out of the deal."

She stared at him, dumbstruck. "Why would he do that?"

Rob grabbed her ring finger and shot her a pointed look. "Because he loves you, dummy. It certainly wasn't because of me. He knows what a screw up *I* am."

"You're not a screw-up," she automatically leapt to her brother's defense. He shot her a *get real* look and despite her foul mood, Amanda giggled.

"We both know that's a load of bull," he said. "But I'm going to do better. You'll see."

Amanda dropped her head in her hands. "Oh Rob," she groaned. "I really screwed up today." Deserting Jake in his time of need was bad enough, but after what she'd just heard, she wasn't sure she'd ever forgive herself.

He rubbed her back. "What's wrong? What'd you do?"

She looked up at him, barely able to choke out the words. "We fought last night and it's a long story, but basically, I came to see you this morning instead of staying home. I intended to meet up with him, but after everything that happened between us at the restaurant, I was late; so late that I missed it completely."

She looked over at Rob and was surprised to see him looking slightly amused. "What? This isn't funny."

He crossed one leg over the other, resting his ankle on his knee. Then he waggled his foot and looked like he was trying hard not to laugh as he said, "I don't know. For some weird reason, it feels good to actually see a dent in your armor. It's sort of fascinating to finally see you as the one who might need a little help. You know?"

She smacked his foot. "Tell me what to do."

"You know what to do. Tell Jake you're sorry."

"I called him two hours ago and left the world's longest message. He hasn't called back."

Rob rolled his eyes. "So go find him. Make him listen. Tell him you love him. He'll forgive you. You only missed a meeting."

"The most important meeting of his life," she whispered. "I'm afraid he'll blame me if his business doesn't get funded."

He stood and yanked her hand to pull her up off the sofa. "He'll forgive you. Now go."

Chapter Eighteen

By the time Amanda arrived at Cook County Hospital, more than three hours had passed since she'd called Jake. Her visit with Max could technically be considered stalling, but she needed more time to figure out what she'd say before she went to see Jake. And she still hoped Jake would return her call, but with each moment that passed, it seemed less and less likely.

She took the elevator to the third floor and then walked down the hall toward Max's room. Encouraged by her conversation with Rob, she felt almost light-hearted. He was right. She just needed to swallow her pride and apologize for missing the meeting. After everything he'd gone through to fix the situation with Rob, it had to mean something. Maybe Kate was right. Maybe Jake did actually want to make their relationship work. She couldn't think of any other reason he would help out the way he had.

The door to Max's room was open and as she drew close, Jake's voice drifted into the hallway.

Her footsteps slowed. She couldn't hear what he was saying. After a few minutes he paused and Max murmured something in response. She stopped outside the door and tried to decide if she should go in or leave and come back later.

Before she had time to decide, Jake said, "That's right. This whole engagement and marriage thing between Amanda and me was a fake." She froze, rooted to the spot as he continued. "We did it to get access to my trust so I could start my business. And she did it because to help her brother. But you know how I feel about marriage. It's the last thing..."

Amanda felt dizzy and her thoughts were racing so fast, she tuned out the rest of his words. A fake. Jake had told Max the truth. She'd never be able to face Max again. And even worse, any hope of a second chance was gone. After their argument the night before and her no show at his pitch, she couldn't blame him.

A harried-looking nurse rushed by, carrying a clipboard and a tray with meds. She stopped and said, "You can go in if you'd like; visiting hours don't end until eight."

Amanda blinked and backed away. "I...no, uh...thank you."

She turned and started toward the elevator. After a dozen steps, her walk became a jog and then turned into a full blown sprint, as if the gates of hell had just opened and the devil himself was in hot pursuit.

Her feet pounded down the hallway, past the elevators and toward the red exit sign at the end of the corridor. She threw the heavy metal door open and it banged against the concrete wall, slamming closed behind her. She dashed down two flights of stairs. She slowed as she got to the bottom, where she sank down onto the bottom step. She should have known things wouldn't work out. She should've listened to her gut instead of to Kate or Rob.

She drew her legs in to her chest and buried her face in her knees, curling into a tiny little ball as she tried to keep the tears at bay. She sat there for a long while and then stood and dusted herself off.

Outside, she hopped in a cab and gave the driver the address. As they sped off, she reached into her purse and pulled out her cell. Then she punched in her friend's home number. It rolled to voicemail and she hung up and dialed Kate's cell. Come on, Kate. Pick up! But a few moments later, the call rolled to voicemail. When she heard the beep, she got right to the point. "Something's happened. I need your help. I'm on my way over."

Amanda hung up and let her head drop back to rest on the seat, clutching the phone in her hand like a lifeline as she gazed out the window trying to figure out how her world had collapsed around her so completely.

* * *

Two hours later, the cab pulled up to her building and she dragged herself out. After spilling her guts to Kate, she felt exhausted and emotionally raw. Even worse, Jake still hadn't returned her call.

The thought caused tears to well again. She blinked them back as she trudged across the lobby and into the elevator. She fumbled with the key a bit, but finally the door unlocked.

As she shrugged off her coat, she frowned. Had she left the television on? Then she heard a faint, off key whistle.

Jake!

Her heart skipped several beats as she walked slowly into the living room. Jake sat on the sofa, his long legs stretched out as he watched the evening news. It was just like she'd fantasized after their break-up.

He stopped whistling when he saw her.

Her voice was just above a whisper as she said, "What are you doing here?"

He looked slightly sheepish. "Rob gave me his key. One of the benefits of being in partnership with him," he said. He reached for the remote and turned off the television. "I wanted to talk."

She swallowed hard. "Jake, I...I'm sorry that I..."

He held up a hand, his expression enigmatic. "No apologies."

She nodded. She didn't blame him for not wanting to hear her lame excuses. She perched on the edge of the loveseat and said, "How did your presentation go today?" *I'm so sorry I missed it;* she added silently, her eyes pleading with him to understand.

"It went really well. Surprisingly well. Until you sent the video, that is." He stood; his eyes didn't waver from hers.

A shiver ran down her spine and her heart pounded. *Idiot! I shouldn't have sent it. What the hell was I thinking?*

She scrambled for the right words. "I uh...I was. . ." She swallowed hard and cleared her throat as she tried again. "I was trying to help." She should've known better than to send the video without checking with Jake first. There'd been too much riding on her actions to gamble. Her eyes pleaded with him to understand, tried to convey what she couldn't find the words to say.

His gaze never wavered from hers. "Well, you didn't help," he said, pausing for what seemed an eternity. "You cinched the deal." He pushed away from the wall and sauntered toward her. "Apparently, Rand's group has never signed a deal after just one meeting; until now."

She clasped her hands in front of her and jumped up. "You got the money?"

He nodded.

She squealed and launched herself at him, flinging her arms around his neck. He laughed and swung her around. After he set her down, he stepped back and said, "And they gave me far more than I ever dreamed they would. I won't need additional funding for at least a year."

Her heart kicked with joy. "Oh Jake, I'm *so* happy for you!" Then she paused. She had to say something, anything to make him understand she hadn't intended to miss his meeting. "Jake, I'm sorry I didn't come this morning. *Truly* sorry."

"Judging from the look of that shoe"—he gestured to her ruined pump lying next to the loveseat—"you tried pretty hard." He looked like he was fighting back laughter.

Despite herself, she smiled ruefully. "Trust me. You have no idea."

"I got the gist from your voicemail." He grinned and then his face took on a more serious expression. "Listen, I couldn't have done it today without you. The pitch would've turned out very differently if you hadn't helped with the presentation. And then, when you sent that video..."—he brushed a strand of hair off her cheek—"how did you do it, by the way? The video, I mean."

"George did it. That's what we were talking about at the party on Saturday. He's one of the creative directors at the agency. He's genius."

"You mean I have Gorgeous George to thank for my good fortune?" Jake rolled his eyes. "Great."

He looked so dismayed Amanda laughed in spite of herself. "If you must know, he wasn't too pleased to help you either, but he owed me a few favors. I cashed them in."

He cleared his throat. "Give me his number. I owe him, big time."

She smiled at his begrudging admission. Under other circumstances, she suspected the two men would've been great friends. Maybe they still could be. But as soon as the thought occurred, she reminded herself it didn't matter anymore. She and Jake were over. Long over. The sobering thought reminded her of Rob's visit earlier.

Her eyes scanned the room. When she located the white envelope, she picked it up and handed it to Jake.

"What's this?" He frowned as he opened it.

"I wanted to pay you back the advance you gave me a week ago since the deal's off and all," she said. "Thank you for what you did with Rob. I don't know what you said to him or what went on during your visit. All I know..." She choked up, her eyes filling with tears again. "All I know is I saw something in him today that I've never seen before."

He shook his head. "I didn't do anyth—"

"You did. Rob told me. And I don't know how to thank you. You were right about everything. But I just couldn't believe it; never would have believed it until I found out the hard way this morning."

Jake slid the check back into the envelope and gazed down at her. "You had to know I did it for you. It was all for you."

She nodded and looked away. Until she'd screwed everything up.

"I hope you don't mind we'll be partners in his restaurant," he continued. "I figured it might be good for him for a while. Just until he figures out how to run a business on his own and knows enough to avoid the pitfalls he fell into with this last one. I just wanted him out of the mess."

"I'm truly grateful," she said. "But you don't have to stay partners. I mean, now that our deal is off, I'm sure it's the last thing you want to do."

"I want to." His voice was gentle, but firm. "And why do you keep saying our deal is off?"

"I went to the hospital earlier, Jake. I heard what you said to Max." She turned back to face him.

Jake frowned. "What did you hear?"

"I heard you tell Max it was all a fake. And I'm glad you did. I'm *relieved*," she said. "I *hated* lying to him, deceiving him. And I'm so glad you went to see him."

He stepped toward her. "What else did you hear?"

"Nothing; I left right after. I didn't want to disturb you and in all honesty, I'm not sure I'd ever have the nerve to look Max in the eye again now that he knows the truth."

He stood in front of her. "You missed the best part," he said softly, tipping her chin up until her eyes met his. "You missed me telling Max I want to marry you for real. You missed me telling him you're the love of my life. And you missed him telling me in his most know-it-all-voice, he already knew that part." Jake grinned and brushed her hair from her cheek. "I meant what I said at the party, Amanda. I want this thing between us to be for real; to be forever."

Her heart thumped. "But, I heard you say the deal was off—"

"The deal is off," he said. "I don't want a fake engagement, a fake marriage or a fake anything else with you. From this point onward, I'll only settle for the real deal."

Her mouth dropped open.

He bent onto one knee and picked up her left hand, pulling off the over-sized Tiffany engagement ring that had become a despised symbol of their outlandish deception. He tossed it onto the sofa without a glance and pulled a ring out of his pocket.

"Jake," she said. "That ring—"

"That ring is going right back to Tiffany's tomorrow morning. I don't want any reminders of the past week."

A smile tugged at her lips as hope bloomed in her heart.

"Amanda"—he cleared his throat and gazed up at her . He held a delicate ring between his fingers—"this is my grandmother's wedding ring. My grandfather gave it to her almost fifty years ago and now I...we both...want you to have it. I want to spend the rest of my life with you and even that won't be enough." He held the ring at her left finger. "Amanda Wilson, will you marry me?"

Amanda's hands flew to her mouth.

"I know after everything we've been through, after how I ended things last year, after the way I've behaved this past week," Jake said, "I know I have no right to ask. And I know I have a lot to prove to you in terms of my ability to make a commitment. But I promise you, if you'll just say yes, I'll spend the rest of my life making up for all of it."

She nodded; feeling like her heart might burst.

Jake's face broke into a broad grin and he slid the ring onto her finger. Then he stood and pulled her into his arms. She melted against him and rested her cheek against his chest and closed her eyes. Kate was right. Dreams really can come true.

After a while, Jake pulled away and reached into his pocket, pulled out a slip of paper and handed it to her. She glanced down at it and then up at him. "What's this?"

"Paris." He smiled, his eyes crinkling at the edges.

"I'm not going to Paris. The deal is off, remember?" She shook her head. "Besides, I have to get back to work. Fun and games time is over and it's back to the office for me."

"We're going to Paris." He fanned the papers to display two boarding passes. His eyes searched her face. "That is, if you'll let me go with you. I'm hoping you do, but mostly, I want to make sure you get that year in Paris you and your mother always dreamed of."

"No." She shook her head more vehemently. "I don't need Paris. I have everything I need, more than I ever *dreamed* of having, right here with you."

"The best things in life aren't about *needing*, remember? They're about wanting." He set the tickets on the coffee table and pulled her close. "Someone I love told me that not too long ago."

She picked up the boarding passes and her brows shot up in surprise. "This flight leaves in five hours!"

He grinned. "Yes, it does. Your dream comes true in just five hours."

"Jake, I told you. Paris isn't important to me anymore. It was just a silly girlhood fantasy. It's not practical and I need to get back to work and—"

"It is important to you. It's *always* been important. It's a dream your mother placed in your heart; a dream to be cherished and its worth moving heaven and earth to accomplish it—especially since she's gone." He pulled her close and kissed the tip of her nose. "Don't ever say it's not important, ever again."

She blinked back tears as she looked up at him. "It *was* important. But you're *more* important. I already have more than I ever dreamed of."

He frowned. "You make it sound like you need to choose between me and Paris. You don't," he said. "The dream meant enough for you to hold onto it your entire life, until you lost them. It was just six months from becoming reality when your parents died." He shook his head and tipped her head up so she looked him in the eye. "You're going Amanda. You *have* to. And I'd like to go with you, because if something—*anything*—matters that much to you, then it's important to me, too."

A lone tear slid down her cheek and her lips quivered.

He looked at her in concern. "What's wrong? I thought this would make you happy."

Her voice was thick and as a few more tears weaved a path down her cheek; she brushed them away. "I *am* happy."

"You're sure?" He looked confused. "I can cancel the tickets."

"I want to go." She brushed the last of her tears away. "I do, if you'll come with me."

"Of course, I'll go with you," he said. "I'll just go back and forth while I get the business started. But I'm sure I can coerce Kate into coming over and staying awhile after the baby is born."

She smiled up at him. "Thank you, Jake."

"Don't thank me." He shook his head. "Paris has always been part of the deal."

She smiled and kissed him. "I never expected our deal to make my dreams come true." She kissed him again. "But it did. *You* did."

He laced his fingers at the small of her back and the look in his eyes curled her toes. She never believed he'd look at her like that, ever again.

"You've fulfilled dreams I didn't even know I had." He pulled her close and kissed her until she felt breathless. "I love you, Amanda. I never stopped loving you. You lived beside me every day in Iraq. I couldn't have made it through without you."

She looked up at him. "You're right."

He frowned. "About what?"

"It's hard for me to ask for or accept help. It's hard for me to admit I can't do everything myself. I realized that today. You'll need to be patient with me." She melted into him for a long time and then finally, pulled away, laughing as a thought occurred.

He gazed down at her. "What?"

"I was just thinking." She giggled. "After you ditched me and left for Iraq, I started to think of you as the devil."

He pursed his lips and gazed up at the ceiling, appearing to consider her words carefully. "I've been called worse," he said as his blue eyes locked with hers. "By *you*, if my memory serves." He arched a brow. "Chauvinist, ass, devil; did I miss anything?"

She giggled. "I'm sure I'll come up with a few others down the road."

His smile crinkled the corners of his eyes. "No doubt, but I'll do everything I can to prevent you from needing to." His lips captured hers. After a few breathless moments, he pulled away. "What about now? Do you still think of me as the devil?"

She bit her lower lip, tilting her head as she gazed up at him through her lashes. "Yes, I believe I do." Her gaze shot down the hall toward the bedroom. "But it kinda works for me."

He chuckled. "Tease."

"Does the devil wanna come out to play? Or should we spend the next few hours packing?"

"To hell with Paris," he declared. "We'll leave tomorrow."

"Now you're talking." She winked at him.

Jake's blue eyes grew dark and he gave her bottom a playful little swat. Amanda yelped and giggled as she sprinted off toward the bedroom with Jake in hot pursuit.

Their engagement deal was no more. What they had now was the *real* deal. A forever deal.

**Check out more great stories from Abby Matisse.
Visit www.abbymatisse.com to stay up on all the latest.**

***

The Sweet Home Chicago Series Continues

A romantic comedy series about a group of Chicago-based friends and the mayhem, mishaps and misadventures they encounter on their journeys toward love.

What Happens in Paris (Sweet Home Chicago #2) Available February 2013

Jake and Amanda are about to discover that a lot can happen between yes and I do. Especially when so much has been left unsaid. Follow Jake and Amanda's journey as they venture to Paris, plan their wedding and–once the post-engagement glow fades–find themselves dealing with the aftermath of a year spent apart, their sudden reunion and the family dramas and personal demons that tore them apart in the first place. In their case, what happens in Paris will most definitely not stay in Paris.

Everything She Wants (Sweet Home Chicago #3) Available July 2013

This prequel to "A Deal with the Devil" features Amanda's best friend, Kate Montgomery. She's a strong-willed and feisty southern belle from an eccentric but upper crust, Birmingham family who finds herself having to choose between the rich and rakish investment banker she's always lusted after and the handsome, but penniless young attorney she's finding it impossible to resist. In the process, she must decide whether she'll dutifully follow the path expected of her or find the courage to forge her own.

***

Introducing The Princesses of Las Olas

A new series featuring the pampered, fabulous women of Las Olas Boulevard and the unexpected twists and turns of fate that help them discover who they are, what they want and how to carve out a life that really matters.

Caring for Cressida (Princesses of Las Olas #1) Available Soon!

Cressida Ann Wentworth had it all. Or, so she thought. Until her skirt-chasing, money-hiding, slime ball of a plastic surgeon husband walked out on her, that is. Alone and fearful, it doesn't take long to realize that–in the pampered and posh Southern Florida enclave of Las Olas–she's just committed the trifecta of unforgivable sins. She's penniless, single and on the wrong side of thirty-five. Now facing the harsh reality of carving out a new life on her own, she'll discover who she is, what she's made of and what she really wants–now that she's no longer the well-tended wife of Dr. Calvin Wentworth. In the process, she'll learn that–improbable as it may have seemed at the time–being dumped wasn't the end. It was just the beginning.

Made in the USA
Charleston, SC
07 October 2012